Caffeine Nights Publishing

Deadly Focus

RC Bridgestock

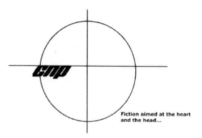

Fiction aimed at the heart
and the head...

Published by Caffeine Nights Publishing 2011

Copyright © RC Bridgestock 2011

RC Bridgestock has asserted their right under the Copyright, Designs and Patents Act 1998 to be identified as the author of this work

CONDITIONS OF SALE

Published in Great Britain by Caffeine Nights Publishing

www.caffeine-nights.com

British Library Cataloguing in Publication Data.
A CIP catalogue record for this book is available from the British Library

ISBN: 978-1-907565-08-3

Cover design by
Mark (Wills) Williams

Everything else by
Default, Luck and Accident

To

Our family who lived with us through the real crime

And support us in fiction

For law enforcement officers - the true heroes - who strive for justice for the victims and their families

Deadly Focus

Chapter One

Nine-year-old Daisy Charlotte Hind was proud of the striking, red, curly hair that cascaded down her back in a haphazard fashion. She was often teased and called names like *Carrot Head* or *Copper Top,* but she didn't care. No one had hair like hers at school. It was special, her mummy told her, just like she was.

Being a bridesmaid for the first time was so exciting; Auntie Sam and Uncle Tom were getting married, and they'd told her all she had to do was look pretty. That couldn't be too difficult, she thought. Daisy loved all the attention the wedding entailed. The grown-ups laughed at her as she stood on the kitchen table being fitted for her dress.

'Stand up straight now,' the dressmaker mumbled with pins in her mouth as she altered the hemline. 'Look forward. Don't look down. Let's have a twirl now. Gorgeous.'

The bridesmaid dress was ready at last, and Mum had picked it up. Daisy thought she would just burst with excitement as she skipped home from school that day.

The dress hung proudly on the living room door as Mum and Daisy walked into the house.

'Yippee,' she said with glee as her mum took off its plastic wrapping so she could try it on. Daisy bounced up and down with joy, her arms waving feverishly in the air as Wendy lowered the dress over her head.

'Oh, wow, it fits a treat,' Wendy said, carefully fastening the tiny buttons on the lace collar.

'Quick, Mummy, I want to look in the mirror,' Daisy said, hopping from one foot to the other as Wendy tied the sash.

'Stand still, will you, for goodness sake,' she said as she turned Daisy around. 'Gosh, you look so grown up.' She was caught unexpectedly by the emotion of seeing her daughter taking an important step toward independence.

Daisy flew up the stairs in her long, silk, jade-coloured dress as fast as her little legs would carry her. She spun round in front of a mirror, making the skirt balloon out.

'I'm going to be a bridesmaid, I'm going to a wedding,' she giggled. Her black school shoes and old socks looked a bit scruffy, she thought, but she had been promised they were going shopping for some silver sandals on Saturday, and she was going to wear tights just like a grown up on the day. She really was the 'princess' Grandma called her.

'Mummy, it's so … beautiful. Can I go and show Grandma, please?' she begged as she ran down the stairs.

Wendy looked out of the window. It was cold and growing dark, but Irene lived only a few hundred yards away. What harm could it do? 'Go on then, as long as you don't stay long,' Wendy said. 'But be careful not to dirty it,' she told her daughter. Daisy grabbed her duffle coat from the banister at the bottom of the stairs and ran out of the door before her mum could change her mind.

'Don't run,' Wendy called out into the night as she watched Daisy go. The girl's hair flew like a kite behind her as she ran around the corner and out of sight.

The street was well lit. Wendy stepped back inside and closed the door. The house felt warm after the bitter cold wind that rushed up the street. She shivered as she pulled the lounge curtains closed and went upstairs to do the same in the bedrooms to shut out the night.

She started to prepare tea, humming softly. Trevor would be home soon. He was working a day shift at the fire station, so she planned to bathe Daisy and get her tucked up in bed by half-seven. It had been a busy and exciting day and Wendy was looking forward to a quiet evening with Trevor, curled up in front of the telly with a glass of red wine. Coronation Street was on twice tonight.

Grandma Irene lived on her own; she was seventy but Daisy made her feel so much younger. Her husband had been dead for ten years, and all of the community activities she'd joined in didn't begin to fill the hole dear Syd had left in her life. As Daisy had grown, she'd gained a friend, a little girl who lit up her days and talked her to distraction. She idolised her granddaughter.

A rap came at her door and although she didn't normally open it after dark the tiny voice shouting excitedly through the letter box was unmistakably Daisy's.

4

'Grandma. Open up, it's me.'

Grinning, Irene lifted the latch and pulled off the chain, and the little girl fell in, stumbling over the threshold in her haste.

'Be careful, sweetheart' she said as she grabbed her arm.

'Look, Grandma, I'm a real bridesmaid now.' Daisy squealed with delight as she threw off her coat, stretched out her arms, and proudly spun around to show off the dress in all its glory.

'Oh, Princess' Irene exclaimed, clapping her hands with joy. 'You look beautiful.'

'I can't stay though; Mummy said I had to get straight back. We've got to keep my dress under a plastic cover to keep it clean.' she said.

Irene smiled. 'Thank you for coming to show me, darling. Here, shall I see what I've got in my cupboard for you?' she asked, opening the door of her dresser.

'Thanks, Grandma,' Daisy said as she struggled back into her coat. She took the sweets eagerly in her hand and gave Grandma Irene a fleeting hug.

'Bye bye, sweetheart, see you tomorrow after school,' Irene said, kissing her on the cheek.

Daisy stopped and waved to her grandma, who watched from her doorstep as the little girl turned the corner into Rochester Road. *Bless her,* thought Irene as she closed the door and locked out the cold. *She's such a good little girl.*

Daisy was almost home when a ferocious blow from behind shattered her skull. She never touched the ground. Her falling body was caught, scooped up, and thrown through the side door of a van. She was gone. Her tiny footsteps and quiet singing voice were no more. Warm, dark-red blood oozed from the head-wound, prevented from splashing to the floor only by the spread of her bridesmaid dress. The vehicle was quietly and swiftly driven away, its prey on board. There was no one in sight, nothing to bear witness to the fact that such a brutal, evil attack on a child had just taken place.

Wendy was getting cross. Daisy had been gone for at least twenty minutes. *Where the hell is she? She'd better not have got chocolate on that dress,* she fumed. Wendy knew her mum was a beggar for treating the little girl. As her anxiety began to mount, she looked out of the window. She stood at the door, but there was no sign of Daisy.

'Have you got an excited little bridesmaid with you?' Wendy said, trying to disguise her irritation over the phone. Irene hated it when Wendy got cross with Daisy. *She's just a little girl* she would say, and *you were just the same with your Nana when you were young.*

Her mother broke her reverie.

'Our Daisy? She left here ages ago. I watched her. She didn't stop a minute. Said you'd told her not to be too long.'

Wendy felt as if someone had just thumped her in the stomach. She dropped the phone and ran frantically to the door. The street was empty but for a few parked cars. The eerie silence in the street was suffocating. Her steps pounded the pavement as she ran down to the corner of Rochester Road.

'Daisy, Daisy, Daisy.' she called. Her voice got louder and louder until her screaming echoed for streets around.

'Oh my god, oh my god, where is she?' she whispered, warm breath visible in the air as she continued running. Her heart beat quickly within her chest, sinking against her stomach, making her feel sick. She hammered at Irene's door, frantically shouting for it to be opened. She flew past her stunned mother. Wendy ran into every room calling Daisy's name. There was no time to talk. Irene was left shaking in Wendy's wake as she screamed out for her daughter and ran back towards her own home. Launching herself through her front door, Wendy snatched the telephone off the hallway floor. Breathless, her heart pounding, she dialled 999 with a shaking hand. Impatient, she tapped her foot and closed her eyes, willing them to answer.

'My daughter's gone … please help me.' Tears streamed down Wendy's face. Her body shook. She slid down the wall and sank to the floor with the telephone grasped tightly in her hand. She sobbed, her body doubled in agony. The only explanation she could think of was that someone had taken

Daisy. Spluttering out her name and address, she gasped, sure she was about to faint, trying to listen, digest and answer the questions the operator asked. Over and over she begged them to be quick before being told the police were on their way. Hearing the dialling tone, she rang Trevor's mobile, although she was sure he wouldn't answer. She looked at the clock. He'd be on his way home. He picked up.

'I know I'm ....' He was stopped suddenly as Wendy's frantic voice spewed down the phone.

'Trevor, Trevor, oh my god, please come quickly. Daisy's gone. Oh god, Trevor help.' She didn't hear his response but knew he had heard her. She didn't ring off, the phone fell out of her hand and she sobbed heart-wrenching sobs.

Blue lights appeared outside their home, illuminating the lounge. Trevor's car screeched to a halt.

'Wendy,' he cried as he ran in. The door was ajar and he could hear her hysterical weeping.

'Trevor, somebody's got her ... somebody's taken her.' She sank into Trevor's shoulder as he bent down to his wife. He picked up the phone, put it on its cradle and gently helped his wife to her feet. She cried into his chest, her hands clawing the front of his jumper as he held her.

'Tell me what's happened,' he said gently, brushing her hair from her tear-stained face.

'She wanted to show Mum her dress.' The image of her daughter in her bridesmaid dress was imprinted in her mind. 'She hasn't come home. I've looked for her ... everywhere.' Trevor caught his wife as her legs buckled beneath her.

'Come on, sit down,' Trevor said leading her to the settee where she collapsed, head in her hands. Trevor sat beside her, holding her tight and rubbing her back.

'This can't be happening. She can't just 'ave vanished.'

Somehow Wendy managed to find the words to blurt out to the police what had happened. Repeating it over and over again.

'What can I do?' Trevor begged the officers. 'Some bastard's got her. She can't be far away.'

7

The evening sky changed colour with the arrival of each additional police car's lights. The search between Daisy's home and her Grandma's was chaotic. Every house in the street was lit. People banged on their neighbours' doors and shouted through their letter boxes to ask for help to find Daisy. Rochester Road had houses to one side only. On the other side was a slope topped with a ten-foot wall, and beyond was a railway line. There was no way she could have got over that, although people crawled with torches up the embankment. Cries for Daisy rang out in the darkness.

A young PC brought a distraught Irene up to Wendy and Trevor's house so that they could comfort each other. As far as anyone knew, Daisy had vanished into thin air. Every minute that passed caused the family more anxiety, more concern, more panic. Their eyes clung to the hands on the clock. When would it end?

'She's a good girl. She would never run away. She was so happy. I gave her sweets and watched her turn the corner from my door. She was skipping. It's so, so cold,' Irene panicked. The police officer tried to reassure her as Irene twisted her hands together in worry. All of a sudden she clasped her chest and grimaced in pain as she struggled to breathe, rubbing her arm furiously. Her face turned grey, clammy to the touch, and the quick-thinking officer who sat at her side didn't hesitate to ring for an ambulance. Wendy rushed to her mother's side and cradled her in her arms.

'Trevor, get Mum some water, could you?' she asked anxiously. The paramedics were quick with the tests, and before anyone knew what was happening Irene's face was covered with an oxygen mask and she was being carried on a stretcher into the waiting ambulance. Wendy grasped her mother's hand tightly for a second as she was taken past. The doors were closed. Sirens amongst the flashing blue lights ensured a clear path was made for the ambulance to get through the crowds that were gathering.

'I should go with her,' Wendy wailed as she watched her mother being taken away. 'Where's my baby?' she sobbed at the police officers. 'I want my mum.'

Chapter Two

He pulled up his collar and fastened the buttons on his black leather coat as he stepped out into a cool evening in the village of Tandem Bridge. The rain had stopped but the streetlight's reflection in the surface water glimmered. It had only been a few days since bonfire weekend. The aroma of burning wood and spent fireworks still filled the air. Jack Dylan took a few paces towards the kerb. There was a light tap on his left shoulder. Instinctively he turned. A sudden, almighty blow to his face sent him reeling into darkness.

The bittersweet taste of blood filled his mouth, tears sprang to his eyes, and the excruciating pain made him stumble to his knees. Stunned and semi-conscious, he shook his head in an attempt to clear it. Blood sprayed in what seemed like slow-motion across the front of his coat and the paving slabs. He could hear shouting as he attempted to pull his broad frame upright. His vision and senses slowly returned and the pavement felt cold and wet to his touch. Reaching up to his aching face, blood covered his hands. Through watery eyes he saw the outline of a man being grappled to the street by two uniformed officers. He blacked out.

Dylan woke in hospital, stretched out on a bed covered by a blanket. A muslin cloth covered the lower part of his face. He tried to comprehend what had happened. The attack was vivid yet over in a flash. If his attacker hadn't been stopped, Dylan might not have survived. Who the fuck had done it and why? God, his mouth hurt. *What the hell do I look like?* he wondered, groaning as he reached up to touch his face.

'We'll give you something for the pain, love. I'm afraid you're going to need a few stitches, though,' the nurse said, placing a sympathetic hand on his arm as she adjusted the cloth to cover his eyes. He was in no rush; it was comforting to be still for a while. The quietness around him and the cloth over his face lulled his eyes shut. The darkness made him sleepy and he let his mind drift. It reminded him of being a child when he'd hidden under the stairs with his mum, brothers, and sisters. They'd covered their heads with the coats that hung there to shut out the flashes of lightning and muffle the sound of thunder, or they'd hid there from the rent man who'd banged on the door for the overdue rent on the estate, which he did regularly.

Dylan was a stocky man who commanded presence by his stature, hard on the exterior and relentless in pursuit of right, but underneath he was a kind-hearted person who longed for a home life. His nickname in his younger years as a police officer had been 'Basher'. In those days he always seemed to be fighting. At the age of thirty-five and with fifteen years of service he'd had a few close calls locking up criminals, but this twat had totally surprised him. Thirteen years as a detective and now a Detective Inspector, he was annoyed he'd been caught out. He recalled his first night on the beat and that damned uniform. Razor sharp creases, a helmet that rubbed his forehead. Detachable starched collars; none of that stretch fabric of today. Studs held them on and had pressed into the nape of his neck, painful and annoying, but he was so proud of wearing that uniform. His parents would have been, too, if they'd been alive.

Dylan's first shift started at 22.00 hours. He was walking alone, new boots gleaming, identifying him as a rookie even if nothing else did. Harrowfield town's main street bustled with life on a night; overspills from the pubs, laughing and shouting filling the air spasmodically. He remembered he'd been told to try to walk with the authority that the uniform gave him, shoulders back. He'd checked to see how he looked in the shop windows as he passed. His reflection looked grand.

The two parts of the Pye radio were kept in his breast pockets. The left hand held the receiver to the ear while the right hand used the transmitter. Fortunate if both worked and a sitting duck if anyone tried to attack him as both hands were occupied. He tried to remember everything he'd been taught back in training school, but what would he do if anything happened, he'd wondered? His nervous mind had mixed up all the rules and regulations, trying to put them in some kind of order.

Twenty minutes on the beat and thirty yards ahead there seemed to be an unusually large gathering of people. A few more steps and he could see they were giving a wide berth to a man screaming abuse, his voice blanketing all others. Obviously no one wanted to be near him.

'Fucking bastard. Fucking come on,' he growled. He had the appearance of a minotaur and was the very last person on earth you'd want to pick a fight with. A giant of a man snorting like a wounded animal. *Who's rattled his cage?* Dylan wondered. *They obviously weren't too bright.* As Dylan got nearer, it became clear that it was his police uniform that was acting like a red rag to this bull. He was shouting at him. The minotaur thundered towards him. Dylan shouted for assistance over the radio while that giant of a man launched himself at him like a bull at a gate. Dylan was suddenly beneath him, fighting for survival. Fortunately for him help had been just around the corner that time too.

He was jolted back from his reminiscences by a sharp pain in his lip, which made him wince. A soft hand reached into his and another rested on his arm. The nurse, he thought.

'Sorry, it'll hurt but I can assure you it's necessary,' said a man's deep voice. It hurt all right and not just a bit. Dylan's eyes watered like hell. Ten minutes later the doctor had finished and the cloth was removed from his face.

'You're very lucky there's no permanent damage. No kissing for a while though,' he said, writing up his notes. 'The stitches will dissolve in about a week.' The doctor was very matter-of-fact, head down as he concentrated on Dylan's file. The nurse helped Dylan sit upright, and he swung his legs to the side. He didn't feel very lucky. As he walked from the cubicle, waiting for his painkillers to be prescribed, he saw his reflection in the window opposite. *Mick Jagger with tassels on,* he thought. He tried to smile. It hurt.

He was climbing into his car, looking forward to Jen's warm bed, when his mobile rang.

'Boss? Dawn. Looks like we've a nine-year-old girl gone missing. Snatched off the street tonight. I'm at Harrowfield nick.'

Before she could say any more, he'd interrupted. 'Be with you in ten minutes.' He rang to let Jen know he'd be late.

Nothing new there. He'd been called out to robberies, suicides and four murders in the last two months. She was on the phone so he left her a message. *Only me, gonna be late. Nine-year-old girl missing. Be in touch when I know more – love you.* He knew she wouldn't be pleased, but there wasn't a lot he could do about it.

'Evening, boss. Bloody hell,' Dawn said as she got close enough to see his lip. 'You overdosed on the Botox? Or been kissing wasps again?'

Not many people would have spoken to Dylan like that but Dawn knew him and his sense of humour well. He grimaced.

'Bet you gave as good as you got.'

'No, actually I was decked, went straight down, and didn't know who or what had hit me. Luckily some officers were nearby,' he managed to mumble.

Dawn was a good Detective Sergeant; Dylan knew that it would be a runner if she'd called him out. She reminded him of Dawn French, a larger-than-life fleshy woman, robust, and with a great sense of humour.

'Hope they didn't bail him,' Dawn said sarcastically.

'No way.' He shook his head. She gave him the update on the child. They briefed the uniformed and specialised officers who'd make initial enquiries. It was short and to the point. He needed them out there to find Daisy. He ordered the search of houses in the area, including attics and cellars. If the owners consented it would be easier, but he told the officers from the search team to let him know if anyone refused.

'We have to be a hundred per cent sure she's not being kept against her will,' he told the uniform task force of thirty officers. Dylan wanted more. 'Get me information that we have on people in the area. The creeps, the sex offenders,' he commanded Dawn. 'Team leaders, debrief at midnight. Let's bloody find her,' he said, raising his voice as officers left to saturate the area of Rochester Road.

Dylan called the Press Office. He desperately needed a press release to be put on the Press Office news line for the attention of all media: *Police are searching for a missing nine-year-old girl, who was last seen in Rochester Way at 6.15 this evening.*

As he got to grips with the teams, Dawn, apart from making coffee, had been scanning the log of events so far. They were both ready to attend the scene.

'I'm glad it's you, Dawn, this isn't sounding good.'

'No. Do you get the feeling it's an opportunist or someone watching?'

'Could be either. Let's go and see what weird and wonderful people live around Rochester Road.'

They both looked over the short distance that Daisy had walked, a route she should have been safe taking. There were teams of officers checking, searching, and rummaging through houses, cars, and sheds. Anywhere, in fact, where a nine-year-old girl might be. Torch lights flashed everywhere. The search by the officers was organised and as thorough as it could be. Members of the public were offering help and it was gratefully accepted. What Dylan didn't want was frenzy, hectic panic. A lone shout of *Daisy* rang out in the night, which in turn started an echo as other people shouted the little girl's name. The packet of pastilles given to Daisy by her grandma was found on the pavement 150 yards from her own front door. The area around the sweets was taped off for 30 square feet.

'That's where she was grabbed,' Dylan muttered to Dawn as he pointed to the pavement.

Dylan and Dawn arrived to sit with Daisy's parents, to go over once again what had happened. Trevor held Wendy as she wept. His eyes swam with tears that he brushed away as they fell to his cheeks. They sat huddled on the settee, trembling. Dylan was unsure whether it was with fear, shock, or a chill from the open door. The officers searched their home, a necessary, intrusive routine, but very upsetting for the Hinds. Wendy showed Dylan and Dawn the most recent picture of her daughter.

'She looks so small, doesn't she? Just like a Victorian doll. Pale skin, red curls,' she said stroking the picture. 'She was so, so excited, it's her first time, you see, being a bridesmaid.' Wendy sobbed, staring directly at them, her breathing erratic. She took a big gasp. 'Where is she?' she pleaded. 'She isn't stupid. She wouldn't wander off. Why, oh why did I let her go?' she wailed. 'I watched her go down the road. Mum watched her come back. She's just literally vanished into thin air. Oh, where's my baby? Please find my baby,' she begged as she rocked. Trevor sat perfectly still, speechless, his head in his hands. Suddenly Wendy jumped, startled, as she remembered. 'Mum? Oh, my god, I've forgotten Mum. Is she okay?'

Dawn contacted the hospital and was told Irene had suffered a mild heart attack but seemed to be doing well. She was responding to treatment and was comfortable.

'Thank you, god. Oh, poor Mum.' Wendy looked to the ceiling for some divine intervention as if trying to make sense of it all. A short while before they'd been a normal family, taking great pride in their daughter as she tried on her bridesmaid dress, and looking forward to a family wedding. Their lives had gone from sheer happiness to total hell.

'Where's my baby, my little girl? Please, please find her, she needs me,' Wendy repeated over and over again, swaying to and fro as Trevor tried to comfort her.

Dylan and Dawn were draped in the sadness that consumed the room. The couple's hurt was almost tangible. Both spoke to the Family Liaison Officer (FLO) when she arrived and then introduced her to Daisy's parents. Janice Henderson, salt of the earth, people said. Dylan knew she was an experienced officer. She needed to be for this one. Although there were supposed to be two FLOs on child abductions, the request that Dylan had made to Force Control had been turned down because there was no one available to take on the role. He'd tutted in disbelief. What was the police force coming to?

'That was bloody awful,' Dawn said as they left Janice with the Hinds and walked out onto the street.

'Horrendous. It's not looking good is it?' Dylan said shaking his head. His eyes were downcast, his hands in his coat pockets as they strode out into the freezing night air. 'Some bastard took a big risk and got away with it. She could be anywhere. We'll have to be sure she isn't still round here first. I want every corner of this area searched before we move on.'

In each house searched, the officers would have to look into every possible place a young girl could hide or be hidden. This would include suitcases, cupboards, drawers, and boxes. There were thirty-five houses to search in the immediate area, Dylan was told. Nothing would be left to chance. As well as the searches, direct enquiries were being carried out of the registered sex offenders living in and around Tandem Bridge. There were sixteen. Each and every one would be subjected to interrogation and their flats, houses, or wherever they lived would be searched. This would hopefully be by consent, but if not, then there would be a warrant requested. Nothing would stand in the way of this little girl being found. Daisy's friends would be contacted to see if she'd spoken to them. It was a priority line of enquiry for Dylan. Daisy went to Tandem Bridge Middle School, as did the majority of children in the area.

It was now the early hours of the morning. Wendy and Trevor looked pale, numb with shock, their faces etched in pain. They kept asking if they could do something, anything, to help. All they knew was that their little girl, their only child, was gone. A few hours before excitement had filled the very room they were in. Trying on that bridesmaid dress was a long-awaited dream come true for Daisy.

'Where is she? I need to know where she is. Daisy has never been out at this time of night before. She'll be so frightened. She'll need me.' It was going to be a very long, painful night for them, and they wouldn't sleep, they couldn't. The search team would continue through the night. There was now a large police presence in the area, which would remain sealed. Although Dylan and Dawn were now going home for a few hours, they would be back at first light, when the briefing of more officers would take place. Daisy needed to be found, and quickly.

Dylan didn't even remember the drive to Jen's house. Unlocking the door as quietly as he could, he found Jen's golden retriever, Max, was waiting in the hallway. Dylan mumbled a hello to him through his swollen lips and Max's tail swished the walls. The dog was always pleased to see him. *Sanctuary,* thought Dylan, as he slipped into bed next to Jen's warm body. She stirred.

'I'm knackered. Love you, Miss Jones,' he said sleepily as he rested his head on the pillow next to Jen as gently as he could so as not to wake her. He drifted into a deep sleep, waking intermittently either due to the pain from his lip or thoughts of Daisy and whatever evil bastard had taken her.

Chapter Three

At 6.20 a.m., just over twelve hours after Daisy had been reported missing, the police received a 999 call from a distressed lady who had been walking her dog on wasteland near to Dean Reservoir, approximately seven miles from Daisy's home.

'Please help. I've just seen what looks like a child's body. I'm sorry I can't go any nearer, could you send someone please? Quickly.'

A police car arrived at the location within six minutes. There was a biting wind. Mrs Day stood on the open moorland, bewildered, pale and shaken, with her mobile phone still in her hand. She was a smart lady of about forty years, dressed for the weather in boots, jeans, and an anorak. Nearby was her red Mini Cooper. Inside the car was her liver and white Springer spaniel.

'I had to put Belle in the car. She wouldn't stop barking, that's why I walked towards … it,' she told the officers. 'But …I … couldn't. I'm sorry. It made me feel sick.' She held her hand to her throat, a hankie grasped firmly in her hand. She was visibly shaking. The older officer placed an arm around her shoulders.

'Mrs Day, you've done really well just ringing in. Are you sure you're okay? Do you need a doctor?'

'No, no thank you, love. It's, it's just such a shock, you know?' She shivered.

The officer guided her to her vehicle where he sat her in the driver's side, then he retreated to the passenger seat. Speaking to her gently he took notes in his pocket book as he asked her where she had walked and where she had seen what she thought was a body.

She pointed. 'Just over there. If you walk straight forward you'll see it for yourself.'

The younger officer followed the route Mrs Day indicated. Some twenty-five yards ahead, away from the road, he saw it.

The body was face down and had a blue plastic bag secured over its head. He immediately contacted the control room and then checked the body for a pulse. There were no signs of life. Using his radio he requested the attendance of paramedics on the off chance anything could be done, but deep down he knew it was futile. They could at least make the pronouncement of life extinct. He called for the attendance of senior CID and uniform supervision. Using blue and white crime scene tape, he started to create a line from the roadway to the body, indicating the pathway Mrs Day had taken. He wrapped the tape around trees to begin sealing off the area, preserving it for a later search.

The officers would record what they had done and why: they had no doubt it was a murder. CID arrived and a detective swapped places with the uniform officer to sit with Mrs Day. He told her that an ambulance was en route.

'I'd only been parked about two or three minutes when Belle started barking continually at one spot, which is so out of character for her. I looked to the place where she was yapping, saw it, and dialled 999,' Mrs Day told him.

Seated in the security and quietness of Mrs Day's car, the two watched the paramedics arrive. They saw the negative nods of their heads and they watched as the paramedics retreated from the scene.

'Are you sure you're okay to drive?' asked the detective. 'We'll visit you later at home to take a statement if that's okay with you.'

'Oh, I'll be fine. Thank you. You've enough to do here. I'll see you later,' Mrs Day said.

Dylan's mobile and pager awoke him as they danced a duet on his bedside table. His face ached. As he yawned his lips cracked and flaked like old paint on dead wood. He picked up his phone. A bright, sharp, wide-awake voice on the other end spoke.

'Detective Sergeant Dawn Farren asked me to contact you, sir. I'll ring you back in a few minutes to give you chance to come round, shall I?' Before he could speak, the caller hung up. Jen had gone into autopilot, so accustomed to the routine when he got called out and their sleep was disturbed. He smiled inwardly as he got a glimpse of her naked body before she covered it with her dressing gown. She turned as she switched on the big light, looked at him, froze, and then said, 'Oh my god, Jack, what's happened?' She burst into tears as she rushed to his side of the bed. 'Just tell me that one day you'll walk away from it all,' she begged, holding him so tight her knuckles were white.

'Don't worry, love, nothing will ever come between us. Definitely not the job. I love you, Miss Jones,' he slurred, trying to stretch his mouth open as he reassuringly stroked her hair.

Jennifer Jones worked at Harrowfield HQ in the admin department, which is where their eyes had first met. Their hands had accidentally touched putting the post in their pigeonholes. Passing the coffee cups had brought about electricity that he couldn't ignore. He was like a lovesick teenager and he knew it when he began changing his routine just to catch a glimpse of her. He'd asked about her discreetly, but no one seemed to know much about Miss Jones other than that she lived alone. What he did know was that she was a stunner, and he wanted to know more. No one had guessed about the relationship so far, which was a miracle in the police force, but that's the way he liked it. *Let's face it,* Dylan thought, *my life is sweet F.A. to do with anyone else.* Dylan told Jen he wanted to protect her. To be honest he didn't know if that was his real reason, but he did know that he stood on a lot of toes in both the criminal world and at the police station, and he didn't want her to bear the brunt of any backlash he may have coming to him. There'd been a few close calls, but for now their secret was safe. His thoughts were interrupted by the shrill of the phone.

'Don't think you're going anywhere without telling me what's happened,' she said, waving a finger at him now the initial shock was over. Jen moved swiftly. As he watched, his suit, shirt and tie come out of the wardrobe in double quick time. Reaching for the pen and paper he always kept by the bed for occasions such as these, he caught sight of the digital clock. It was 06.50 a.m. He yawned and licked his swollen lips before speaking, but a sharp pain with a burning sensation caused him to gasp.

'Hello, boss. Body found at Dean Reservoir a short time ago.' Dylan listened and took notes. 'DS Farren wants you to meet her at Harrowfield nick.'

Jen placed a steaming cup quietly beside him on the bedside table and planted a kiss on the top of his head. He took a sip of the coffee. 'Shit,' he squealed as the cup stuck to his lip.

'Pardon sir?'

'Yeah, tell her I'll be there ASAP.'

He dressed quickly. Dylan had basically moved in with Jen although he'd kept his flat on at HQ Training Centre for appearances' sake.

'Don't worry, love, the idiot who did it is locked up,' he said as he picked up his briefcase. 'I'll ring you when I know what's happening.' With that he gave her a hug as he flew out of the door. She watched the lights on his car as he reversed out of the driveway. She sighed. It depressed her to see what the job did to him. No sleep, a busted lip and not knowing what horrendous sight was awaiting him: that was just for starters today.

Dylan and Dawn travelled in his car to Dean Reservoir. He travelled the road often, as did his fellow workers, because it was a short cut between Harrowfield nick and Tandem Bridge Station. The blustery winds made it feel cold and the clouds were grey and heavy, threatening rain. However Dylan was pleased that the traffic was surprisingly light.

'Can we have the helicopter up, to attend the scene for an eye in the sky view and aerial photographs, please?' Dawn asked the officer in the control room via the radio. 'A body tent and windbreaks would be good too. They'll need to be the sturdy ones. The wind's really picking up here.'

'I'll contact operational support and get back to you,' came the crackling reply.

'Fell walking isn't my speciality, boss, and no way am I going to get my new boots covered in sheep shit,' said Dawn looking down at them, horrified at the prospect.

'You girl. I've got my wellies in the boot, but you're not having them.'

'You'll just have to carry me, then, won't you?' she said cheekily.

'Impossible,' he remarked, laughing, which made his lips stretch tight and sting. 'Ow,' he said.

'Serves you right.'

Dawn was married and had met her husband Ralph while they were still at school. She'd been a waitress and he'd been a trainee chef. Her Achilles' heel was food, which she never apologised for. 'You are what you eat,' she would often say, 'And boy, do I eat.' Ralph was now the head chef and owner of a restaurant they'd named '*Mawingo'*, Swahili for 'up in the clouds', after a place they had visited on their honeymoon. It had far-reaching views across the Yorkshire countryside, and a fantastic reputation. She assured Ralph she didn't love him for his culinary specialities, but it was a hell of a bonus.

Access to Dean Reservoir was difficult. Salters Road was a narrow, single track tarmac road with few passing places. It was littered with potholes and corroded edges, definitely not a road on which you could travel at speed.

'I'm glad it's your bloody car we came in,' said Dawn as they bumped along the uneven surface. The road was on a slow incline to such a height that you could see over the historic village that lay below in the valley. They travelled up the hill and the road opened up to a huge expanse with long distance views of moorland. It was nice in summer, but in winter it was bleak, barren and uninviting. The hills in the distance were dark silhouettes touching the sky. The clouds rested on the ground and the trees beyond appeared to float as if suspended in the sky. It was an awesome sight. If it had been painted it would have looked unrealistic on canvas. To the left of the road was a coppice of trees; some evergreen, some bare, which shielded the reservoir ahead. The trees were bending as though exercising in the strong wind. There were no homesteads nearby. It was a lonely scene. As they travelled the desolate road a few sheep wandered around near to the walls. They could be seen huddled together in the distance, desperately trying to shelter from the elements, the only visible sign of life around. Dylan had ensured the road was closed off to all traffic where the outer cordon started. It would ensure that the Press with their marvellous zoom lenses could not get close enough to take photographs of the body. He knew once they heard about it they would be there like a shot.

'Do you think it's Daisy?' Dawn asked.

Chapter Four

The wind roared across the moor, flattening the long grass and teasing the trees in its path. They stopped in the gravelled car park alongside the marked police vehicles. Dylan's car door was almost ripped off its hinges as he opened it onto the rough open terrain. There were deep dark holes filled with bits of twig and clumps of heather underfoot. The crime scene tape flapped about like the tails of a kite in the wind. The weather could at any moment turn perishing, Dylan knew only too well. Outdoor clothing was a must. He was immediately impressed with how the first two uniformed officers at the scene had acted on their own initiative and made a mental note to send a report to their supervision to praise them. *Future CID material,* he thought to himself as he began clambering into his protective suit. Leaves curled and twisted, sweeping the ground around him.

'Bloody hell,' he shouted over the wind as he fought to keep the suit in a position that meant he could get his leg in. The SOCO van pulled up beside him and, more by good luck than management, Jasmine was on call. Jasmine could have only been a size eight, but her ability made up for her lack of muscle.

The two detectives who'd attended the scene were DC John Benjamin and DC Vicky Hardacre. Dylan was pleased to see them; John was an athletic young black lad who was a gentleman and a bloody good detective in Dylan's eyes. Vicky was a young girl, single, tall, blonde, quite attractive, always upbeat. She was outgoing, loud and brazen, but in Dylan's experience she had a heart of gold. While he allowed Jasmine to get on with the photographs and digital filming, Dylan and the others sheltered as best they could from the icy wind at the side of the police van.

'How the hell are you, boss?' Vicky shouted to be heard over the noise of the blustery weather.

'Good, Vicky, and you?'

Dylan's phone rang. His hand was so cold he fumbled when trying to get it out of his pocket and missed the call.

'Bloody mobiles,' he grunted. It rang again. He opened the van door and stepped inside. Hearing anything in the howling wind was impossible.

'Judith Cockcroft's the on-call pathologist and she can't get to the scene for another three hours, so she'll see us at the mortuary at eleven,' he said climbing out a few moments later. Dylan was anxious to see if the body had red hair and needed to know if it was a girl, but he couldn't see anything from where he stood. They were all sadly confident that it was going to be Daisy as they got the nod from Jasmine and started towards the body.

'Hell. Watch out where you tread, the ground's uneven,' Dylan warned as he stumbled. His ears burned with the cold so he pulled the hood of his paper suit up in an attempt to keep warm, then took a pair of gloves out of his pocket and shuffled from one foot to the other, rubbing his arms as he stood looking down at the body. It was white, marble-like against the matt background of brown, coarse moorland grass. He knew they were lucky to find her so soon. Dylan looked up as he felt a few heavy spots of rain on his face. The wind continued to whip him and he turned his back to it.

The torso looked doll-like in the vast expanse. A mark on the child's buttock stained her skin. The clumps of heather had guarded her from the elements, so incredibly she hadn't deteriorated rapidly. Dylan no longer noticed the weather as a waft of lavender passed under his nose. His senses were heightened. Everyone was still, their focus on the little girl, oblivious for a while to anything or anyone around them as they took the sight in. Dylan asked Jasmine to move the body slightly. Now they could see the two marks, one visible on each buttock. They were dark and appeared to be cigarette burns. Jasmine photographed them independently, close up. The little girl's legs were parted. She looked like a mannequin, rigid and inflexible. Seeing an adult's dead body was always a shock to the system, but seeing a child's dead body was worse, Dylan reckoned. It drew you to it with a quiet sadness. A life not lived. They were the worst you could be called to, the injuries sometimes so horrific, so unbelievable, and so appalling on someone so innocent.

Moving his eyes slowly up the body, Dylan could see only her left hand; her right one was beneath her.

'Bloody hell, the end of her little finger is missing,' said Dawn. It looked like a clean cut, a black bloodstained stub. The killer was obviously calm and calculated, but why take part of a finger? What was the significance?

The blue plastic carrier bag covered the whole of her head and neck to her shoulders but a few red hairs spilled in tendrils beneath it.

'Daisy?' Dawn said in a whisper.

'It's got to be, hasn't it?' said Dylan. 'We won't remove the bag here. We'll wait 'til we're in the mortuary.' They laid a clear, sterile plastic sheet next to the body and lifted her the few inches it took to get her off the ground. Very gently they rested her upon it, not attempting to turn her again. It was folded over, each end sealed and taped. She was ready to be moved from where she had been dumped like rubbish.

The rain was coming down with a vengeance now and lashed across the landscape; it was icy and beat the group relentlessly. Quite fitting. The weather was as angry and resolute as the team for such a waste of life. A tent was being erected over the area where she'd been found, to protect it from the elements and to try and keep as much of the scene preserved as possible.

'I'm satisfied this is just a dump site. It's not the primary murder scene. We'll need soil samples,' Dylan said, talking to the team as well as making a mental list for himself. 'The weather will undoubtedly do its damage, but any opportunity to examine some of the ground is better than none.'

The mortuary attendant arrived with the HM Coroner's black transit van to take the body back to the mortuary. The plastic sheet containing the little body was placed inside a body bag that the mortuary attendant brought over to the officers. It was similar to a large holdall with four handles. Single-handedly, John carried the light weight to the waiting vehicle. Daisy was now in safe hands. The rain continued to beat down as the doors closed, unforgiving, pelting the ground in anger. There was no sign of Daisy's coat, shoes or bridesmaid dress.

Dawn stopped for a moment and brought out a multi-coloured embroidered handkerchief from beneath the blue latex glove that covered her hand. She was left-handed and dabbed her mouth with the hankie, an action that was similar to that of using blotting paper. Dylan had seen a vast number of beautiful hankies used by Dawn over the years. He knew she was hungry because she dribbled. She had once confided in him after a few glasses of red wine that she'd no control over it. It was only slight, almost unnoticeable, but she thought she looked like a salivating dog.

Fortunately coffee and sandwiches arrived. A warm drink was welcome. They took off their protective suits, put them into evidence bags and got into their vehicles. The windows steamed up as the engines ran, heaters on full. Dylan sipped his drink, warming his hands. He stuffed his stocking feet under the blast of the warm air from the heater until his toes tingled as the feeling came back in them. *Caffeine at last.* The swelling and numbness of his mouth caused coffee to run down his chin.

'Want a hankie, boss?' Dawn smiled as she bit into a teacake. He declined, shaking his head.

'You bring me to some weird and wonderful places,' she said, shivering so much her teeth chattered. 'Why do you think the killer used the plastic bag over the head and cut off Daisy's fingertip? What's all that about?' she asked him as she took sips from her steaming plastic cup.

'We'll find out when we get him, Dawn, and we will get him.'

'We will,' she echoed.

Dylan handed her his drained cup, wiped the inside of the windscreen with his gloved hand, put the car into first gear and slowly crept forward to the uniform car, raising his hand in thanks to its occupants. The uniformed officers would stay and keep a watchful eye on the scene while they followed the body to the mortuary for continuity.

'I wouldn't want to be here even if I was dead,' Dylan said as they arrived. No matter how many times he went to the morgue it never got any easier.

Chapter Five

He texted Jen from the sanctuary of the car park to tell her he'd be home late. *I'll be waiting* came her reply and he smiled to himself.

'What you got to smile about?' said Dawn.

He tapped his nose. 'You're not in the need to know,' he said, concentrating on dialling the superintendent. She pulled a face and continued to make up her pocket book.

'The Super says good luck, and we've to keep him updated,' Dylan remarked sarcastically as he hung up. 'For all the blasted good that does.'

Mortuaries never seemed to be modernised in Dylan's experience, definitely nothing like the ones he saw on TV. Harrowfield mortuary was an old ivy-laced, detached building in the hospital grounds. The interior was even less inviting. It felt grubby. Jen had once asked him to describe the smell, but he couldn't find the words. The odour seemed to be rejected by his body as if he shouldn't inhale it. However today it hit him the minute he entered. He could taste warm metal and smell rotting flesh, old garbage, and an abattoir on a balmy day. He reached in his coat pocket for his extra strong mints and popped one into his mouth. Dylan had learned never to go to the mortuary without them. He walked down the corridor past the curtained window of the viewing room. The room where families got one more opportunity to see their loved ones, albeit laid out on a trolley. It was glossed up as formal identification, but in reality it resulted in the outpouring of emotion, the chance to say goodbye. Ironic that in something as terminal as death people still needed closure. Dylan walked across the vestibule to the upstairs office. He'd spent hours at this place over the years, too many, he reckoned. He took a deep breath, as once again he knew he'd have to put on his professional mask of the man in charge for the others. The young rookies in attendance didn't need to see his repugnance. He had to look after them, reassure them, consoling them that at least they got to walk out, not many people did. Dylan knew that downstairs at the rear of the building was the old marble examination table with its fluorescent light hanging above it like the light above a snooker table. In the adjacent room there were fridges three tiers high, where the bodies were kept.

Les, the mortuary assistant, was in the office already, dressed in his coverall, wellingtons and plastic green apron.

'I might have known it'd be you disturbing us, Dylan,' he said as he switched the kettle on. 'You're like the grim reaper these days.'

Dylan laughed. 'You'll never be out of work while I'm working, Les. I don't seem to be able to go to bed these days without someone calling me out to a body.'

Judith Cockroft, the pathologist, appeared as the clock struck eleven.

'Glad to see it's not only me that's run ragged, Dylan.' she said. Then, on seeing his facial injuries she added, 'You can tell me how you got that as we progress.'

'I wish I got paid as much as you though, for my pain.'

She smiled broadly at him as she took off her coat, hung up her bag and started to put on her green suit and apron, washing her hands, and tying her gown as she talked. 'So, what 'ave you got for me today?'

Dylan outlined the circumstances of Daisy's disappearance and then moved onto the body of the small girl. He told her about the position of the body, the bag over her head and the missing fingertip.

'Daisy had long red hair. It can be seen beneath the carrier bag and we don't have another missing girl in the area,' he said.

'Seems highly likely then.' She sighed deeply.

DC John Benjamin nodded to Judith, Les and Dawn as he entered the room with Vicky in tow.

Dylan placed his coffee on the floor at the side of his chair as he sat and took his policy book from his briefcase.

'The arrangements have been made for the scene to be protected,' John said, sitting down beside him. 'The underwater search team are ready to look in the reservoir for the clothing like you asked, sir.'

'Thanks for that, John,' Dylan said as he put his pen to paper.

Coffee consumed and suited up, they went down to the examination room to be met by the sight of the young girl's body on the table.

'It's Daisy,' said Dawn in a matter-of-fact way.

'You don't need to state the bloody obvious,' Dylan snapped. Seeing the youngster on the slab had turned his stomach, but watching Dawn's eyes fill with tears he was sorry for his outburst.

Jasmine busily took photographs, Vicky collated exhibits that were handed to her by Judith, and John assisted.

The officers watched and listened intently. The body was unwrapped and the plastic sheeting used to cover her was carefully peeled away. She'd been placed on the table face down, just as she had been found. Her fragile, tiny frame hardly filled a third of the slab. For some reason it felt chilly in the mortuary. Dylan shivered; it was cold and eerie. He recalled how Wendy had described Daisy's excitement and joy as she'd left home to visit her grandma.

The only voice was Judith's calm expressionless commentary. 'Not sexually assaulted,' she stated into her Dictaphone. 'No signs of any penetration,' she said as she took vaginal and rectal swabs. 'Two circular burn marks, one to each buttock, which look to me like a cigarette burn. Let's remove this awful carrier bag before we do anything else,' she said pulling the bag off the head and handing it to Vicky. As she did so a mass of red hair cascaded onto the slab. Dylan heard an intake of breath, but from whom he couldn't tell. At the rear of the head near the top there was a large indentation filled with blood. A closer look made possible by Judith moving the hair showed that her skull had been smashed.

'She's taken a fierce blow,' she remarked. Jasmine photographed as Judith measured the wound.

'Two inches in diameter.' She held her breath as she stretched to hold the ruler to the wound. Dylan considered what weapons could have caused the trauma while the little girl was turned over by Les and Judith. Daisy was easily recognisable now from her picture. Her eyes were wide open, staring, piercing, her red hair spread across her upper torso.

'What beautiful hair,' Judith remarked as she gathered it in gloved hands to cut samples. She looked closely at red marks visible where Daisy's eyebrows had once been.

'Fucking hell,' whispered Dawn.

'Someone has attempted to shave them off,' remarked Judith, looking up from the body to Dylan. There were no other obvious injuries to the body, but the usual samples of blood; nail clippings and scrapings were taken, tenderly. Her internal organs were checked and weighed. Dylan noticed that the mortuary had lost the smell that it had had when they entered and he wondered why. The emotion in the room was tangible as Judith closed Daisy's eyes. Her hair and body was washed and she looked peaceful. The little cherub was at rest, as if asleep. But this child would never wake. Dylan's emotion changed to anger. He badly wanted the bastard that could do this.

'Right, let's have a hot drink. I think we all need it,' said Judith.

Dylan knew her well enough to know that the sight of this little girl on the mortuary table had touched her.

Out of their protective clothing and back in the office, Professor Judith Cockroft completed her notes. As she sipped steaming black coffee, she remarked how unusual the case was. 'The blow to the head was a massive one and in my professional opinion would have caused death instantly.'

Thank god for small mercies, Dylan thought.

'A round, heavy object with a diameter of two inches was used. Daisy's left little fingertip has been severed cleanly and her eyebrows have been roughly shaved with a razor or perhaps a craft knife,' she continued. 'Two marks to her buttocks are indeed burn marks, probably caused by a cigarette after she died,' she concluded. Although Judith spoke to everyone in the room, her comments were addressed to Dylan. As Senior Investigating Officer, he would have assistance from a number of experts throughout the enquiry, but it was his personal responsibility to find the killer.

'I must go. I've got a meeting at the hospital in ten minutes,' Judith said as she rose from her chair. 'Let me know how you get on won't you?'

'Sure,' said Dylan. 'Thank you.'

She picked up her bag, threw her coat over her arm and bade the team goodbye; then, with a wave of her hand, she was gone.

'Okay everyone, we'll run this one from Harrowfield HQ. Number one: Dawn, rally up the staff that's on duty. Whoever we need, bring them in. Number two: arrange a briefing for two-fifteen this afternoon. I'll speak to the Press Office. Number three: conference at five. That'll give them the chance to get it out on the evening news. Right, see you back at the nick.'

The officers slid their chairs back on the tiled floor and prepared to leave. Dylan walked over to Les. 'Thanks for the hospitality once again, mate.'

'Hope I don't see you too soon,' Les smiled.

Dylan pressed a five pound note into his hand. 'For the tea fund.'

'No. No, it's all right.' Les pushed Dylan's hand away. 'Nobody else from your lot bothers. It's only a couple of cups of coffee.'

'I'm not bothered what they do. That coffee's a lifesaver and I don't want there to come a time when there's no caffeine available,' Dylan laughed.

John and Vicky were busily collating and discussing with Dawn the exhibits that were to be taken back to the station when Dylan returned to the group.

'Dawn, I know you're still on the Johnson murder, but I want you as deputy SIO on this one. Have you any problem with that?' he asked.

'No, none thanks. I want to nail the bastard as much as you,' she replied. 'Look I'll help with the exhibits and cadge a lift back with Vicky and John. See you at the station eh?'

Dylan knew she was a bit narked at him but he also knew she'd get over it. He didn't do apologies.

31

Dylan walked slowly back to his car, pondering over the post mortem. Using the phone hands-free, he had a chance to ring Jen as he travelled back to the station. He wanted to let her know he was leaving the mortuary and that he was dealing with another murder.

'How's the lip and are you coming to mine tonight?'

'I'm okay,' he laughed, amused by her rush of questions. It was lovely just to hear her voice. If he closed his eyes he could smell her scent and see her smiling face. She was his sanctuary, his lifeline and his *normal*. Without her he could never maintain the pace and the workload he'd had to endure lately. It's not that he didn't enjoy the challenge, but each murder took a little bit of something from him. He saw the worst side of life, man's inhumanity to man, and the arrogant, evil bastards that caused mass trauma twenty-four seven, but was clever enough to know it was bound to eat away at anyone.

'Will you be coming for tea? I'm cooking your favourite, liver and onions,' she said. Her joviality brought a wry smile to Dylan's face. Although he saw some awful sights he never lost his appetite and she knew he'd enjoy the meal if she made it for him.

'Yeah, that would be great.'

'Make sure you have some fruit. There's a banana and an apple in your briefcase if you get hungry. Oh, and if you need it after being at the mortuary there's a clean shirt hung with your blue suit in the wardrobe. Keep in touch and remember I love you.'

'I love you more. You might see me sooner than that. I'll be at Harrowfield nick shortly.'

Twenty minutes later he pulled up outside the main entrance of Harrowfield HQ. His reserved parking space was taken.

'Fucking hell, not again,' Dylan said, slamming the palm of his hand on the steering wheel. He knew the Peugeot parked there belonged to Detective Constable Hornby. He was going to get the biggest bollocking of his life when Dylan got hold of him. Dylan reckoned if Hornby had been as committed to police work as he was to football he'd have made a good officer. He had lost count of how many times he had warned him before about parking in the DI's spot. The bay was allocated for an easy exit and access to the police station for Dylan, DI and force hostage negotiator. He could be called upon at any time to a life or death situation, so it was important that he could get in and out of the station quickly. Dylan parked behind the Peugeot, stepped out of his vehicle, put on his coat, and collected his briefcase from the boot. It was so full it wouldn't close, but the sturdy handle held firm. It was always with him wherever he went. Like Dr Who's TARDIS, the space inside seemed to go on forever.

He walked through the foyer of the police station and today, for some unknown reason he noticed how shabby it looked, with its battered and scraped walls. Due to modern day culture and the lack of respect some people had for the police, the seats were fastened to the floor, not discreetly, but with large metal brackets and ugly bolts, and there was a protective screen surrounding the front counter. Progress? He mused.

'Afternoon,' he shouted to the front counter staff as he swiped his warrant card in the lock, allowing him access. Just through the door on the left was a stable door, which was the property store.

'Afternoon, Harold,' shouted Dylan in his deep, authoritative voice.

'Afternoon, Mr Dylan, sir,' Harold replied in his high-pitched whine. 'Always nice to see you,' said the property clerk, his head popping over the bottom half of the door. 'It usually means something serious has happened and I'll be getting a lot of property for my store though,' he moaned.

'And no different this time, Harold.' Dylan smiled. 'Nasty murder overnight. You'd better make some space for the exhibits and be sure they've all got labels on before you accept them. You know what policemen are like when they're rushing.'

'I will, Mr Dylan, sir. You know you can rely on me,' said Harold. His last name was Little. *A little man in size as well as name, he's no bigger than a jockey,* thought Dylan.

Dylan's aim was the cells as he strode out down the corridor, a man on a mission. Eventually he was going to solve the mystery of who had hit him and why. Nobody hit Jack Dylan and got away with it. He wanted answers, he wanted them now, and someone was going to feel the force of his anger. He would soon come face to face with his attacker and he couldn't wait.

Chapter Six

Dylan swung through the double doors of the custody suite and they flapped wildly behind him.

'Morning sir,' the sergeant said, throwing his legs off the desk as he jumped out of his chair. 'Shit, boss, he didn't half give you a whack, didn't he?'

Dylan instinctively put his hand to his face 'Who the hell is he?' he asked as he romped into the cell area. The sergeant ran to keep up. 'I hope you haven't given him a fucking cooked breakfast. Let me see if I know the bastard,' he said searching the names of those chalked on the custody board.

'No can do, boss.' The sergeant shook his head.

'Come on. I only want to look. I'm hardly gonna smack him here now, am I?'

'I would if I could, boss, honest, but he got bailed on the instruction of him upstairs. The superintendent must be obeyed,' he said, rolling his eyes. Dylan turned and vanished before the sergeant had time to blink. He ran up the stairs in a blind rage, ignoring everything and anyone he passed. Dylan could feel the steam coming out of his ears. Superintendent Walter Hugo-Watkins, the divisional commander, was going to feel the full force of his anger.

Watkins was a graduate entry. A cloak and dagger Freemason, or so he thought, but everyone knew of his ambition to become a Grand Master. He was a thin, lanky man, with a matching moustache. His short, dark hair was always groomed to perfection. Watkins was a self-important man who only had twelve years in the job and couldn't understand why he wasn't a chief constable already

Dylan saw him as soon as he flung open the door, morning paper open in his hands behind his power desk. Before he could lift his head to see who or what had the audacity to enter his office without an appointment, Dylan threw down his briefcase and grabbed him by the throat, lifting him into his adjoining en-suite. Watkins' Grecian 2000 smashed on the pristine white tiled floor and the liquid trickled along the grout.

'You fucking piece of useless shit. Some low life wounds one of your officers and you fucking bail them. I should fucking deck you.' Dylan released him, throwing him forward, and stood back. Watkins wasn't worth losing his pension for.

'You can't speak t … to … to me like that. You'll be … er … disciplined,' Watkins stuttered as he tried to regain his composure, brushing his shirtfront and adjusting his tie.

Dylan glared at him. 'Fucking do it.'

'My hands were tied,' Watkins protested. 'Force policy states that … er …. What about the murder? What's happening?' He picked up the papers that Dylan's briefcase had caused to slide to the floor.

'Come to the fucking briefings if you want to find out. Don't think this is finished. Wanker.' Dylan stormed out, intentionally knocking the china cup and saucer that was Watkins' pride and joy to the floor as he pushed past him.

Dawn sat in the SIO's office next to the briefing room, coffee waiting, as Dylan stomped in, slamming the door behind him. 'Before I retire I'll have that supercilious, useless bastard,' he said slumping down noisily in his chair. 'Can you believe that tosser bailed him?' he said picking up his mug and gulping his coffee. The hot coffee burnt his lips. 'He bailed the twat that attacked me to make space for container prisoners. "Force fucking policy" he said.' Dylan grimaced. 'Can you believe that?' Unable to sit still, he paced the office. Gulping more coffee, he confessed, 'I've just had him up against his office wall.'

Dawn's mouth fell open. 'You haven't chinned him?'

'No, I stopped, fortunately for him. He asked about the murder. When's he ever done that before? So I told him to come to the fucking briefing.' Dylan took off his jacket and flopped in his chair, elbows on the desk. He sipped his coffee more slowly, holding the mug with both hands.

Dawn stood. 'I've an idea. Be back in a minute. I'll find out about the bloke who attacked you,' she said tapping his shoulder soothingly as she passed. 'Briefing in ten, boss, try to compose yourself whilst I'm gone,' she called with a backward glance.

The hot drink helped to soothe him. He'd enjoy telling Jen about what had happened tonight. He smiled. Although he knew she would worry, she did understand how the likes of

Watkins and a few of the other hierarchy created havoc for everyday policing, simply because they had never worked at street level. He couldn't remember seeing one of the top brass at any of his incident rooms showing an interest, and it disappointed him greatly. Dylan had been awarded numerous commendations from the courts for outstanding police work, and he ensured the deserving members of his team, including the civilian support staff, were also rewarded. When serious crime was occurring, the bosses disappeared into the woodwork. When the awards were being presented they reappeared like returning migratory birds for the photo call, dressed in their best uniform, shiny buttons and crowns. *Then again,* he thought, *on the positive side if they stay out of the way they can't meddle.* He didn't know which was worse. The thought satisfied him for the moment. He rang and gave a report to the Press Office, not to be released until deceased's family informed.

The body of a young girl was found earlier today at around 6.20 a.m. near to Dean Reservoir. Although similar to the missing girl from Rochester Road, she has yet to be positively identified. Enquiries are ongoing. End press release.

'All you need to know about your attacker is in here, boss,' Dawn said as she entered the office, handing him an envelope. 'After the briefing,' Dawn said as he made to break the seal. She was right. Briefings were of paramount importance to the investigation, and he needed to be focused. He placed the envelope in his briefcase. Like *scene attendance*, some people thought naively that *briefings* were unnecessary, but he knew different.

The conference room doubled as a briefing room; there was no separate facility at Harrowfield Police Station.

A murder was a major disruption to any police division, affecting resources, staffing levels, budgets, and performance. Because of this, SIOs were despised and murders were just a nuisance: they produced only one crime for the monthly figures, which didn't aid performance, that being all that mattered for Home Office targets.

Dylan and Dawn walked into the room and took their seats at the front. The hum and chatter ceased. Jasmine followed, out of her unflattering protective clothing and in tight jeans, long dark hair trailing down her back. She caused heads to turn. Dylan looked around the room noticing experienced officers. He knew they liked to cherry pick what they dealt with, but not on Dylan's enquiries. There were also officers who were new to major investigations and he knew they would require guidance. These officers would have to be paired with someone with a required level of knowledge.

Dylan stood and introduced himself and Dawn for the benefit of the few who didn't know them. The room was full. He was about to start when uniformed Chief Inspector Fleet hurriedly entered and stood with her back to the door. Moira Fleet was a stocky woman in her forties with short, dark hair that made her look masculine.

'Sorry I'm late. I've only just been asked by Mr Watkins to attend on his behalf,' she said. Ruddiness flecked her complexion. 'He had an urgent appointment at HQ. Divisional Commanders or something.' Dylan nodded and glanced at Dawn who smiled knowingly.

'Can everyone hear at the back?' he called. Heads nodded to reassure him people could. 'There's an evil killer out there. I want him or them to be found quickly. I don't want people dragging their feet. Neither do I want anyone holding back. If you've any ideas or concerns, speak to us. I don't bite so don't be shy. Jasmine, will you please start the DVD of the scene where little Daisy was found.' While the DVD played, Dylan emphasised the important parts for the audience, pausing the DVD every now and then. In most murder enquiries, not everything was disclosed to the officers, especially at the first briefing. Some things were held back that only the killer would know. On this occasion, however, Dylan gave them all he had.

'I've given you one hundred per cent of what we know. Your working days will be twelve hours long until you're told differently. Any questions?' he asked. There was silence. The room emptied quickly. Dawn dabbed her mouth, he glanced at his watch, and saw it was two-fifteen.

'Canteen, Dawn? Then we'll make sure all the priority lines are ongoing.' As they walked towards the door he saw DC Hornby out of the corner of his eye, lurking in the corridor.

'I'll see you up there in a minute, Dawn. Hornby: a word,' Dylan shouted, grabbing the man's collar and ushering him into the empty snooker room. 'I've warned you before. Not only will your balls hurt if I have to tell you again but you'll be back pounding the beat before you can say "Jack the Ripper". Do I make myself clear?' DC Hornby nodded. 'Fucking move it then.'

'Sorry, boss.' A red-faced Hornby scuttled out of the room. He knew full well where he had left his car.

Dylan had a reputation for being a hard man on the streets as a young detective; perhaps foolishly, he'd backed away from nothing and nobody. He hadn't changed; he wouldn't let anyone get one over him and he wouldn't stand for any nonsense either.

Dawn had finished her meal when Dylan reached the table in the canteen, with his briefcase full of work by his side. He discussed the imperative lines of enquiry he wanted so Dawn could brief the investigation teams; CCTV and house-to-house enquiries were an obvious priority. Dawn returned to the briefing room. The canteen was busy. He sipped his coffee and nibbled at his ham sandwich while he updated his policy log and read a few reports. He saw the banana and apple Jen had somehow managed to squeeze in and it made him smile. The canteen table was now a makeshift desk. He picked up his mobile.

'Hiya, love, just a quickie,' he whispered.

'That would be nice,' she said, a smile in her voice.

'I should be so lucky,' he said. 'Just touching base. I'm only in the canteen if you're passing?' he said hopefully. 'I don't know what time I'll get to yours tonight, maybe half-ten or so.'

'That's fine. Just let me know when you leave and I'll have something ready for you to eat,' she said. 'I love you.'

'I love you, too.' He put the phone down on the table and nodded across to the property clerk who was leaving the canteen, iced finger in hand. *How mouse-like he is,* Dylan thought.

Updating his policy book, Dylan had to state the reasons for his decisions and outline the lines of the enquiry. Although laborious, he always completed the policy logbook in his own style. Succinct, but the reader could see what had taken place and how the investigation had progressed, what decisions had been made to establish what had happened and boy, were they like the Bible when defence barristers like pit bulls tried to rip the evidence or procedures to pieces. He walked over to get his mug topped up from the counter and felt a light touch like an electric shock on his hand from behind. It was Jen: he knew it without looking.

'Hello, sir,' she breezed as she asked for some milk. He turned and smiled.

'If you've any trouble with the murder team's travel and subsistence forms you let me know, Miss Jones,' he said loudly for observers to hear. 'God, you're beautiful,' he whispered. He slowly walked back to his table watching her leave. Her long blonde hair spilled over the shoulders of her clingy blue shift dress. As she reached the door she turned. He was transfixed. She looked at him and gave him a smile. It wasn't a game; it was their relationship, which no one else could feed off.

'Have you looked at the contents of the envelope?' Dawn asked on her return as she leaned on the back of his chair. He pulled the envelope from his briefcase. 'You'll need that,' she said, pointing to the strong coffee on the table. 'Call of nature, be back in a min,' she said and disappeared.

Glancing over his shoulder he was puzzled as he saw her rush out of the canteen. He pulled the photocopied paper from the envelope and saw, in large letters across the page: 'VIOLENT, APPROACH WITH CAUTION, WEAPONS'. Dylan looked at the passport-sized picture of his attacker. He had two black eyes, a shaven head and a tattoo on his neck. Michael James Moorhouse, thirty-one years old, six feet one inch tall with twenty previous convictions for assaults, robbery and firearms. He'd been released from prison six weeks earlier after doing five of a nine-year sentence and was already on bail for an assault on a taxi driver. The file had been updated recently and now read: 'Bailed pending further enquiries re: wounding of a police officer – Detective Inspector Dylan'.

'Fucking piece of shit shouldn't even be walking the streets. Bloody Watkins. Why do we fucking bother?' he said out loud slamming the papers on the table. Although he had heard of Moorhouse, their paths had never crossed. *Great. Local psycho, that's all I need,* he thought as he felt his blood pressure rising. *If I see him first I'll be in there with a fucking pickaxe.*

Dawn strolled back and stood against the table. 'Is it safe to come back yet?' she asked before sitting down. Dylan stared at her. 'You always have to pick on the biggest twat don't you? I've had a word with the Serious Crime Squad and he ought to be under surveillance. You got away reasonably lightly; the next person might not survive. Apparently he saw you come out of a court building and thought you were the one who'd sent him down last time. That's his story, anyway, according to the detective who interviewed him.'

Dylan sat staring at the paper in front of him. 'Bailed for six fucking weeks. Don't they have any common sense?' He gently touched his swollen lip and flinched. 'Honestly, is he gonna turn up at court? Is he, hell,' he said as he stuffed the paperwork back into the envelope. He thought about it for all of a minute. 'He can wait. Let's get on with this job. We have a murderer to find.'

Down two flights of stairs to the incident room, the Home Office Large Major Enquiry System (HOLMES) team were setting up their computers.

Dylan and Dawn's next call was to the Hind family to tell them about Daisy. There would have to be a formal identification. He couldn't save them from that and there was no easy way to tell them. Dylan would never let anyone else inform the families. Not all senior investigators felt the same, but even though it was one of the hardest parts of his job, he wouldn't sidestep it. So many times before he'd had to tell loved ones of a death and about the deceased's horrific injuries, and he often needed to tell them again at a later date for it to sink in. Dylan knew he couldn't shield them from the pain and he never tried. That was all part of the grieving process. It never got any easier; he was the bearer of the worst possible news. They would cling to his every word and rely on him, trust him to find the killer, and eventually, when it was all over he would have to break the bond he'd forged. What did they call it at HQ, an 'exit strategy'? Like the opening and closing of a door. How simple they made it all sound. His was the knock at the door that no one wanted or believed. Dylan never knew how anyone would react because everyone reacted differently. He wondered what he had to face this afternoon. How does anyone react when they're told their worst nightmare has come true?

Chapter Seven

They arrived at 3.15 p.m. The house was quiet and the atmosphere heavy as Janice, the police family liaison officer, let them in. Wendy and Trevor stood to greet them, anxiety etched into their faces as Dylan and Dawn entered the room.

'You've found her haven't you? She's dead isn't she? She's dead. Oh, my god she is dead.' Wendy held a hankie to her mouth suffocating the sound of sobs. Trevor stood behind his wife protectively, cradling the back of her head against his shoulder. Tears ran from his eyes and dripped from his chin.

'Tell us,' he whispered.

'Please sit down,' Dylan said. They immediately did, as if the quicker they sat, the sooner they would know. 'Earlier today, the body of a young girl was found near Dean Reservoir. We have recovered her to the hospital mortuary. She appears very similar to the description of Daisy. I believe it is her, but I'm afraid I'll need you to formally identify her.'

The couple sat shaking, holding hands. They looked dazed and numb.

'What're we waiting for? Let's go. I want to be sure. I need to know. I want to see Daisy one more time,' sobbed Wendy, hugging a cushion to her, as she stood.

'Can we both see her?' asked Trevor softly.

Dylan nodded; he'd already made the arrangements. The reaction was expected. They hadn't asked what had happened, how their little girl had died. It was as though they didn't need to know, and they didn't want to hear.

Jack Dylan and his officers were regular visitors to the mortuary. For Wendy and Trevor, it was a place they never wanted to have to visit or even to imagine visiting, even in their deepest nightmares.

The drive took only twelve minutes without rush hour traffic. Wendy crumpled a pack of paper tissues in her hand. Her tears were silent but her pain was tangible. The silence made the journey seem like an eternity to Dylan. As they reached the mortuary doors, Trevor and Wendy hesitated for a moment. She gasped as she stumbled. Trevor tried to hold her. He was doing his best to comfort her. Dylan could see he was in fear of collapsing himself and stayed close to them just in case he was needed.

'Please don't let it be Daisy,' muttered Trevor.

'Let me wake up. Now, please,' Wendy quietly begged. Dylan knew they would be reunited with Daisy soon, if only for a short while. She would no longer be lost to them. Dylan wished there was something he could do to ease their pain. He knew there wasn't.

Dylan remembered every inch of the viewing room. Scrutinizing the décor was his way of distracting himself from the bodies. He knew it was a similar size to a box room and had an entry and exit at opposite ends so that you could walk through and pass the body. It was sparsely decorated with an odd bunch of plastic flowers in a vase in one corner and a dark wooden cross on the back wall. The smell of potpourri wafted in the air. There was nothing else but a trolley upon which Daisy's little body would be draped in a starched white blanket, her face exposed. The room would feel peaceful, even religious, as choral music played quietly in the background. On another wall there were three windows at about waist height and from where they stood in the corridor outside, they could only see the drawn black curtains. Pulling the drapes back allowed them to see the body.

'Are you ready?' the attendant asked Wendy and Trevor.

On a nod, the curtains were pulled back slowly with a sash cord, similar to unveiling a plaque. Dylan didn't know whether that was done as a matter of respect or whether it was to lessen the shock. Nothing could have prepared Trevor and Wendy for what they saw inside. They gasped sharply.

The room was dimly lit, which helped sometimes to hide any deterioration or bruising to the body, in an attempt to minimise the trauma. Some bodies had to have make-up applied to reduce the shock to the loved ones. Dylan knew of a mortuary attendant who knitted clothes for toddlers and babies, so that their parents would have a lasting memory of the child in peace and tranquillity, rather than being dressed in a hospital robe. Marjorie, another mortuary attendant, took hand prints and footprints of babies for the bereaved parents as a keepsake, something extra for them to cling to. Everything possible was done, and with sincerity and respect.

'Oh, no,' said Wendy, bringing her hand to her throat. Her knees gave way and her face crumpled in pain. Dylan and Janice reached out together instinctively to catch her.

'What have they done to her? Why? Why? Why?' she wailed, as uncontrollable tears rushed down her cheeks like a waterfall. She turned into Trevor and buried her face in his chest, beating him softly with her clenched fist. He held her. Janice put her arms around them as the onslaught of emotion poured from them. From beneath the brilliant white sheet that adorned Daisy's body peeped a few strands of unmistakable red hair. She looked angelic.

'She was so happy … she'll never, never be a bridesmaid now, will she? Please can I touch her?' Wendy sobbed, turning to Dylan.

'Of course,' he replied. 'I'm sure she'd want you to, don't you?' He tried to smile as he suppressed his own emotions. Janice held Wendy's hand as she led them into the room. Trevor followed cautiously, as if his feet were walking through treacle. Wendy looked waxy as if every ounce of life had been sucked out of her.

Jack Dylan had lost his parents when he was in his twenties, through illness. He wished they were alive, but he was so glad for the time he'd had with them. These days murders were inevitable, with a society less respectful and more violent. Nowadays, sadly, it was simply a talking point like any other occurrence. Life was cheap.

The officers stood outside, watching. Wendy and Trevor needed space, a few moments alone with their little girl. Dylan saw Wendy drop to her knees; she leant her head against her daughter's arm, clasped the child's hand in hers.

'Mummy's here, darling,' she wept. 'You're safe now; everything will be okay. Don't you worry.'

Trevor's hand was on Wendy's shoulder as he stroked Daisy's head. He was rooted to the spot.

'You would have been a beautiful bridesmaid, darling. Mummy and Daddy love you so, so much,' he said, almost zombie-like. The atmosphere was chilled and the smell of rose petals was strong in the air. Dylan didn't dare look at Janice and Dawn; the tears swimming in his eyes threatened to overspill. The death of a young child rocked him to the very core. To do his job he needed to be in control, to be focused.

Dylan disliked his bosses. With few exceptions, they neither saw nor wanted to know about this side of a homicide investigation. He simply wanted the bosses to show some interest and support for the officers who had the arduous task of dealing with the horrifying remnants of violent crime. Just turning up at the briefing or even debriefing would have been enough for him.

'I need the toilet.' Wendy suddenly rose from the floor, and ran to the door. 'I'm going to be sick.' Janice chased after her as she rushed down the short corridor and steered her to the toilets. Frantically she ran into the sanctuary of the cubicle. She was retching violently. The foul-smelling liquid sprayed the bowl and beyond as she fell to her knees on the cold, tiled floor. A hand slowly and gently held her damp fringe from her face. Janice's other hand stroked her back.

'Sorry. I'm sorry.' Wendy coughed into the bowl.

'It's okay, it's alright,' Janice soothed as she stretched over her to get her some toilet paper to wipe her mouth. She turned her around, put the seat down for Wendy to sit on and helped her from the floor. Her breathing gradually slowed down and her face regained some colour.

'Oh, god. I'm so sorry; it's on your suit as well.' Wendy attempted to brush the lapel on Janice's coat.

'Don't worry. I've had a lot worse than that, believe me. Are you feeling okay now?' she asked bending over her, still gently rubbing her back. 'Let's get you cleaned up and get this over with, eh?' Wendy splashed her face with cold water in the worn basin as Janice cleaned the front of her coat as best she could. 'Are you ready now, love?' Wendy stared into space, looking into the old speckled mirror above the sink, and nodded.

Later, hands firmly clasped around cups as they drank hot, sweet tea, Jack Dylan promised them, 'We'll find the person who did this no matter how long it takes. You have my word. Daisy died from a head wound, she was hit with something once, and was killed instantly. Her body was found on grassland near to Dean Reservoir.' He spoke slowly and clearly. It was so quiet he could hear the sound of the group breathing. 'She wasn't hidden, but she was naked,' he continued.

'The dirty, evil bastard. I'll kill him when you find him. God help me, I'll kill him.' Trevor spoke through clenched teeth, his face growing red and contorted in anger, tears spilling from his eyes. 'Please god, tell me he didn't do that to her. Tell me he didn't,' he cried.

'No. No. Give me time to finish, she was not, and I repeat not, sexually interfered with in any way.'

Their sigh of relief was audible and rippled around the small office at the mortuary.

'She had a few other small injuries which were caused after she died. The tip of the little finger of her left hand was removed, it looks like someone attempted to shave off her eyebrows, and what looks like two cigarette burns have been made, one on each of her buttocks.'

'What? In god's name.' Trevor's eyes were red, wide and staring. Dylan could see he couldn't comprehend what he was hearing. 'Why the hell would anyone do that? He tortured her? I'll kill him. Find him. I'll do the rest.'

Wendy was quiet, still, and she just stared. She had withdrawn into her innermost thoughts as if she couldn't take any more. Dylan explained about the Press and that sometime tomorrow he would give out Daisy's details, but not until he had heard from them that all their relatives had been informed. It was time for Janice to take them home. Daisy's death, the death of their only child, had damaged them, perhaps beyond repair. Their lives had been changed forever.

Dylan drove Dawn back to the nick to collect her car. 'You're quiet, you okay?' he asked.

'Yeah, I was just thinking. Imagine your only child being taken from you in such a savage way. Life can be so cruel,' she sighed.

'And without warning. You never know what's around the corner, eh?' he said thoughtfully.

He pulled up at the side of her Suzuki Swift, both of them submerged in their own thoughts.

'You keep smiling,' he said as she got out of the car, leaving the door open as she walked to her car. He reached over the passenger seat for the door handle to pull it shut. For the first time ever he was worried how a murder was affecting Dawn. 'Hey, and don't be bloody late in the morning. I need a top deputy on this one,' he shouted after her. She turned and glanced over her shoulder, managing a brief smile that didn't reach her eyes. Dylan felt for the Hinds, but he also felt for his team. They were human after all. They had feelings and this one hurt. He wondered, like Dawn had said on so many occasions, how people found the strength to cope with such personal devastation. 'Somehow evil walks amongst us,' he had once read. *Very poignant*, he thought. He was tired, but strangely pleased that Daisy had been found. At least it wouldn't be a case of the family searching for years. He was frustrated and concerned that nobody was locked up or even in the frame, but Dylan wasn't a quitter. He was determined to find the murdering bastard. The pressure on him over the next few days and weeks would be immense.

His thoughts turned to Jen. She had a lot to put up with. He never seemed to see her these days. She ran to meet him at the door with Max when she heard his key in the lock. He didn't know how he'd coped going home to an empty flat before he'd met Jen, and he held her tightly. Knowing how lucky he was made all the difference. He savoured every minute with her.

'I'll run you a bath, love. My mortuary man,' she screwed her nose up, smelling the rot on him as she reached up for a kiss. She had already showered, and had on her light pink silk dressing gown, her hair clipped back. She smelled of *Rive Gauche* and looked beautiful to Dylan. Clothes dumped; sat in the bath, coffee in hand, Jen sponged his aching back. He lay back, closed his eyes, and purred like a contented cat.

'I worry about you. How do you work at the pace you do? See the things that you see and not be affected by it?' she asked, her head in the crook of her arm rested on the bath's edge, as she continued to sponge his body.

'I don't think about it a lot,' he whispered contentedly, guarded.

'But how does a man as gentle and kind as you turn into the hard-faced detective? It's unnerving, as though you just flick a switch. Sometimes I wonder if I know you at all when we're at work, you're so ... different.'

He opened his eyes and looked at her. 'Okay, you want to know how I felt inside today? It was awful, really bloody awful. Daisy's parents collapsed on us. The poor little girl had been stripped, her eyebrows shaved, she'd been burned. I saw how it affected the whole team.'

'And you?' She sighed, laying a comforting hand on his shoulder.

'I can't let the team see, can I? Superhuman Jack Dylan, I think not. The sight of her tore me apart; she could've been a child of my own.'

'You are superhuman, to me.' She smiled at him lovingly and stroked his damp face.

He got out of the bath, coffee cup still in hand, and drained the cup as she dried him. Boy was he pampered. Jen was trained in massage, reflexology, and Indian head massage, as well as being a hairdresser: he'd truly hit the jackpot when he'd found her and he was never going to let her go.

'Right, Jack Dylan, time for bed. I want your undivided attention. No more talk about work. I need you.' She teased him with a loving kiss.

He slapped her bum as she turned to hang up the towel. 'And I need you too,' he said, kissing her softly on the back of her neck.

'Bed, my boy,' she ordered jumping on the bed and tapping the space beside her.

Their lovemaking was always fulfilling. He still hadn't got over the newness of her and knowing that work could call him out again that night, he turned into her curves, snuggled up and slept.

He awoke at half past six to the smell of bacon and before his eyes a breakfast tray appeared.

'Morning, sleepyhead, your hair needs cutting,' Jen said ruffling his hair. 'You look like Tin Tin in the morning when your hair stands up in the middle like that.' She laughed, playing with the hair on the top of his head. He smiled at her sleepily. She busied herself around the bedroom, drawing back the curtains and collecting the washing from the laundry basket. His clothes were draped neatly on the wardrobe's plinth to the side of the bed: dark navy suit, crisp white shirt and striped tie. *God, is she organised,* he thought as she dropped a kiss on his forehead, and then he tucked into his breakfast.

He dressed and was ready for another day, wondering what it would bring. Stroking Max at the door he gave Jen a kiss and held her in his arms.

'I do love you, you know,' he said very aware that when the job was running he abandoned her.

'I know. I just worry about you, that's all,' she said stroking his lapel as he held her close. 'I would like to spend more time with you instead of sitting here waiting for you to come home. I hate watching while they pile more and more work on you. I mean, four murders in as many months. And I can't even tell anyone we are together. You know I can't lie. What if someone asks me outright? Oh, I know the reasons why, all the gossip, and you're only looking out for me, but I'm proud to be on your arm, Jack.'

'I know, love, and I'm proud of you too. If it comes out we'll deal with it. I know we won't be able to keep it secret forever, but for now it's our secret,' he said kissing the tip of her nose.

'Don't push yourself, Jack, that's all I ask,' she said as she pulled away from the embrace. 'Remember you're no good to anybody dead.'

Chapter Eight

Dawn was already in the office when Dylan arrived. A phone was ringing and she reached over her desk to pick it up, nodding as he entered. He took his jacket off and swung it over the back of his chair, unlocked his desk and methodically reached for the papers in his in-tray. Dawn was silent, he noticed, as she listened intently to the caller. Closing her eyes she handed the phone to Dylan. 'I think you'd better take this, sir,' she said.

'Boss. Just letting you know that Grandma Irene died about two hours ago. We've just called the doctor out for Wendy. She's not good and to be honest Trevor isn't much better.'

'Flaming hell, Janice, that's terrible. Do you need any help? I'll get on to HQ again.' He looked over at Dawn who held her head in her hands.

'No, I'm fine, honest, boss. It's just so bloody sad. Can you imagine losing your daughter and your mother in less than twenty-four hours? It's just surreal.'

'God, I know. Look, I'm being hounded by the Press. I've got a conference at eleven. They want me to name Daisy. I need to know if the family have been informed and I suppose the same goes for Grandma. If you could tell them I'd be grateful for confirmation as soon as possible, and explain how it'll help get the media's support. Pass on my condolences, will you?'

'No problem, sir. I'll have to speak to Trevor. Wendy is just out of it. She's saying her mum has just gone to get Daisy. I'll get back to you shortly.'

'Thanks. If you need anything, don't hesitate to give us a call.' He didn't replace the phone on its cradle when Janice rang off, but held it to his cheek. Dylan was thoughtful. 'Can we arrange one of our team to assist Janice with the family liaison, Dawn? I'll ring HQ and bollock them. What's the point in having Home Office guidance and force policies if they don't adhere to them?' Dawn cringed as she listened to him tell the person on the other end of the phone at HQ in no uncertain terms that they needed another FLO immediately.

Meanwhile, she arranged for DC Susan Raynor to back Janice up until further assistance arrived.

'Talk about the proverbial straw that broke the camel's back. Irene dying will really destroy the Hinds. They seem to be such a close family.'

'Thank god they are,' said Dawn.

It was a high profile case, a child dead; the media were in a frenzy, desperate for information. The telephone rang and Dawn answered it. 'Press Office for you, boss. It's Rachel,' she said, as she handed it over the desk.

He covered the mouthpiece, 'Coffee,' he mouthed to Dawn. She made a one-fingered gesture at him. 'Do it,' Dylan said firmly.

'Okay, okay I'm going,' she said getting up. 'Male chauvinist,' she called as she blustered out of the door. He smiled. 'Pig,' she mimed through the glass.

'Hi. Rachel. Sorry about that. Staff problems. Now, press conference at Harrowfield HQ still on for eleven, if you can confirm it to the media? I'm still not in a position to name the girl to the public until I know family members have been contacted. I'm just waiting for the FLO to confirm. Maybe by eleven we'll have that confirmation.'

He told Rachel about Irene's death.

'Heavens, that's terrible. And national TV and Sky are chasing you for interviews, obviously its high interest, a child murdered, and now her grandmother dying.'

'Can you get over to Harrowfield a bit before eleven? I need to discuss my approach and what I'll say at the conference with you.'

'Yeah, I'll be with you in about half an hour.'

He was worried about how the papers would sensationalise it. He could see the headlines now: NAKED BODY OF YOUNG GIRL FOUND, GRANDMA DIES OF SHOCK. He knew he had no control over it, but he felt for the family and the community. Fear would blanket the village and surrounding areas. He made a quick call to Jen. Luckily with a phone on her desk he could ring her whenever he wanted.

'Just to let you know, I'll be doing the press conference and TV from about eleven so you know where I'll be. More sad news, Daisy's gran died this morning.'

'Never. That's awful. The family won't be at the conference then?'

'No, I don't think so. Janice is with them and they've called the doctor out to Daisy's mum. They're just devastated. Who wouldn't be?'

'God, I'm not surprised.'

'So, love, the media won't be happy, but they'll just have to put up with my dulcet tones.'

'Nobody better.'

'Not sure about that. Speak to you after. By the way, last night was the best. I love you.'

'You too.' He could hear her smile. He knew she was sitting wading through her paperwork only a couple of floors away, but it felt like miles at times like these when he just wanted to hold her close. Jen had a handful of friends in admin, which helped her pass the day. She involved herself in voluntary work, organising events for charity outside of work. She said it had helped her cope when he was working. Jen often spoke of feeling lonely while he worked long hours and he didn't know how to resolve that. She was vocal in telling him she hated the police because of what she saw it doing to him and he had to agree that he would be tossed aside like a worn car tyre, unwanted, unfit for purpose, in time. He'd simply be replaced without a further thought when it came to him retiring. So why did he do it?

Dylan had had his boost from hearing her voice and he felt ready to get to grips with the media issue, what he would say and what he wanted to get across to the public. Dawn had handled the team briefing and got the team out and about on enquiries.

'Who you been talking to, to put a smile on your face?' Dawn asked as she joined him.

'Ah, it was a wrong number. Funny how weird people act when they ring a DI by accident,' he lied. 'Coffee and toast for us, Dawn,' he said standing up from behind his desk. 'My treat as you made the coffee.'

'I should think so.'

'I've just spoken to Janice to let her know Susan Raynor is sorted to back her up,' said Dylan as they walked to the canteen.

'And I told the troops in the briefing the evil bastard had caused the death of Daisy's gran. God knows how Trevor and Wendy are coping.'

'Rachel's on her way from the Press Office to discuss any issues before the press conference. Do you want to be present for that?' he asked.

'I'd like to be there for the meeting, but you're on your own with the Press. One singer, one song,' she laughed.

'It would be good experience for when you're applying for the next rank.'

'When I have to do it I will, but for now they're all yours.'

'Okay, no problem, if you're chickening out,' he teased.

'They'll probably focus all their cameras on your mouth anyhow.' Funny, he'd almost forgotten about that.

A short while later Rachel arrived and all three sat and discussed how to handle the media side of the enquiry. The phone rang. It was Janice.

'Sorry to keep you waiting, boss, but I've just got the green light from Trevor. Poor thing, he's been on the telephone all morning to family and friends, but at least it's kept his mind occupied.'

'Is that for both Daisy and Irene?'

'Yeah, both. They're asking if it's possible for them to have a joint funeral and burial. Seeing as Daisy adored her gran so much, they'd like them to be buried together. I told them I'd look into it for them. Auntie Sam's wedding has been postponed and is unlikely to happen this year. She just couldn't go through with it.'

'It's sad, but you can understand. It's a really nice thought about them being buried together. We'll do what we can. Let them know that Daisy's murder will be headline news in the papers and on the news tonight, will you? And be careful, some of the nationals may try knocking at the door; they seem desperate for an exclusive. Don't let them near. Any problems, ring us.'

'Will do, boss. Thanks.'

'By the way, Janice, you're doing a great job,' Dylan said sincerely.

'Thanks. It's nice to be appreciated. I'll get back to it and tell them about your call.'

It was standing room only in the conference suite. The photographers let loose their flashes. Dylan entered the room and sat behind the desk at the front. It was a lonely job being an SIO. He knew he would have their undivided attention while he spoke, and then the room would erupt, with questions being fired at him from every angle. The clock struck eleven and, as the flashes stopped, Dylan started.

'Daisy Charlotte Hind was a little girl of nine, the only child of Wendy and Trevor. The evening she went missing, she'd simply gone to her grandma's home a few hundred yards down Rochester Road, onto Rochester Way, to show her the bridesmaid dress she was wearing. She'd never been a bridesmaid before and was overjoyed to have been asked by her Auntie. She didn't stay at her grandma's. She was straight in and out as her mum had told her. Grandma watched Daisy as she walked back home until she turned out of her sight into Rochester Road.

'We know little Daisy didn't make the next few hundred yards to her door. Her naked body was found on wasteland near to Dean Reservoir some twelve hours later at 6.20 a.m. yesterday. She hadn't been hidden and was about twenty-five yards from the road. She'd been wearing a grey duffle coat, black shoes, and a jade green bridesmaid dress. None of these items of clothing have been recovered. She hadn't been sexually assaulted and she died from a single blow to her head. Due to the ferocity of the blow, she would have died instantly. This was the brutal and callous killing of a young, defenceless child by a calculating murderer who needs to be caught.

'It's also with great sadness that I can tell you that her grandma, Irene, having heard that her little princess, as she called her, had been snatched from the street, collapsed with chest pains. She was taken by ambulance to Harrowfield

Hospital, where she suffered a fatal heart attack earlier this morning.

'I appeal to anyone who has the slightest suspicion about a partner or family member to contact us. We would also like to hear from anyone who was in Rochester Road or Rochester Way yesterday evening and who saw either Daisy or anyone acting suspiciously. Finally, anyone who was in the area of Dean Reservoir yesterday. Has anyone any questions?'

A show of hands told Dylan he'd have to curtail the question and answer session otherwise he would be there all day.

'Jim Blake, *Daily Mirror*, what's Grandma's last name?'

'Barker.'

'*Harrowfield Times*, how many officers are working on the case?'

'Around forty, at this time.'

'*Tandem Bridge Echo*, how are the parents coping?'

'Unless we've lost a child ourselves, I don't think any of us can understand the pain and misery they're going through. Daisy's mum has had to receive continued medication to help her cope, and with the news of her mum dying too.' Dylan shook his head. 'We can only imagine the trauma this evil killer has caused.'

Dylan held up an enlarged photograph. 'We have pictures available of a bridesmaid dress similar to the one that Daisy was wearing.

'As you can imagine, we've a vast amount of work to do, so thank you.'

Dylan continued to be bombarded by questions, although none could be heard clearly with everyone talking at once. He held up his hand in an attempt to halt the noise. The room became less frantic as people began to listen once more.

'I'll be available for one-to-one interviews later, thanks again,' he said as he rose from his seat. The TV stations lined up. The local radio and the papers all wanted their own individual photographs or footage to use. Dylan patiently ensured they were all satisfied before he left the arena. It just might help to gather the information that he would need to lead him to the killer, who knew? An hour later he returned to his office, hoarse.

The incident room was already a hive of industry. The tapping of fingers on keyboards was like rain on a windowpane. Searches were continuing and these had now extended to the reservoir and surrounding areas. Dylan sat quietly in his office, scribbling down notes as he thought about the lines of enquiry. *Where are Daisy's clothes? Soil samples, vegetation samples could link the killer to the area. Possible routes of access to Rochester Road and Rochester Way? CCTV, garages en route? Who are the 'creeps' the 'weirdos' the strange people in the area? The locals will know who they are. Sensitive searching of Daisy's room. Enquiries at Daisy's school - Harrowfield Middle School. Did she know her attacker?* Dylan knew people wanted results, not words. His thought process was disturbed by the telephone ringing, and it made him jump.

'Is that DI Dylan?' asked the sharp-tongued voice at the other end of the phone. 'This is Avril Summerfield-Preston, the Divisional Administrator.'

'Yes,' he replied absent-mindedly. He'd seen Avril flouncing about the upper floors of the station for as long as he could remember, but he didn't know her or in fact what she did. She sat on her own in a corner at meetings and never offered her opinion, which he'd thought odd for her position. He'd never seen her talking to anyone socially, probably because everyone thought she was arrogant, abrupt and a joke as part of the senior management team. Avril appeared to be a loner and gave the impression she thought she was above everyone else. She was a strange woman. She tried with her appearance, he'd give her that, but even dressing in Chanel wouldn't have given her style or stature. She was just one of the unfortunates of the world. 'Beaky' was her nickname around the station, due to the fact she had an enormous nose. Her ears protruded through mousy, thinning hair that always looked as if it was in need of a good wash. Her overpowering perfume arrived before she did, and Dylan couldn't decide whether she used it to cover up a rather embarrassing perspiration problem or not.

'My property store is full to capacity because of your murders.' She broke his reverie, speaking as if Jack Dylan had committed the murders himself. 'It's a Health and Safety issue, Inspector, that I want sorting immediately. I don't want any more exhibits going into the store.' By this time, he had held the phone away from his ear and promptly hung up. He wasn't going to be spoken to or dictated to by a jumped up administrator who never went out of her office and had no idea of real police work. The telephone rang, and he'd no doubt it was her trying again, so he ignored it.

There'd been a rumour about her and Superintendent Walter Hugo-Watkins, he remembered. Allegedly, she'd been seen leaving his office and walking down the corridor to her own office unaware that her dress was tucked in her knickers. He smirked to himself. *It takes all sorts,* he thought, *but what a boring pair they'd make. Then again, perhaps a match made in heaven.* He smiled, then shook himself: he'd much more important things to think about. The Hinds wanted to know if they could plan the funerals. It was a fast decision for anyone to make, but then again he knew that everyone dealt with life and death differently and focusing their mind on something positive was a good thing. He spoke to the coroner stating that it may help the Hind family to come to terms, or give some closure to the deaths, if they could be buried as they wished. They had no immediate suspects and so far the enquiries were unyielding.

The days rolled by, unnoticed due to the pace of work. He worked, he ate, and he slept but not always in that order.

Chapter Nine

Dylan opened the door. Max ran to greet him, nearly knocking Jen flying in the narrow hallway.

'Hiya. Someone is pleased to see you,' she laughed placing a kiss on Jack's head as he bent to stroke Max. 'Kettle's on, you eaten?' she asked as he followed her into the kitchen.

Before Jack could reply, his mobile's shrill tone made him jump. He pressed 'receive' and they looked at each other in anticipation.

'Sir, I've been called out to a shooting at a flat on the Greenaway Estate. A friend of the occupant couldn't gain entry and noticed a strange smell. Entry has now been forced and there's a dead man in there with head injuries and a gun at his side.'

'Are you at the scene?' Dylan asked. Jen turned away before he could see the disappointment in her eyes. Busily she made him a warm drink.

'No.'

'Well fucking go then. Get suited up and ring me back when you're standing by the body. It sounds like suicide.' He threw his phone on the table.

Jen swung round. Dylan didn't speak like that to anyone, not in her presence anyway.

'Well, the man is fucking useless,' he said noticing the look on her face. 'He hasn't even been to the scene, how the hell can he describe it to me?' She ignored his outburst and concentrated on making him something to eat. There was one thing for sure. He would be going back out to work soon.

'I'm sorry, Jen,' he said, rubbing his forehead, unsure if the apology was for the outburst or the language. He ached; his eyes were struggling to stay open. 'He'll be ringing again. He won't make a decision. He's pathetic.' He stood behind her and turned her round to give her a cuddle, closing his eyes with the comfort of the embrace. It wasn't like him to get mad and lose his temper. In silence, he ate the omelette that Jen had prepared for him. As they sat together at the dining room table Jen looked at him closely. She noticed his face was grey and puffy, dark circles ran around his eyes, and darkened either side at the bridge of his nose. For once he looked older than his years. The phone rang. He picked up slowly and put it to his ear, his elbow resting on the table. His head was bowed to the receiver, eyes closed. Detective Sergeant Wigglesworth attempted to explain the sight that greeted him.

'Well, sir, half the head is missing,' he said. 'There's a gun on the floor near to his right hand. I'm not happy. It might've been staged to look like he's done it himself. Someone could have easily locked the door behind them on the way out. We don't know who he is. Sir, will you be attending? I've told control I think it's suspicious.'

'Come out of the scene.' Dylan exhaled loudly. 'Make sure SOCO are there and doing the necessary photographs. I'm on my way.'

'Thank you, sir.'

Dylan put the phone down, threw his head back against the chair back-rest, and closed his eyes. Jen knew by the set of his mouth that he was raging. One of his pet hates was people who wouldn't make a decision. Passing the buck wasn't an option in Dylan's world.

'Years ago they'd have put officers like Wigglesworth against the wall and told them to go and find a bloody job they could do,' he muttered under his breath. He pushed himself up from the table and picked up his briefcase and jacket. He'd been so sure he would be called out he hadn't bothered changing out of his suit.

'Sorry, I won't be long, love. From what he's told me already I know it's a suicide,' he said.

She had never known him to be wrong.

She stayed seated at the table, fuming inside. 'You're tired. You should leave him with it, and then he'd have to sort it himself. He gets bloody well paid and then wants someone to hold his hand. I know you'll go,' she said, 'But there're times like this when you should say "no".' He gave her a silent, reassuring hug and kissed the top of her head, too weary to argue, knowing she was right.

His anger kept Dylan from falling asleep at the wheel. The subservient DS Wigglesworth harped on about the strangeness of the body as he met Dylan in the car park leading to the flat.

'It just doesn't seem to fit somehow, suicide,' he said shaking his head to and fro, trying to justify calling the DI out. Dylan couldn't bear to look at him, never mind discuss it with him. He suited up in silence and strode to the steps leading to the scene like a man on a mission.

'Should I wait outside, sir?' DS Wigglesworth enquired, hovering nervously behind him.

'No, you bloody shouldn't. Follow me.'

Dylan forced himself to be amiable, but the DS had no common sense. Wigglesworth had made the mistake of telling Dylan in the past he didn't want to be a detective. He was just gaining experience to tick the box before moving up to the next rank, which infuriated Dylan.

The scene was a flat on the top landing of a two-storey maisonette. Most of the windows and doors on the estate were covered with a rusty brown metal mesh informing everyone of the lack of occupancy. Rainbow-coloured graffiti covered the walls, and cans that once held alcohol or aerosol spray adorned the staircase and lobbies. Bits of paper and old cigarette butts littered the floor, but the smell of cat urine and dog excrement overpowered the reek of tobacco. The overflowing bins and blocked waste pipes soured the air as Dylan walked along the damp landing.

Inside wasn't much better. To say it was a 'shit tip' was an understatement. An overpowering combination of stale smoke, chip fat, sweat and cheap scent hit him as he stepped through the door. What made it worse was the heat. It was roasting, with the electric three bar fire on full in the lounge. Empty beer bottles and cans adorned the floor. An ashtray that overflowed with tab ends sat on the arm of a grubby chair. Ash covered the cushion like dandruff. The curtains were closed and the room's only light was from a TV in the corner that flickered silently to an empty arena. Dylan stepped over a mattress strewn with dirty clothing and blankets. Ahead of him he could see dirty dishes piled high in the kitchen. Empty cans and used bottles covered the worktops. Immediately he saw the deceased's body wilted on a chair, his head tilted back against the wall and a shotgun next to him on the floor.

Dylan moved close to the body. True, there wasn't much left of the head. It finished at the lower jaw. The remnants of blood-splattered brain and bone decorated the wall behind, as well as the ceiling above. He thought it looked like a pressure cooker had exploded and spewed its contents of rice pudding and jam everywhere. Not pleasant. Stuck to the ceiling, surrounded by the bits of flesh, was one solitary eye, staring down at them. Unusual, uncanny, but not something that distressed Dylan.

'Have you told me everything?' he asked Wigglesworth. Dylan's eyes scoured the room.

'Yes, sir, of course, sir.' His eyebrows furrowed as he looked at Dylan.

'Just making sure because you're being watched,' he said pointing to the ceiling where the eye peered down eerily.

'Oh, my god,' Wigglesworth said running away, his hand to his mouth. That would teach him for calling him out. Dylan smiled; he had a warped sense of humour, sometimes, but in his job he needed it. A closer look at the body revealed a metal bar down at the man's feet. It was a thin rod about half an inch in diameter and about three feet long. DS Wigglesworth rejoined him, his face ashen.

'Feel better now?' Dylan enquired nonchalantly, but he didn't wait for a reply. 'Okay, it's suicide,' he announced. 'The man has sat down on the chair, put the barrel of the single-barrelled shotgun in his mouth, and used the metal bar to push the trigger. *Bang*, all over, and the devastation left behind you can see. Help SOCO search for ID will you? I want photographs of any tattoos he's got and then I want the eye recovered.'

'Re … co … ver the eye, sir?' Wigglesworth, said swallowing hard.

'Yes, to return it to the body where it belongs. Nobody else wants to have to suffer seeing that. Photograph it first in situ. Let me have copies. It'll be a good one for training on how to identify suicide. I want a report with your findings on my desk first thing tomorrow and do the report for the coroner. I need a firearms officer to secure the weapon and recover any further unspent cartridges so they can be disposed of safely. I'll leave it with you, as they say,' Dylan said, looking over his shoulder as he turned to leave.

He thanked the scenes of crime officer. It was not uncommon for Dylan to leave a DS with a body such as this: he knew the likes of Dawn or Larry Banks would have got on with it and told him about it the next day at briefing. Being a detective was all about making decisions. Tonight's scene, although gross and not something one would choose to view, was at the lower end of the scale as far as nauseous and evil were concerned, and quite straightforward.

He returned to Jen's to get some much-needed sleep so he was ready for whatever the next day might bring. He knew from experience that could be anything. He liked the unpredictability of the job. Most SIOs would work continuously when a job was running, their rest days increasingly never taken. Silently they went on their 'days owed' card in their desk drawer. This was evidence to show they had worked a day when they should have been off. HQ was quite happy for Dylan to work his rest days, but didn't like it when he tried to take time out. He knew he had four months in days owed on his card.

'Breakfast together. What have I done to deserve this honour?' Jen said, stroking Dylan's neck as he sat at the table.

'It was a suicide last night,' he mumbled, mouth full of cereal. 'He'd blown his own head off. DS Wigglesworth just couldn't hack it. He threw up when he saw the eye on the ceiling. Serves him right for calling me out.' Jack smiled, gulping from his mug of tea liked a pleased child.

'That's awful. I'm not surprised he was sick, most people would be, but it does serve him right. Don't get me going on that one this morning. What you up to today?' she said, snapping her lunch box together and throwing him a banana and an apple to put in his briefcase.

'I need to catch up with the Hodgson murder trial to see where they're at with that one, before getting to Daisy's murder. We've had no luck yet.' His voice sounded flat as he put on his suit jacket and picked up his briefcase.

'I wonder how many people talk about murders and suicides over breakfast,' Jen said, as she put on her coat and reached up for a kiss goodbye, squaring his tie. He smiled; what could he say?

'Might see you later at work, Miss Jones,' he called as they both walked to their cars.

'Have a good day. You'll find the murderer, you know you always do,' she called.

Easier said than done, thought Dylan.

Chapter Ten

Dawn always had an infectious glow about her and Dylan was pleased to see her smiling face in his incident room. The smell of toasting bread drifted in the air to greet him.

'Looks like you certainly put the frighteners on Michael Moorhouse for head butting you,' Dawn said as she accepted a slice of toast and dripping from a plate that was being passed around the busy office.

'Why, what makes you say that?' he said as he snatched a slice from the giggling typists.

'Dooh, well, he did blow his head off last night. Was it suspicious, is that why you went?' she said wiping the fat running down her chin with her hankie.

He stared at her open mouthed: he hadn't realised that the body he'd been called out to was the man who'd attacked him.

'No, not suspicious at all. Just a DS who couldn't tell a suicide when he saw one. Do you know, I didn't stay long enough to find out the deceased's name? I'm obviously losing it, Dawn I didn't recognise him.'

She nearly choked. 'Not surprising really, he'd no bloody head according to the report,' she laughed.

'At least he won't get the chance to hurt anyone else.' He touched his lip instinctively. It still felt lumpy. Jen would be relieved. He texted her: *You know that low life gorilla that did my lip? He was the body I went to last night.*

And you forgot to tell me? she immediately responded.

I didn't recognise him

That's not like you

I'd a good excuse, since he'd no face.

LOL Talking of gorillas you should be at the dentist at 10.

You know how to make a grown man cry, don't you?

The mention of the dentist made him cringe. He hated the dentist. He shivered as he remembered as a child being dragged on two bus rides across town by his mum, having had no breakfast. His mum feared he might bring it back with the anaesthetic, bless her. The only good thing about the excursion was sitting in the waiting room reading the old comics that his parents couldn't afford new. He could still hear his stomach growling. Feel his legs shaking uncontrollably, whether with cold or fear he didn't know. He recalled a huge, high, cold chair where a metal clamp was put in his mouth to wedge it open. He wondered if he recalled correctly a half-deflated black rubber ball being slammed over his nose and mouth, or if it was just a nightmare. Dylan could still conjure up the smell of gas and recall the hissing that it made as he drifted down a never-ending tunnel of swirling distorted images. The voices of the dentist and his nurse he'd heard get louder and drone off as the gas took effect, unrecognisable as human as he fell into oblivion. He always woke with tears streaming down his face as he fought to climb back through the fog. Blood oozing down the edges of his mouth, gauze stuffed in his cheeks making him look like a chipmunk. Fortunately he was always released before the blood running down his throat choked him and he would stagger out of the room only to hear '*next*' being hollered for the unsuspecting poor victim. Those days were long gone, but he still didn't like the dentist. He'd go though, just to please Jen.

This morning the waiting room was quiet. Leaflets littered the table in the middle of the room. A fire glowed in the fireplace and the sun streamed in through the windows. Not a lot had changed over the years, he thought, as he picked up a summer edition of *Homes & Gardens*. He had just got nicely seated when the nurse appeared.

'Mr Dylan, the dentist is ready for you now.' Great, waiting around always made him nervous.

'Good morning. Just a check up this morning, I see by your notes,' said the dentist cheerfully, shaking Dylan's hand as he walked into his lair.

'Don't know what's good about it,' Dylan smirked apprehensively.

'Oh, you're a comedian, Mr Dylan,' the dentist laughed as he tilted Dylan's chair back, pulled his mask over his nose and mouth, and shone the light straight into Dylan's eyes. Was his dentist a sadist?

'Let's have a look. Relax your tongue,' he said whilst hooking a saliva ejector into the corner of Dylan's mouth. 'Keeping you busy I see. Are you getting any nearer to catching the perpetrator? Relax your tongue, no, relax it,' he said, pressing down on Dylan's tongue with the back of the mouth mirror to make sure he did what he was being told. 'Nasty scar on your lip, Detective. Did you get that in the line of duty, eh?'

Dylan wondered why it was that dentists always asked questions when they had their hands in your mouth, knowing full well you couldn't reply. Did they really expect you to answer back? Dylan found it uncomfortable enough having water spitting up into his face, running down the side of his neck, an instrument down his throat, never mind making idle conversation.

'Relax your tongue. Nearly done now, Mr Dylan. Well done.'

Dylan tried hard to relax and keep focused on the map of the town of Harrowfield and its surrounding areas on the ceiling of the surgery, the area he was having searched for Daisy's killer clearly visible to him. My god, why hadn't he thought about it before? The body had been found on the back road used daily by him and his colleagues between Harrowfield Station and Tandem Bridge. Was that significant?

'Okay, all done,' the dentist said triumphantly as he ejected Dylan abruptly into a sitting position. 'Swill your mouth out, please. Have you ever considered crowns on those front three teeth?' he asked. 'It'll only take a couple of hours, just two appointments. That front tooth is not going to hold out much longer.'

Crowns. Crowns. Had he ever considered crowns? Had he hell. Ten minutes in the chair was enough.

'I'll give it some thought,' was all he said as he headed for the door. 'See you in six months,' he called as he fled.

'He wants me to have crowns,' he told Jen from his mobile phone.

'Wow. How good would that be? Film star teeth.'

'In your dreams and his.' Dylan scowled.

Jen laughed. 'You big baby. Of all the awful things you see and do in your job you're frightened of the dentist?'

'I'll think about it,' he heard himself saying for the second time today. 'Speak to you later.' But he was already defeated; she would persuade him, he knew she would.

Driving back through the town, Dylan realised that Christmas was looming. The streets were adorned with lights and gaiety. It was quiet, so he parked his car on the high street. He was impulsive. Shopping for Dylan was no different to making decisions on a murder enquiry. Once he made up his mind, he went with it. Heading straight to the jewellers, a two-toned gold bracelet took his eye for Jen.

'Can I help you, sir?' asked the young female assistant.

'Yes, I'll take that one please.' He pointed the bracelet out in the window display.

'Would you like it gift-wrapped?'

He nodded. It was a good job he wasn't a shopaholic, he thought; he'd just spent five hundred quid in five minutes flat. A card, now, and his Christmas shopping would be finished. He recognised one of the assistants in Central Cards: Marjorie Sykes. Some years ago she'd been a police typist, he recalled, but she didn't appear to know him. She was still a smart, middle-aged lady and although she'd been an excellent typist, had been required to leave, if his memory served him correctly. He smiled as he remembered why. No one had known of her prejudices until a prosecutor was reading the case papers that she'd typed. The statement by the officer in the case read: *You flipping custard go flip yourself,* the man shouted. *Hiss off, I'll fight any of you fruckers.* The swear words used by the defendant had been changed for somewhat milder ones by Marjorie. Although causing amusement, she was told in no uncertain terms that the words needed to be verbatim for court. She insisted that she didn't like to hear such language and she certainly wouldn't type it. Nothing would make her compromise her values or beliefs. He thanked her and wished her a merry

Christmas as she took his money for the card. It must have been so difficult to think of the alternative words, he chuckled to himself as he walked out of the shop.

As he put the shopping in the boot of his car, his mind turned to the families who he knew wouldn't be relishing the festive season. It would be a horrendous time for the Hinds. A time of loneliness and tears, even though family would surround them. Their hurt would be even more acute because of the time of year, if that was at all possible.

Back at the office he put Jen's present into an empty printer-paper box and wrapped it again. *She'll never guess what it is now,* he thought, smiling as he rang her office number.

'Jennifer Jones, can I help you?'

'You certainly can, Miss Jones,' Dylan grinned. 'I'm sitting in the office quietly for a change, and thought of you.' She was silent, so he knew someone was nearby and she couldn't talk. 'I've arranged a drink with the team at six o'clock in the bar. Just buying them a beer to say thank you for their work on the Johnson murder enquiry. You remember the robbery that went wrong? The young father that got stabbed?'

'Fantastic, result, yes. I'll see you there.' He could hear the happiness in her voice.

Waiting to go, he started to read over the papers regarding the position of the enquiry into the Daisy Hind murder. It was so warm in the office he could have happily laid his head on the desk and fallen asleep. He noticed the map of the town on his wall was exactly the same as the one on the dentist's ceiling and he tore it down, screwed it up and threw it in the bin. He didn't need a constant reminder of the dentist.

The Lounge buzzed as he approached. The team's triumph was tangible and he felt the pats on his back as he walked to the bar and ordered a drink.

'Ladies and gents, your attention please.' Dylan shouted to be heard. The drone became a murmur and then no more. 'Thank you for all your efforts in getting two murderers sentenced to life today. You've given the family the best present they could've hoped for this Christmas, in the circumstances. This is what the job's all about and you can feel proud of yourselves. A chain is only as good as its weakest link and we didn't have one.' He held his glass high. 'Well done everyone. There is money behind the bar, so have a drink on me.' A raucous cheer went up.

Dylan made sure he passed Jen on the way to the toilet. She was standing in the corridor speaking to DS Larry Banks. He always felt a twinge of jealousy when he saw her talking to other men. He saw her laugh, throwing her hair back as she did when she laughed with him.

'Think I'm in there, Jack,' Larry said as he joined Dylan at the urinal.

'You think so, mate?' was all he could think of to reply, as they both headed to find her at the bar.

'Let me get that, Jen,' Larry said hurrying forward to take Jen's empty glass from her. Dawn walked in his path and Larry stepped over, kissing her on the cheek, which enabled Dylan to catch Jen's arm.

'Leaving at eight?' he whispered. She nodded silently in agreement.

Dylan left and paced the kitchen of her home waiting for her return. *That bloody letch. How dare he think he'd a cat in hell's chance with Jen? Of all the conceited ...* he raged. Her key turned in the lock and he realised seeing her that Larry had every right to fancy Miss Jones. Dylan's Miss Jones. He walked towards her and held her in his arms.

'Larry thought he was in with a shot. I was jealous,' he told her with his best little boy wounded look.

She leaned back, laughing. 'As if,' she said, but didn't break the embrace.

'I'm rather proud of myself today, actually,' he said as he stepped back so he could look into her eyes. 'I managed to get your Christmas present.'

'How the hell did you 'ave time for that?' She giggled. 'I haven't even thought about yours yet.' But he could tell she was pleased by his act.

'Ah ha. I made time for my girl. Now, Miss Jones, I think it's time for bed,' Dylan said, slapping her backside as she took off her coat and hung it behind the door.

'Now that is the best decision you've made today,' was her reply as she ran up the stairs.

Chapter Eleven

There is always a *review* of detected and undetected murders: the detected ones to see if there is anything that would assist in future investigations, the undetected to identify areas that may assist the present enquiry ensuring nothing has been overlooked.

Headquarters select personnel for major incidents so the ratio is the same for each Division, thereby least affecting their performance and ultimately the force as a whole. SIOs have to fight for staff in the first instance and carry on fighting to keep them, as divisions constantly demand to have them back. This murder was no different. Divisions consistently send their lazy bastards first; why send your best? On the other side of the coin, an SIO won't return first those who are doing a great job, the ones with the energy and desire to be on the murder. Dylan silently thanked the gods for Dawn. He realised how lucky he was to be working with such a professional. It took at least some of the burden off his shoulders.

Daisy's review would take place four days before Christmas, a week away. The timescales didn't concern Jack Dylan; with the help of the computerised systems, the preparation of a review file in the established format didn't take long to produce. It consisted of a written summary of what had occurred, accompanied by photographs and a DVD. He would use these props to set the scene. A document averaging some twenty pages in length would be copied for each member of the review team and cover all aspects of the enquiry. After the presentation, the review team would take their copies away and, alongside the murder team, would sift and search through what had been done and consider what else could be done, if anything, to aid the investigation. Dylan would wait for the comments and ideas. He never thought of feedback as negative; he didn't care who came up with an idea as long as it helped to catch the killer.

An assistant chief constable, a chief superintendent and an SIO, along with another four officers with specialist knowledge, would be on the review team. The positive side of this was that for a short time at least, an ACC would take an interest in the murder. The chief superintendent would probably just be getting a tick in a box for the next round of promotions. They didn't experience the demands of a murder enquiry.

It was a few days to Christmas, but he wasn't in the mood for celebration. He knew he was being totally unfair to Jen. She loved Christmas; decorating the tree, the smell of pine cones, the shopping, wrapping the presents, writing out the cards. She loved just about everything that surrounded it. For the first time she wasn't going home to the Isle of Wight to be with her parents, and that was because of him. She'd made her first Christmas cake, and the mince pies. Dylan wanted to make it special for her. It's not that he didn't enjoy Christmas, but this year, if Daisy's murderer wasn't detected, he knew he wouldn't relax. His conscience wouldn't let him.

Dr Francis Boscombe, the offender profiler, worked for the Home Office and had travelled up from London on the train. He was a clean-shaven, balding, plump man in his fifties, about five feet ten inches tall and dressed in baggy cord trousers, a blue shirt and a dark brown battered tweed jacket that was obviously comfortable to wear. He listened intently to what Dylan and Dawn told him and visited the scene with them. He pored over the mortuary photographs, made notes at the scene, and studied the limited background information. He now knew as much as the officers on the case. In his opinion, the offender was male, possibly a local, and had a good knowledge of the area. He considered him an opportunist. He thought it possible that this type of murderer would take away items as trophies. It was also clear to him that the killer had displayed Daisy's body. By not hiding her, it was obvious that the killer wanted her found.

'What's he trying to tell us?' he said to himself out loud, obviously puzzled. 'He certainly wanted her seen.' This concerned him. 'Just my first impressions, Dylan, you understand. I can't be sure this is a one-off. He could kill again. Only time will tell, I'm afraid. Please keep me updated; any little occurrence could change everything and I might be able to help you further. It's a strange one, this,' he said, scratching his cheek with his weather-worn hand. He had stated some obvious things to the officers but he had also re-confirmed Dylan's own views. 'The murderer appears to have been methodical and organised in his approach, an orderly person. Now I've a train to catch.'

Dylan answered his mobile as he and Dawn watched Boscombe's train leave the station.

'Boss, Janice. The Hinds have received a Christmas card. It says in capital letters, "HAVE A GOOD ONE", but inside is something like a small piece of flesh wrapped in clingfilm. It's possibly Daisy's fingertip. I can just make out what seems to be a finger-nail.'

'Bloody hell, how gruesome's that? Look we're on our way. I want SOCO there as soon as possible,' he said as he looked at a puzzled Dawn.

'Consider it done, sir.'

Chapter Twelve

Twenty minutes later Dylan and Dawn were at the Hinds' home. Although it was a horrible thing for the family, from an inquiry point of view it was a positive one. The killer was giving them a chance to identify him. Trevor and Wendy were grey and their eyes were hooded and dark. Wendy was visibly shaking.

'The card, the envelope, postmark, and stamp all will be forensically examined. It's another opportunity to trace whoever's responsible,' Dylan said as he tried to reassure them. 'Somebody, for some reason, wants to cause you more pain.' Dylan only had to look into their faces to see how much they were hurting.

'I want you to both think very hard. Have either of you upset or argued with anyone, no matter how slight or trivial you may think it was? Absolutely anyone? Someone out there wants to kick you when you're down. We need to find out who and why.'

'We've done nothing to anyone. We haven't, honestly, have we, Trevor?'

Trevor shook his head. 'We don't deserve this,' he said, quietly.

A short time later, as Dylan and Dawn wandered down the Hinds' path back to the car, Dylan turned to a deflated Dawn. 'Think positive. We have another chance to find some evidence. Let's just hope forensic turns something up from the card. Mind you, we won't get anything until after the Christmas holidays, which is a flaming nuisance.'

Back at HQ, Dylan was informed that the Assistant Chief Constable would now not be available on the morning of the review. Whilst no explanation was given, his apologetic secretary told him that she would try to re-schedule the ACC's January appointments, to meet at his earliest convenience. Dylan wondered what could be more important than a child's murder. He had learnt his lesson in the past, cursing and swearing when someone had let him down only to find out later they had been involved in a serious road accident. Since then he had always bitten his tongue unless he was aware of the facts. If there was no good reason however, it was time to watch out and *pin your ears back.*

Staffing levels over the Christmas period had been staggered to give everyone time with their families, although officers would continue working round the clock to find Daisy's killer. Other agencies closed for seven days, therefore forensic inquiries and the like would remain static throughout. Dylan reassured the Hinds that none of them, including himself, would rest until Daisy's killer was found. They would have on-call staff at all times and whilst Dylan planned to take Christmas Day off, he would still be contactable.

It was hard to get into the Christmas spirit after the last few weeks and with nothing, not even a glimmer of hope, in the investigation into Daisy Charlotte Hind's murder, Dylan was at an all time low. He was tired. He wasn't sleeping properly, waking up at four in the morning and tossing and turning, wishing for morning. He hoped Christmas would re-charge his batteries.

Dylan left the office. It was early, but he was useless to anyone in his current frame of mind, so he decided to have a drive to try to clear his head. Feeling irritable and needing to let off steam, he put the car in reverse, put his foot down, and sped out of the police yard. At the very last second he saw the van and braked suddenly.

'Fucking hell,' Dylan gasped, as the skid brought his car to an abrupt halt without the anticipated 'bang'. The property clerk driving past the entrance to the gated yard had nearly been annihilated.

'Sorry, mate,' Dylan said as he wound down his window to apologise to Harold. 'My fault entirely, my mind was elsewhere.'

'It's okay, Mr. Dylan. Don't you worry yourself. No one's hurt,' said Harold. His voice quivered and his face was flushed. 'You're a lot busier than me. You … you go first, sir.' He waved Dylan on and slumped against his steering wheel.

Dylan's heart rate finally found its equilibrium and he realised he was driving towards Harrowfield Middle School. On the sports field he could see a soccer match taking place. He stopped, shivering as he got out of his warm car to watch. The cold, fresh air felt good and he breathed it deep into his lungs as he stood on the touchline near the penalty box. It was a fast game between Harrowfield and Bradley School. Both teams looked exhausted, socks rolled down, 1 – 1 on the scoreboard. Someone shouted, 'Five minutes remaining.' Dylan felt quite excited. The sound of the referee's whistle pierced the air. He was pointing to the penalty spot.

'Come on, Harrowfield,' came the shout of a supporter. There was a lot of booing from the Bradley School end, as Malcolm Meredith, Harrowfield's PE teacher and coach, walked on the pitch to speak to his team. He looked calm and confident. He pointed to a little thin lad with a red, elfin face, who stood shaking on the periphery of the group. 'Chris, you take it. Goalie's left,' he advised.

Chris opened his mouth as if to say something, showing the navy blue brace on his teeth.

'Your best striker?' Dylan asked Meredith, who had come to stand beside him on the touchline.

'Spencer? Nah, he's been off injured most of this year. Plays centre forward and never scored.'

'Poor lad. Why'd you give him the pressure shot then?'

'He's a capable player. It'll give him confidence, if he scores,' Meredith answered as he clasped his hands together and jogged on the spot. 'Come on, Chris,' he cried through gloved, cupped hands.

Christopher Spencer pulled his socks up over his thin, mottled legs. The referee called him forward. There were shouts and screams from the crowd.

He put his head down and ran forward, blasting the ball to the left of the goalkeeper. The keeper dived the wrong way. The teacher was right. It was like slow motion. The ball went in.

'Yes.' Dylan threw up his clenched fist and cheered along with the crowd.

Chris turned and ran back towards his teammates, who mobbed him. The coach ran on to the pitch with other spectators and lifted Chris high, swinging him around and round. Dylan smiled. *Great kick, well-done lad,* he thought. *That took 'bottle'.*

Christopher Francis Spencer, aged ten, scoring a goal, a penalty, maybe the winner, it was surreal. This was a dream come true. He couldn't wait to tell his mum and dad. A few minutes to go and the team were on a high. Christopher couldn't stop smiling; he didn't ache or feel the cold anymore. He didn't even mind the brace he'd recently had fitted and was still getting used to.

The final few kicks of the game, and it was a corner for Harrowfield, safe at Bradley's end. The ball was crossed, a hard kick. Up went Christopher and it hit him on the side of the head, knocking him to the ground.

That hurt, he thought, turning his face from the mud as he fell. He heard a loud cheer and raised his head. The ball had gone in the back of the net. He couldn't believe his eyes. He was dragged up from the ground by many pairs of arms. The referee blew his whistle. They were in the final. Two goals for Spencer. He was a hero. He was lifted to shoulder height and chaired around the pitch.

Dylan got into his car and drove, feeling guilty all of a sudden. He was never going to catch Daisy's killer watching a football match now, was he?

Chapter Thirteen

This is the very best day ever, thought Christopher. He was bursting to tell his dad. How he wished he'd been there to see it. The changing rooms were noisier than he had ever heard before.

'Great game Chris, well played,' said Meredith, picking him up in a bear hug.

Dylan drove to Jen's, switching his car radio on for the first time in as long as he could remember. He felt relaxed, positive.

Chris collected his kit and stood at the entrance to the ground, wishing he had some credit on his mobile so he could ring his dad. No sooner had he thought it than his mobile started vibrating.

'Dad, guess what? We're in the final and I scored,' Christopher shrieked down the phone, shaking with excitement. He grinned from ear to ear.

'That's fantastic, son, gosh, I'm so proud of you.'

'You should have seen me.'

'Listen, Christopher, I've got a flat tyre and I can't get hold of Mum, so I'm going to be late picking you up. I'll be there as soon as I can, stay at the usual place.' Christopher heard his dad chuckle, knew he was smiling. 'What a player, eh, son?'

Christopher stood and daydreamed. Would his name be in the papers? He imagined the headlines. SPENCER PUTS HARROWFIELD MIDDLE SCHOOL INTO THE CUP FINAL or CHRISTOPHER FRANCIS SPENCER A HERO. He wasn't bothered which they used.

Most people had gone home. All the Harrowfield players and supporters left, shouting and whistling to Christopher as they passed. Mr Meredith pulled alongside.

'Do you need a lift, Chris?'

'No thanks, sir, my dad's picking me up.'

When Martin Spencer arrived fifteen minutes later, there was no sign of his son. He tried ringing his mobile, but it was out of service. *Where can he be,* he wondered? It was totally out of character for Chris not to be where he said he would be. Martin got out of his car and wandered around the sports field, checked the changing rooms. The doors were locked and bolted. He drove around the area, looking for his son. He telephoned home, just in case. The area leading to the football pitch used by the school was off a small, unmade road. There were a few houses at the end but it was mainly an area where people exercised their dogs. Martin returned home and paced the house.

Where is he, where the hell is he? he asked himself over and over again, scratching his head. 'What was Chris thinking of, going off somewhere? That's why we got the bloody mobile, so he could keep in touch with us,' he said as he pressed re-dial for the umpteenth time.

When Sarah Spencer got home with her shopping, she rang round Chris's friends, but all they could tell her was that the last time they had seen him he was waiting for his dad. Martin and Sarah were worried sick. They reported their son missing to the police at twenty to six.

Dylan and Jen had just arrived at the Farrington Restaurant for dinner. It was a lovely place in the middle of nowhere, on the outskirts of town, far away from prying eyes. Dylan had been promising Jen a night out for ages. Feeling much brighter, he had taken the bull by the horns and booked the table as a surprise. Jen looked gorgeous in a short, floral-print, silk dress and high sling back shoes. She was wearing Jack's favourite perfume; she knew she smelled good too.

It was blustery outside and they had practically blown into the place. The flames of the candles on the tables flickered as the heavy, wooden door closed behind them, but once seated, the room felt warm and cosy.

'Miss Jones, you look good enough to eat,' remarked Jack.

The candles in the brass candlesticks and their soft, warm light gave the surroundings a romantic radiance. The cream damask tablecloth and napkins were perfect for the china, glass, and cutlery set out on them. A fire blazed in the open fireplace, which added to the comfortable glow: its sooty fragrance could hardly be noticed. It was quiet and intimate with only one other couple dining. They were both looking forward to the evening. Jack for once looked relaxed, and handsome in his white shirt and tie, Jen thought, as the maitre'd' pulled out their chairs. They smiled, content with each other as Jack reached for Jen's hand across the table.

'This is lovely. Thank you for bringing me here, Jack,' she said as they were handed the menu and wine list. Jack didn't hesitate to order a bottle of Chateauneuf-du-Pape, Jen's favourite wine.

She looked coy. 'I hope you're not trying to get me drunk, Mr Dylan.'

'And what if I am? I'll drive. You can have a drink for once. Mmm, I think I'll have a sixteen ounce sirloin,' he said, his eyes dancing with delight as he looked at the menu.

'I might have known you'd pick that, but such a big one?'

'Yeah, I'm starving. What about you?' he grinned.

'A big one, but I think I'll have the monk fish,' she teased, looking deep into his eyes.

The dulcet tones of Dylan's mobile cut short the banter. *No, not now*, he thought as he took a few steps over to the reception area. Jen nodded her thanks to the waiter, who looked at her sympathetically and asked if they would like to wait until the gentleman had finished his call before ordering. Jen could see Jack's face from where she sat. She knew in her heart that they wouldn't be eating at the lovely restaurant with the pretty candles. She blew them out in defiance. She could tell by the way he cocked his head and held the mobile to his ear with his shoulder to free his right hand, the way he wrote in his pocket notebook, and the way he listened intently to what he was being told that he would be going back to work soon. His expression was serious as he passed the bottle of red wine that the understanding waiter had corked, to Jen. He opened the car door for her in silence and got into the driving seat. He looked at her and laid his head back.

'I've just got to make another call. I'm so sorry, love.'

'Is it a bad one?' she asked through gritted teeth, a lump in her throat.

'Yeah, a young lad's gone missing.'

She cuddled up to his arm, leaning towards him from the passenger seat of the car while he keyed the number of force control into his mobile. She was angry, upset, sad, and annoyed with herself for being so selfish. She didn't want him to see.

'I hope you find him, safe,' she whispered, as tears of disappointment stung her eyes. She wouldn't let him see her cry; she knew he felt guilty enough.

Jack was in work mode and at once became a different person. He talked on his mobile and Jen knew she had already faded into the background, forgotten for the time being. She hated his job for what it did to their lives.

'Who's the on-call DS? Call them out. On-call CID? All to the CID office for briefing, please. I want the helicopter up and a full search team to the CID office. Close the street where he was last seen,' Dylan instructed.

He marched ahead of Jen into the house when they arrived home. Changed his suit and tie in silence and was on his way with a quick kiss on her cheek, but without a backward glance. She watched as usual as the tail lights of his car disappeared. She drew the curtains to shut out the world and clambered into her pyjamas. Taking her make-up off slowly whilst seated at her dressing table, she picked up her hairbrush and ran it through her hair. She hung up her pretty dress and, with dressing gown and slippers on, she padded down the stairs.

'Hi fella, looks like it's you and me for dinner again. Beans on toast?' She groaned as she looked in the cupboard and remembered the lovely food that had been on the menu. Sitting at the kitchen table, she stroked Max's head, rubbing behind his ears as the microwave whirred. He snuggled up to her leg and placed his head on her knee, appreciating the attention. Food, glass and bottle of wine on the tray, she was followed by Max into the lounge, where she lit the fire and flicked on the TV, mainly for the background noise. The house was so quiet without Jack. *The last thing he needs is another child missing,* she thought as she uncorked the bottle of wine from the restaurant and filled the large glass to the brim.

'To the police service. Thanks again for ruining my evening,' she toasted.

Jen had never been a drinker, but planned to have another glass as an anaesthetic to her heartache. The job was hurting both of them. How long could she keep on worrying about Jack and being left alone, disappointed? If she stayed with Jack she knew her life would be being available for him … when he wasn't working. Did she want it to be like this? She didn't want to be forever watching his car lights disappearing away from her; she knew that. There would always be a murder, always someone going missing, but did that mean she had to suffer because of it?

'One day, Max. One day it'll all change. Do you think?' She pulled Max closer to her.

Chapter Fourteen

The enquiries into missing persons, or 'mispers' as they are known, are well-rehearsed approaches, and although each one is dealt with on its own merits, there is a routine to follow. The tried and tested plan is intended to ensure thoroughness, so that nothing is overlooked.

Two uniformed officers had attended at the home of the Spencers, a male and female, the available unit. They had recorded what had happened and obtained a recent photograph of Christopher and a description of what he had been wearing.

Christopher Francis Spencer was four feet tall, of average build, with very short light brown hair. He was wearing a navy blue tracksuit that advertised Adidas on the right breast, white T-shirt, and size six blue Adidas trainers. He had with him an Adidas navy blue sports bag, which would have in it a blue towel, his football kit, and maybe a juice drink. Christopher was a normal kid. His only distinctive, identifying accessory was the newly fitted, navy blue brace on his top teeth. It was totally out of character for him to go off, he had just spoken to his dad, and was elated about the football result. Instinctively the duty inspector wasn't happy. This boy going missing felt totally wrong. Christopher's description went out immediately. Searches using dogs would take place and the helicopter would be up within the hour. CID was requested along with a DS who'd called out a DI. It wouldn't be long before the Press were out like vultures, asking questions because of the police activity.

Dylan arrived at Harrowfield Police Station at seven o'clock. He was sure he'd heard the name of the missing boy before, but dismissed the thought as quickly as it had come to him. Dylan looked at the lines of enquiry to see if they were sufficient. What contingency planning had been put into place for the search to continue overnight? Had they already cleared the ground beneath their feet? Dylan swore by the golden rule. Had the detectives already searched Christopher's bedroom? Did he have a computer? Dylan knew how important it was to try to understand the family and get a background for Christopher himself. What sort of family were they? Which school did he attend? What did the school know about him? Who took him for football? Where is that person? Dylan tried to keep an open mind as he worked through what was already known about Christopher, but his mind was racing at a hundred miles per hour. He needed answers to lots of questions and the night was drawing in. He sent his detective sergeant and two detective constables, one a specially trained family liaison officer, to the family home, having first briefed them that the purpose of their visit was to gather information.

The on-call detective sergeant was Larry Banks, and he joined Dylan in the office. Dylan had worked on a number of occasions with Larry the lad, as he was known. A lot of police officers had nicknames; it went with the job. He was six feet tall with neatly combed back, jet black hair. Some thought it was dyed, but Dylan wasn't sure and frankly didn't care. What he did know about Larry was he was always impeccably turned out, he was forty-five-ish and divorced twice with no children, and he somehow managed to afford a luxury riverside apartment and a bright blue Audi sports car. He always wore slip-on leather shoes without socks; the rumour being that, as his socks had once been his downfall when he'd to leave some married lady's bedroom in a hurry, not wearing them meant he had less to worry about if he needed to make a quick exit. If he wasn't on the pull or in the gym he was in his favourite haunt, the pub.

Children, in Dylan's experience, were found in all kinds of places. A small girl who went missing had only gone to the bottom of the garden, climbed into her pet rabbit's hutch and fallen asleep, much to her parents' relief. Others he could remember had done much the same thing in attics, cellars, sheds and garages. However, experience was telling Dylan that this one felt different.

In the darkness enquiries progressed, but there had been no sign of Christopher since the match. The cold night and the thought of hypothermia concerned Dylan. Some of the team were still with the family. The enquiry was ongoing and arrangements were made for them to stagger their contact throughout the night. Cell site analysis of activity from Christopher's mobile was instigated, which Dylan hoped would lead to a possible location. The area around the football pitch was sealed, and a tent was erected around the entry where Christopher had waited. Rain was forecast.

Initial searches were negative. The Spencers' house showed nothing untoward, they were just an ordinary family who were out of their minds with worry. Dylan returned home in the early hours knowing that he personally couldn't do any more until first light. Jen was lying awake in the dark as he crept into the bedroom. She didn't turn to face him.

'Hi, love, I'm sorry if I woke you,' he whispered as he pulled back the covers and slid into the nice warm bed.

'You're freezing,' she squealed as Dylan snuggled up behind her. 'You want to talk about it?' she asked turning to give him a cuddle.

'It's a ten-year-old boy, gone missing from a school football match earlier. I saw him score a goal, Jen. I stopped at the school to watch the match for a few minutes.' *Was the murderer watching too?* Dylan wondered. He put his face in Jen's shoulder. There was no more to say.

'Let's hope he turns up, eh?' she said as she held him tight. She was just pleased he was home with her.

Dylan didn't sleep much; his mind was racing. Many times he woke with questions or ideas, and jotted them down on the pad on his bedside table. *Contact the Press Office. Keep a lid on panic in the community. Search sites?* The thoughts went around and around in his head.

The alarm clock read '05:30' in big, red numbers when he opened his eyes. As they were adjusting to the darkness, the phone rang. It was police control. A security night watchman walking home by torchlight had come across a body hung from a bridge over the canal at Lowergate.

'Is it the boy?' Jen asked tentatively, her mouth dry.

'Looks like it,' Dylan said as he climbed out of bed. He turned and leaned over to kiss her. 'I'm sorry, love.' he stopped and cupped her face in his hand, looking into her eyes. 'That's all I seem to be saying these days, isn't it?

Remember I do love you. I know I keep saying it, but I never want you to forget.'

Shit, shave, cuddle, and he was off, while Jen rolled over in bed stuffing her head under her pillow and groaned. *Why, why, why was it always Dylan that was called out?* 'Urgh, she growled in between clenched teeth, crying in anger into the mattress.

'Larry, meet me at the scene as soon as you can.' Dylan spoke on the hands-free phone in his car, anxious to hit the ground running. 'I need the scene sealed. SOCO are on their way, I'm told, and I need an exhibit officer identifying. Do you know if preliminary examinations have been carried out by paramedics?'

Larry yawned. 'Um, yes. Okay, okay and don't know,' he said trying to keep up with Dylan's requests while still trying to see through the fog of last night's ale.

Once suited up, the group led by Dylan walked along the towpath to the bridge, then along the twenty or so footplates that SOCO had laid so no one would trample over any evidence that may be there. There was no sign of Larry, but to be fair he'd got the scene sealed and an exhibits officer on site. A searchlight enabled them to see the hanging body. A shuffle along the footplates told Dylan that Larry was walking in haste towards them.

'Larry, arrange me some canvas screening on poles, would you? The last thing we need is prying eyes,' he shouted not turning to look in his direction.

'Will do, boss,' Larry replied.

He could see the body of a young boy, bright blue nylon rope around his neck. A smearing of something dark was around his mouth and about his face, like mud. He turned away. The body looked like something from another planet. The boy's face was distorted and purple in colour. His dark blue tongue protruded from his mouth. It was elongated and swollen to probably three times its normal size. The boy's eyes bulged out of their sockets: even from a distance; it was a nauseating sight. Dylan could quite understand the shock and reaction of the man who found him.

The occasional splash of the slow-moving water of the canal disturbed the silence, making the quietness of the moment seem eerie. Even though they were fifteen feet away from the body, Dylan could see the boy's head flopped to the right like a rag doll. He shivered. He had seen a few hangings in his time. All had been horrific, but this was by far the worst. Another child's body.

The team walked slowly and carefully onto the bridge itself. It was only about four feet wide. Not big enough for a large vehicle, Dylan noticed. He could see that the rope came up over the stone wall and was fastened to a lamppost at the opposite side.

'The child's got an injury to the top right hand side of his head,' the officer from SOCO pointed out. 'Look, you can see where it's bled.'

'It's not consistent with a fall,' observed Dylan. 'Not suicide. Murder? Someone has taken the time and effort to leave the child's body like this. We're going to have to somehow lift him onto the bridge or lower him into a dinghy.' Dylan pondered. 'And as soon as possible.' He was sure it was just one of many problems that lay ahead.

'The canal is only about two feet six deep here, so we can examine the body in situ using a scaffolding tower then lower it by cutting the rope,' an officer from operational support informed Dylan.

'We'll need two people to lower the body into a dinghy and paddle it to the canal side.' Dylan thought out loud, considering the option. It bothered him, the extent to which the murderer had gone to display the young lad's form. Evil didn't begin to describe it. This was not simply a dump site. Dylan knew the killer had planned everything before he struck and left the body on display in this way, but why?

Chapter Fifteen

Daylight crept upon them, nobody noticed. Christopher's sports bag could now be seen at the opposite side of the bridge. Scenes of crime officers worked busily securing evidence. Dylan told them to cut the rope a couple of feet above the body for closer inspection of the knot and possible DNA.

The suits of those worn would be retained just in case they were required by anyone for evidence at a later stage. Everything had to be recorded, retained and revealed for disclosure to any future defence team, should they wish to examine it. Once the sports bag had been photographed, its contents would also be photographed individually, item after item carefully examined. Dylan left Larry to oversee the recovery of Christopher's body and went to meet the liaison officers outside the Spencers' home, after which he planned to go inside to meet the family and break the sad news. He saw Detective Clive Merton, the FLO for the incident, and PC Frances Hope, who was new in post, just having returned from her FLO training.

The family's worst fear would shortly become reality. Their son dead. And at this stage a lot of unanswered questions. Why? Who? When? Where? He would also have to tell them how their child had died, but not yet. He needed to tell them of the discovery before they heard it through the media. He briefed the FLOs as to the situation at the canal and what would happen later in the day, then he went into the Spencers' house. Martin and Sarah were open-mouthed, just waiting for news, reminding him of hungry chicks in the nest waiting for food. Their faces were ashen with lack of sleep, worry and distress. Inside they sat and then Dylan broke the news. As he spoke, tears rolled silently down their cheeks. Sarah hugged her daughter Jane to her.

'Oh, my god no,' Martin cried. 'Where is he? I want to see him.'

'The boy's body, which we believe is Christopher, is being taken to Harrowfield mortuary. You'll be able to see him there. I'm afraid you'll have to make a formal identification,'

Dylan told them. Sarah cried quietly. As she tried to stand, her legs buckled and she almost dropped Jane. He didn't want to tell them Christopher had been hanged. He knew that he would have to break this harrowing detail at some point, but he could only do that once the facts had been established and the time was right. *When is there ever going to be a right time to tell them that?* Dylan wondered. Once again he found himself trying to console a destroyed family, attempting to soften the impact as best he could. He drew on all his experience in dealing with situations such as these. But in his heart, deep down, he knew that no matter what he said or how he said it, all they wanted was Christopher back.

'Let me assure you both that once I'm in possession of all the facts I will hold nothing back from you. You have every right to know.' He knew how difficult it was, the not knowing, but asked them to be patient while enquiries were being completed to establish what had happened and how Christopher had died.

'I will update you later in the day and, apart from seeing Christopher; you will be able to go to where his body was found if you want.' Dylan was careful not to say 'died' as it was unlikely in his mind that he was killed there. The post mortem would hopefully enlighten him as to what had taken place.

He headed back to the mortuary. Once there he met up with Larry, the scenes of crime officers, Andrew and Mike, and the on-call pathologist, Professor Shirley Wright. Dylan had met her before on other cases. He was glad it was Shirley; he had a lot of time for her.

'The lad had played football for the school. They won and he scored their two goals. Strangely enough I saw him there, but that's another story. After the match, he'd waited for his dad, in the usual place. Dad had a flat tyre and was late. When he got there, Christopher had gone, which was totally out of character. A digital photograph of the boy has been taken in situ.' Dylan handed it to Shirley.

The examination began. Some rounded object, the size of a golf ball or thereabouts, had caused the injury to the right rear of Christopher's head.

'It was a forceful blow,' remarked Shirley. 'It would have rendered him certainly semi-conscious if not unconscious and it has caused a massive hairline fracture to the skull.'

The circular impact mark was measured and found to be two inches in diameter. Petechia, burst blood vessels, covered the whites of the eyes. The noose was carefully cut from around the boy's neck and preserved. The dark coloured substance around and in his mouth was discovered to be excrement.

'Ugh,' murmured Shirley, as it was swabbed and scraped into containers. Was it human? Only time would tell. The smell of the mortuary had taken on the overriding smell of faeces, which rose above the normal distinctive smell of death. This was not just murder. The killer was leaving a message. But why?

'It appears that he's lost part of the brace from his upper front teeth. Some of it is intact, but the majority is missing. There has been bleeding and bruising, which suggests that it was ripped out by force, either by something or somebody.' Shirley continued Christopher's post mortem. He had not been sexually assaulted and his internal organs were all normal. He had been a healthy young boy prior to his death.

'Cause of death, strangulation by ligature,' Shirley announced, as she meticulously recorded weights of organs, and took blood and other routine samples. 'After the blow to the head he would have been unconscious, but the strangulation, the hanging, is what killed him.'

As Shirley washed her hands, she turned to Dylan. 'Best of luck with this one, I hope you catch the perpetrator pretty quick. If I can be of any help, well, you know, don't hesitate.'

Dylan watched the little boy's body being prepared for formal identification, the swollen, protruding tongue carefully pushed back into his mouth. Only hours ago this lad had been a star, on top of the world.

He was always appreciative of the way the mortuary attendants took such care with their preparation for viewings.

Looking at the young lad placed on the slab, Dylan thought how like a doll he was, almost Pinocchio-like. But this doll wasn't about to come to life. Some people say when the soul leaves the body, only a shell remains. It certainly gave Dylan that feeling.

Alarm bells were ringing for Dylan. Christopher Spencer's head injury was very similar to that sustained by Daisy Hind, and his body had been left on display, too. Lunchtime. Time to consider strategy and resolve issues. Examination of the sports bag suggested one yellow and white striped football sock was missing, or lost.

A new policy book had already been started and given the operation name, *Larkspur*. Daisy's incident was named *Foxglove*. Names were given to ensure operational security so there was no mix up between incidents.

There were two extended scenes that required careful fingertip examination, according to Dylan. They were the football pitch area, including the entrance where Christopher would have waited for his dad, and the disposal site by the canal, where the body was found. There was the usual collation of CCTV, the search of the changing rooms and the school locker belonging to the little boy. Malcolm Meredith was the teacher who had taken them for football that day; he would need to be interviewed at length. As far as they knew, he was the last person to see Christopher alive. Schoolfriends, Dylan needed a list of schoolfriends. The list of actions to be completed continued to flow from him, ready to be recorded on computer once the location of the incident room was established. He would run the enquiry from Harrowfield, on the floor below the Daisy Hind murder enquiry.

Dylan stood in the doorway to the new incident room. It contained rows of desks with blank-screened computers. At the front was a dry-wipe board where important details could be recorded and seen by everyone, saving hours of repetitive questions or checks. Empty for the moment, ironically it was like a school classroom.

Enquiries organised, he and Larry met up with the bereaved family for the identification of their son, and told them of their findings.

'Missing at the moment is Christopher's mobile, possibly a football sock, and part of the brace from his teeth.' Dylan told them. This was a difficult time for them; not only had they suddenly lost their only son, but he had also been brutally murdered.

'How does anyone come to terms with such heartbreaking news?' Dylan asked Larry.

'God knows. Their life won't ever be the same again, that's for sure.'

They both knew from experience that this was only the start of the family's misery, and it would be protracted. As if the death was not enough, they would have to endure the investigation, with its peaks and troughs and, if it was successful, the additional trauma of a trial.

Dylan sat with Larry, the family liaison officers and the Spencers. Their family had grown and now included Christopher's grandparents. Martin and Sarah Spencer had been to the mortuary, seen Christopher, and formally identified him. It was surreal; they were in deep shock. In his own way Dylan tried to make things easier.

'Christopher was hit over the head and it is very likely he was rendered unconscious immediately,' he told them. He went on to tell them the facts, as he knew them, unpleasant as they were.

'Christopher's attacker or attackers put a rope around his neck and hung him over the bridge, which strangled him. That was the cause of death. He was not sexually assaulted in any way.' He hoped this would distract them from the thought of strangulation. They did not move. Their facial expressions were frozen. After a moment's silence, Granddad Frank cleared his throat.

'What monster would do this to a young lad? Who could be so evil? Get me the bastard's name. I want to know who he is.' He started to cry.

'Was it older lads … do you … think? Was … he bullied?' asked Sarah, spluttering her words out as she struggled to understand. 'They really, really hurt him, didn't they?' She started sobbing uncontrollably. Martin held her tight to him.

'He looked so lonely in the hospital,' he said as tears ran down his ashen face. 'If only I hadn't had that flat tyre ... the first time he'd scored; he was on such a high when I spoke to him. You don't think ... it had to do with that do you? I told him I was so proud of him. I should have gone to see him play, then this wouldn't have happened. It's all my fault.'

'Hindsight is a wonderful thing, don't blame yourself, it's not your fault.' But Dylan knew blame was one of the first emotions, along with denial. 'The enquiry will be tireless, I can assure you of that. There'll be all sorts of rumour, speculation, and gossip. Don't, whatever you do, listen to any of it. If you need to know anything, ask one of the team or me. Clive and Fran will stay with you and I'll personally keep you updated with any developments as they happen. Is it possible, do you think, that Christopher could have lost or left behind one of his football socks?'

'The kit was almost new; it had name-tags sewn in every piece. He was so careful, and he was proud of his football kit, he wouldn't have ... no, no way,' Martin said.

'Officers will have to go through Christopher's room, I'm afraid. It's routine, no stone will be left unturned and neither will anything be left to chance. Do you think the flat tyre was a puncture? Had you noticed it before, Martin?' asked Dylan.

'To be honest, I don't really know. I've put the spare one on now, so it's in the boot. If only I'd got there on time, it wouldn't have happened. I let him down.'

'We'll take the tyre away for examination. It's likely it was just coincidence, but we'll have a look.'

Under Dylan's instructions any exhibits, however irrelevant they might seem, would be kept. They might prove to be of no relevance to the investigation, but it was better to be safe than sorry.

Over the next few weeks, Dylan knew he would be seeing quite a bit of the Spencers. Their lives would be turned upside down and their background scrutinised. It was necessary for the investigation to show that they were not involved in the murder. The public could then concentrate on helping find the killer or killers. He would discuss the media with them, explaining how they would be used as part of the investigation. He would suggest that, in the next day or two, if they felt strong enough, they should consider a press conference. In his experience, it always seemed to boost an appeal. He apologised for all the things they were going to have to endure, but if it helped catch Christopher's killer or killers, then in Dylan's opinion anything was worthwhile.

He hadn't told them about the faeces in Christopher's mouth. There was plenty of time for that in the future. He would tell them before any inquest or court case, but at the moment he felt they had endured enough.

He asked them to think of any arguments or upsets Christopher had had, any incidents of bullying, anything at all, no matter how insignificant it might seem, that had happened over the past days or weeks. Before leaving, he asked if they had a recent photograph of Christopher, one that they really liked. In the coming days and weeks he would be headline news, sadly for the wrong reasons. Sarah reached into her purse and took out a photo. She looked at it, then held it tight to her chest before handing it over, trying to control her breathing.

'That's a real good one. Everybody says so. He's such a good lad,' she said proudly. Dylan made his apologies. He needed to get on.

Back in the station with a warm drink in his hand, he rang Jen. He spoke to her about the murder and told her what a horrible sight it had been. She told him to make sure he ate, let her know when he was on his way home, and not to forget that there was another day tomorrow.

She sat still when she replaced the receiver, thinking about what he'd been doing all morning and what he'd seen. It sounded like something most people only saw for an instant, briefly, or in a horror film. Where on earth did he get the strength? Another family's child taken and killed. All eyes would be on Jack to catch them, and quick.

Chapter Sixteen

The next morning Professor George Rutherford performed a second, independent post mortem on Daisy Hind that took two hours. *The first one was bad enough,* thought Dylan, *but the second is like rubbing your fucking nose in it.* With Christopher's to deal with as well it was horrendous.

'Thank you, Dylan, I've no further need of the body. I'll drop a letter in the post to that effect for you this evening so that the coroner can release it,' confirmed Professor Rutherford.

It? thought Dylan. The professor had just totally dismissed Daisy as a person and it made Dylan sad. He had, however, raised no matters of concern or disagreement with Judith Cockroft's findings, so Dylan expected the coroner to open an inquest within the next few days.

Back at HQ, Dylan ensured that there was a team looking at Harrowfield Middle School. He needed details urgently. The school might have helpful information regarding Christopher Spencer. *What about the football teacher at the game, what could he tell them? What did the school know about him?* He scribbled notes on a pad as thoughts ran through his mind. *What about the night security man who found him?* The enquiry moved ahead, CCTV in the area had been collected between the two locations; he wondered if it showed anything. Dylan felt frustrated. He was at the match and yet he couldn't recall any of the spectators. Maybe the murderer was one of them. The thought really pissed him off.

This was such a vile crime that it would create ripples of fear not only in the immediate community but around the county as well. The press conference was scheduled and he knew that they would want access to the family, but he wouldn't allow that yet. They would sensationalise the hanging and he couldn't control the story. He could only give them the facts and appeal for information. Maybe the family would be ready by Monday. He was aware that these days more and more families were used in press conferences, but he saw this as impacting the public to gain sympathy, rather than the public seeing a detective sitting there reading the facts. People would hopefully think *there but for the grace of god*. This was a normal family, just like theirs.

Now late, but satisfied the enquiry was up and running, he made for the car to go home. He felt exhausted, but his mind still raced. So many things whirred around his head: *did older boys, bullies, attack Christopher Spencer? If so would he expect more injuries? Did Michael Meredith, the football teacher have any involvement?* His mind continued to chase around. The drive home was slow, as he fought with himself to keep awake. He wound the windows down, languishing in the cool breeze. Home. The relief was immense as he turned off the engine and slumped in his seat with a huge sigh escaping his lips. He'd made it.

'Hiya, mate,' he said as he opened the front door and Max greeted him. He stroked the dog's head. 'My faithful friend.' He smiled, despite his mood. Jen wandered down the stairs.

'I'll make you a drink, love. You go straight up,' she said yawning, 'Do you want anything to eat?'

'No thanks, I'm so tired I feel sick.'

She planted a kiss on his lips. He dragged his legs up the stairs and knew that he would be asleep as soon as his head hit the pillow, a sleep that would be fitful as his mind refused to rest.

The weekend had flown; there was nothing new from the investigation, although the machinery of the incident room was up and running at full capacity, and the lines of enquiry for the detailed investigation were now prioritised. It always took around seventy-two hours to put the foundations of an incident room into place. Detectives were being selected for specialist roles such as exhibits, FLOs and telephone enquiries. The HOLMES team, immediately active, knew what was required and supplied any information that came in, along with a constant source of coffee for Dylan. The remaining detectives on the team were direct enquiry officers, front line staff that went out visiting witnesses, dealing with suspects, and ultimately interviewing the killers. There would be daily meetings and briefings to share information, to learn of new developments and to hear of the main drive for the day. The evening debrief was to collate and disseminate the results of enquiries, usually around eleven hours after the start of the day. Everything was continually recorded: the SIO with his own policy book, and a duplicate log created on the HOLMES enquiry account. Morale and drive were needed, and on a daily basis he or his deputy would attempt to motivate the team. This was easily done when there had been a forensic update or a breakthrough, but became harder as the investigation wore on. The well-worn adage that the next or last action may be 'the one', was always reinforced. In other words, the next call could be the missing link.

Dylan had worn musical ties, socks, and even brought a singing Santa into the incident room to lighten the atmosphere. He had a good sense of humour, which he displayed whenever he got the chance. Dylan told officers at the beginning of every enquiry: 'I expect one hundred per cent commitment and professionalism.' True to his word, if anyone was found slacking or causing embarrassment to the enquiry, they would be removed immediately and would never work on a major enquiry again.

The press conference the next morning with the Spencers was harrowing. They sat pale-faced, ashen with grief, as their lives were catapulted to the fore for public scrutiny, a topic of conversation in homes, workplaces, and pubs across the county.

'This is an extremely disturbing case. Christopher was hit on the head with some force by an unknown object and then was hanged using a blue nylon rope that was placed around his neck,' Dylan told the assembled reporters.

He held up and showed them a similar type of rope.

'I'm satisfied that the murderer or murderers brought this rope with them, suggesting that the hanging may have been premeditated. Christopher was the ideal son, a typical young lad who enjoyed sport and played football for the school, something that he had been doing the day he disappeared. On that day he had scored two goals for his team and was overjoyed. He was a well-liked boy. There is no obvious motive for the brutality of Christopher's death. It has caused great sadness to the school and the community that a child has died in such disturbing circumstances. The total devastation of his parents and family is beyond doubt.'

Sarah's tears were constant, so she couldn't speak. Her head was bowed and her shoulders were stooped. She dabbed her eyes continually with a tissue while at the same time either smoothing her hair or picking at a piece of cotton on her dress.

'Please help us find who did this to our son,' Martin said simply, his voice almost inaudible, his lips and lower jaw quivering.

Dylan concluded the conference, dealt with the interviews, and then spoke to the family.

'Well, that's the Press sorted for now. We want everyone to know about Christopher's murder. Somebody out there reading a paper, listening to the radio, or watching the TV might just give us a call. Regarding the funeral arrangements, there will have to be a second independent post mortem, I'm afraid.'

'Oh no....' Wendy sighed.

'After that examination, I'll get onto the coroner about the inquest and the release of Christopher's body. I can assure you, I am treating this as a priority.'

The family nodded in unison and remained silent.

Dylan didn't personally like press conferences: the cameras, the publicity. Although he was confident, he was always conscious of his dull northern accent. He didn't need this for his ego, but he knew others relished it. They would go out of their way if they thought they could get on TV. Sad. He was always nervous because he did not want to forget something important or say anything wrong, and it was important nothing detracted from the appeal. Often he spent hours talking to the media only for it to be edited to a few short snippets of news.

Back at the incident room, Dylan walked into the debrief. Officers told him that the school Christopher attended was doing all it could to help and had allowed them access to classes and to Christopher's classmates, while offering what support they could to the children. In assembly, the Headmaster had informed the school that the police would be in the building and told those who hadn't heard the terrible news that Christopher had died. He'd assured the children that they could always talk to one of the teachers if they were not confident about speaking to the police officers.

Malcolm Meredith, the football teacher, had been seen by an officer and he told the team that the teacher appeared to be genuinely upset. In his statement he said that he had last seen Chris at the entrance, waiting for his dad, and he was sure he had been the last to leave.

'Where did Meredith go after the game?' Dylan asked the officer.

'The Red Lion to celebrate. It's his local, sir.'

'And the spectators at the match?'

'Meredith said there were quite a lot of people there, families, friends and local people. He knew a lot of the faces, but not all the names. I have the names of the people he did recognise, sir.'

'Did he find a football sock belonging to Christopher in the changing rooms?'

'No, sir. He said no one left anything. He said he always checked to see if any kit had been left after a match.'

'Thank you.'

The debrief over, it was just after nine. He called Jen then drove home thinking about the two murders, about how they could be linked and about Christopher's missing sock. Dylan was sure the killer was taking trophies. Bloody hell, with Daisy's murderer still at large, Dylan would have thought Meredith wouldn't have left the boy alone. Or did he leave him? Had his officer just spoken to the killer? He made a decision there and then that he would get his team to put Meredith under the microscope and collate all the information he could about him. He knew better than anyone else that murderers came in all shapes, sizes, and professions. Dylan needed to find this killer before another child was murdered.

Chapter Seventeen

Mr Cater, the Coroner, was an experienced man in his mid-sixties, slim of build, smart in appearance, and articulate. Dylan thought he cut the perfect grandfatherly figure as he sat at the front of the court on the morning of the twenty-third of December, listening to evidence regarding how, why, when, and where Daisy Charlotte Hind had died. Mr Cater was always thorough and sincere, and he allowed Daisy's family to be present to hear for themselves the full circumstances of their daughter's death. Janice Henderson sat with Wendy and Trevor. Dylan sat alongside the Coroner's Officer.

It was a relaxed atmosphere and the Coroner nodded sympathetically towards Mr and Mrs Hind. Numerous reporters representing various papers from local to tabloids filled the seats. The Coroner's Officer was called to the witness box first to outline the scene surrounding the finding of Daisy's body and her subsequent identification by her parents. He submitted to the court Daisy's birth certificate. Mr Cater now had proof of identification. He read out the statements of the paramedics who had pronounced her dead. After he had finished, Dylan was called into the witness box.

'Good morning, Detective Inspector. Sit if you wish,' the Coroner said in a quiet voice. You could hear a pin drop.

Dylan read the oath out loud and then sat as he told the court how Daisy had disappeared and how she had been found some twelve hours later. 'Sir,' he concluded, 'Two independent post mortems have been carried out and neither party requires Daisy's body to be retained. Therefore there is no objection from either prosecution or future defence to Daisy's body being released for funeral purposes.'

'No known suspect is being sought?' asked the Coroner.

'Not at the moment, sir. An investigation was started when Daisy went missing. Her naked body was found on wasteland near to Dean Reservoir. Cause of death a massive single blow to the head.' Dylan went on to explain her other injuries.

'Thank you, Detective Inspector. I have the relevant paperwork and letters from Professors Cockroft and Rutherford before me.' Mr Cater adjourned the inquest until such time as the offender had been traced and prosecuted. Finally, he told Wendy and Trevor that he would release Daisy's body to them for burial and offered his sincere condolences. Their plans for Daisy and Irene's funeral could now move forward.

Dylan returned to the Christopher Spencer incident room. His focus had to be on the latest murder. Larry was working on some papers at his desk as Dylan walked through to his own office.

'I want to know about Malcolm Meredith. Check we've searched his car. Ask him if Christopher has ever been in it. Get SOCO to fingerprint the interior.'

Larry followed Dylan and stood at his office door, leaning on the door jamb. 'Meredith says he drove his car through the car wash on his way home from the pub the night Christopher went missing.'

'Great.' Dylan put his head in his hands. 'Did he valet it?'

'No, he says not.'

'Did he teach Daisy, do you know?'

'Probably,' Larry replied, yawning.

' "Probably" won't do. He either did or he didn't. We need to be sure. Come on, Larry, we need to put him in or out of this enquiry. Get his car searched and his house as well.'

Larry walked into Dylan's office and sat down.

'Have we got cell site analysis back for Christopher's phone? Recent numbers dialled?'

'No, sir, nothing yet, but they're on with it.'

Dylan studied the piece of paper in front of him for a moment. 'What about Martin Spencer's car tyre? There was a puncture mark on the wall of the tyre, but we don't know the cause. It's a quarter of an inch in diameter, it says here. What do you think? Nail? Screw?'

'I don't know, sir.'

'Because it's on the tyre wall, it's not repairable. Keep it anyway, just to be on the safe side.'

Martin Spencer ran a small tile shop in the town, a one-man business, which was why he'd had to work on the day of his son's big football match. He'd not had the opportunity to see Christopher play football and now never would. *Other dads would've been there*, he thought. He blamed himself: *if I hadn't started my own business, if I'd only closed the shop.*

Sarah was on anti-depressants to help her cope. She blamed herself, too, since she and Jane could have gone to watch him play. It hadn't been such a bad afternoon, weather-wise. Why didn't she think about it? She had never thought about going to his games. Her son played for the school; he must have been good. She should have supported him. She always went shopping on a Friday afternoon, god knew why. She didn't have to. She just always had.

Dylan knew all too well that their lives had been engulfed by Christopher's murder. He had seen it before too many times. The Spencers would be told over and over that hindsight was a wonderful thing, and they could spend the remainder of their lives beating themselves up about it, but it would not bring Christopher back.

He'd been satisfied from early on in the enquiry that neither the mum nor the dad was involved in the killing and that Christopher had not been ill-treated. Dylan wished he could give the Spencers some good news, some positive development. Unfortunately, all the lines of enquiry were unyielding, if not on occasions damn demoralising, so far. But Dylan hadn't been beaten yet by a murder investigation, and he wasn't going to be beaten now. No matter how long it took, he would find those responsible.

In the office, he spoke to both Dawn and Larry, who listened and took notes.

'The murders should really be run separately, according to Home Office guidelines. Both should have a different SIO. Hold on. I'll telephone ACC operations to see what he wants me to do.'

'Ideally that would be the case, Jack,' the voice at the other end of the phone said, sounding laid back and smooth over the loud speaker. 'But we haven't a spare SIO who can take this on and neither do we have an ACC who can oversee it. See how you go and we'll see if anyone frees up. You could always detect them,' he laughed sarcastically.

Dylan put the phone down, downhearted. 'Old, old story. As long as someone is dealing with it ...," Dylan said. He was a realist and knew that no one would ever be freed up, or oversee it.

Dylan would not merge the enquiries, although he would look at comparisons. Should evidence link them, they would be merged immediately. If it didn't, then neither investigation had been derailed and each could remain focused. *Was the murderer one person who knew both Christopher and Daisy?* he wondered.

'Right, I need to know that the teachers at Harrowfield Middle School have all been checked out thoroughly, Larry. Also the caretaker, supply teachers, classroom assistants, and dinner ladies, absolutely anyone who has been at the school. Michael Meredith, the football teacher, was the last to see Christopher alive. That we know, but did he also know Daisy? Did he teach her? I want him interviewed again. I want to know where he was the day Daisy went missing. Dawn, who else would know these two children by sight? Doctors? Dentists? Did they both attend the local church? There has to be a connection.'

'Leave it with us, sir,' Dawn said as she and Larry left the room. Dylan doodled on a pad, listing the comparisons between the murders.

Boy – 10 yrs
Girl – 9 yrs

Harrowfield Middle School
Harrowfield Middle School

Snatched
Snatched

Hit on the head 2" diameter wound
Hit on the head 2"diameter wound

Cause of death: hanging
Cause of death: head injury

Not only child
Only child

Body clothed
Body naked

Dog excrement in mouth
Eyebrows shaved/cigarette burns to buttocks.

Brace removed
Fingertip removed

Daytime
Evening

There were similarities; Dylan couldn't deny it. They were staring at him in black and white. He believed that the murders had to be connected, although he would still not officially link them at this time. He needed tangible evidence. Both murders were disjointed in that neither followed a pattern that could suggest a motive. The naked body, the burns on the buttocks, the bag on Daisy's head and the missing fingertip, while for Christopher, the dog dirt and the hanging. *Why?* The murderer was no doubt organised and calm, but what message was he leaving for them? It would be interesting to hear what the offender profiler had to say now. Would he be able to shed further light on the enquiry? Would he connect the murders? If it were one person, would there be any more deaths? Dylan needed to know how the killer chose his victims, if the killer was a lone individual. He didn't believe these murders were random. Both victims went to the same school. Why taunt Daisy's parents?

Dylan found he had been left numerous messages about the property store, but one concerned him. Harold had gone off sick, but Dylan didn't want anyone else touching the murder exhibits. Just then he saw Detective Constable John Benjamin pass his door.

'John.'

'Did you shout boss?'

'Yeah, just saw you at the last minute, mate. Are you and Vicky going to be at Harrowfield nick today?'

'I think Vicky has some bits and bobs to drop off at Tandem Bridge. Something you need doing?'

'Apparently the property stores are bursting at the seams, so the divisional administrator tells me, and the property clerk has gone off sick with a twisted ankle. Would you just have a look at the stores for me? I know there's a cage within the void area that has the cold case murder files and exhibits in. I thought it might be possible to house our latest two murder exhibits in there and catalogue them at the same time. I want to keep them under the same roof. It'd be so much easier than the attic at Tandem Bridge.'

'No problems boss. I'll get it done this afternoon.'

'That's great, John, thanks. How's the family?'

'Brilliant. Emma's six now and Jake's four. Just don't get enough time with them. You know what it's like when the job's running.' Dylan had heard that before, many times.

'Make sure you make time. There's nothing worse than setting off on a morning before they get up and getting home after they've gone to bed. You miss so much and before you know it they're married and have children of their own.'

'Easier said than done though sometimes, boss,' John sighed.

'Yeah I know. Don't let that nosy administrator know what you're doing. We'll tell her when we've made a decision. It'll be easier that way.'

'Consider it done; I'll get back to you.'

'Cheers, John, and remember, family comes first.'

Dylan left a message for Dawn and Larry to meet up with him the next day after the briefings. He wanted to discuss with them the approach to the families. There was something bugging him, but he couldn't put his finger on what it was, what he was missing. Experience told him it would be something simple and obvious that he wasn't seeing.

There was nothing forthcoming from any line of enquiry. The headmaster of the school couldn't think why anyone would want to hurt Daisy or Christopher. There was no connection between teachers, football, school friends; they didn't even think Christopher and Daisy knew each other. They'd drawn a blank with Meredith, who had a watertight alibi.

Dylan wondered if Boscombe, the offender profiler, could tell him more. He was trying to keep focused. He wanted answers. He needed answers. The pressure was building all the time, and he hoped and prayed there wasn't another child killed. The phone rang.

'Hey you, how ya doing? Home for tea?'

'Hiya, love.' He leaned back in his chair. His shoulders visibly dropped as he relaxed and stretched.

'Should be, nothing new here, but not for the want of trying.'

'It'll break, don't worry. You'll do it. You'll get there. Come on, Jack. This isn't like you. Pick yourself up. You need to keep that team bubbling.'

'Don't worry. I'm fine. It's just so damn frustrating. I want to find that link. What the hell am I missing?'

'Apart from me?' He could hear the teasing in her voice, and he smiled.

'You know what I mean,' he said. 'I'm just worried another child'll be killed.' *Is it me,* he wondered.

Although Dylan was sifting through evidence, his team was out searching, interviewing, and statement-taking. The volume of paperwork in the incident room was mounting daily. Dylan needed to be aware of every piece of information that came in. Ultimately each action would form the basis of the prosecution file. He kept a check on the workload of each individual officer, which was easily done using information from the computer. There was no way he could afford to have anyone slacking. If he'd marked the lines of enquiry 'priority,' he expected them to be treated as such. His team had energy, just no suspect.

The phone rang and it was Janice. 'Sir, Daisy's funeral has been confirmed for the December the twenty-eighth. Will you be there?'

Chapter Eighteen

Jack woke the next day feeling a lot brighter. For once he had slept well, and it was Christmas Eve. He cuddled Jen to him.

'I've a feeling today is going to be a good one,' he said enthusiastically.

'That's more like it,' she said kissing the tip of his nose before she jumped out of bed to get breakfast.

Funny, he thought as he sniffed the air, rising from bed, *no smell of bacon.*

'Porridge for breakfast,' she shouted from the kitchen, as if she had read his mind 'It'll give you a good start.'

'Bacon,' Jack shouted in response from the bathroom with foam on his face as he shaved.

By half past seven he was on his way into the office having had his porridge. The coffee was percolating, and he could smell the strong aroma as he opened the door to the incident room. Before he had time to sit down behind his desk, John and Vicky knocked on his door in unison.

'Morning, you two,' he said brightly.

'Morning, sir,' they both chirped, equally eager.

'The store you asked us to look at,' said Vicky, sitting down in a chair adjacent to his desk.

'Yeah, how is it?'

'Full. But the good news is that we think the murder exhibits will fit easily into the void. The most recent exhibits are neatly catalogued and marked up, on the shelves boxed and labelled, so it'd just be a matter of lifting and relocating them. We could do it in a day.' Vicky smiled.

'Looks like our little property man has been passing his time reading some of the old files, so they'll need to go back to the void anyway,' said John.

'That's brilliant, thanks a lot.' Dylan was delighted.

He stood up and put on his jacket. He needed to speak to the Spencers and the Hinds.

'Larry, you ready?' Dylan called. 'We're going to see the Spencers. Dawn, I'll meet you for lunch and then we'll go and see the Hinds.' Larry jumped up from his chair as though he had been roused from sleep and ran out of the incident room after Dylan.

Sarah Spencer made them a cup of tea and placed a plate of biscuits on the table in front of them. Both she and Martin still looked pale; red, puffy eyes circled with dark rings. Weight had simply dropped off them, made apparent by their clothes, which hung on their frames.

'I won't ask you how you are, it's obvious. Is there anything or anyone that's come to mind that may help with the case? An argument within the last few weeks or months that you've been able to think of?' asked Dylan.

'No, sorry, there's nothing at all that we can think of. We've racked our brains trying to think of something or someone but there really is nothing, nothing at all. Clive and Fran, your officers, have been so good, we feel so useless. We know there has to be an explanation but we haven't got a clue. It's the not knowing. It's just wearing us out,' said Martin, who looked just about all in.

The room they sat in was adorned with pictures of Christopher and his little sister, Jane, school pictures, holiday pictures and party pictures. The most noticeable thing was the absence of Christmas decorations or cards.

'Martin, Sarah, I'm sorry, try not to worry. I know that's easier said than done, but we'll get there, I promise,' said Dylan. 'By any chance did you know Daisy Hind, the little girl that was murdered? She went to the same school as Christopher.'

'No, I don't think so, is there some connection? We haven't watched the news or bothered with papers ever since … it happened. They're just so awful. I'm sorry.' Sarah dabbed at her eyes with a tissue.

'What about her mum and dad, any connection there? Trevor and Wendy Hind?'

Martin looked shocked, sat up straight, and moved forward on the settee.

'Trevor Hind, did you say? I went to school with a Trevor Hind. Was it his daughter that was killed? That's unreal.'

'How well did you know Trevor?' enquired Dylan.

'We were best mates, but we never kept in touch. I don't think Sarah has even met him.'

'When did you last see him?'

'Gosh, about six months ago at the Harrowfield School reunion.' A smile flickered across his face as he reminisced. It was the first time Dylan had seen a smile on Martin's face. It made him look younger somehow.

'Did you go, Sarah?' Dylan asked.

'No, I stayed home and looked after the ki … well, you know,' she said quietly.

'I'm interested. Tell me more, Martin. Where was it? How did you get to know about the reunion?'

'What has that to do with Christopher and Daisy?' Martin said with disbelief. 'It was boring. Nothing happened. I'd a couple of pints, a chat with one or two old mates, and then came home.'

'Where did they have it?'

'The Con Club opposite the school.'

'Were there a lot there, a good turn out?'

'Probably about thirty. I went on the *Friends Reunited* website about eighteen months ago, just out of curiosity. I put in my details, what we were doing as a family, a picture just like others had. I should imagine there'd be pictures on the site from the reunion because folk were taking them. I went to see what my mates looked like after thirty years and to drum up a bit of business, to be honest.'

'So you saw Trevor there? Anyone else in particular that you were mates with from school?' Dylan felt an adrenaline rush. Was this the link that he'd been missing?

'There was me, Trevor, and a lad called Barry Sanderson. We knocked about together. We liked to think we were the three musketeers. "All for one, one for all", we used to shout.'

'Was Barry at the reunion?'

'Yeah, he looked terrible. He's got a drink problem. Poor old lad.'

'Can we look at the site on your computer?' asked Larry.

'You could if it was working, but it's on the blink. I haven't used it since the reunion. I kept saying I'd get it fixed, but with everything else that's happened, it's been the least of my worries,' he said, then he sighed. For a few short moments, he had thought about something other than his little boy. 'There was nothing untoward, it was just a drink.'

'No skeletons in the cupboard from your schooldays that could have anything to do with it?' Larry asked tentatively.

'No, nothing at all. A few boys' pranks I can remember, but no, I'm sure it can't be anything to do with the old school crowd,' he said shaking his head.

They stood to go. 'It's just one line of enquiry. Something we'll look at like everything else. No stone will be left unturned. I promised that and I meant it. If you do remember anything else, don't hesitate to contact us. We'll be in touch.'

Dylan drove Larry back to the nick. They were both deep in thought.

'We need to do some research on the reunion, Larry, as a priority. I'd like you to find out about Barry Sanderson and everyone else there. Draw me a list up whilst I'm over at the Hinds' this afternoon please.'

'I'll get straight on it. See what I can get off the site and from the organiser. Leave it to me.'

'It's about the right time,' Dylan said thoughtfully. 'Lunch? Canteen?'

'Suits me, boss, it'll be interesting to see what the Hind family have to say this afternoon.'

Omelette with salad for lunch, Jen would be proud of me, he thought as he stood in the canteen queue. Larry, however, couldn't resist the full, all-day breakfast, served with extra toast. Dawn joined them at the table and they told her about the reunion.

At the Hind house, Trevor and Wendy were duplicates of the Spencers. Both looked completely drained and distraught. Wendy was still taking medication and looked particularly drawn, her eyes dull and glazed. It was understandable.

'Is there something new, something to tell us?' asked Trevor. They both looked eager for an answer, any answer.

The house was full of cards, they blanketed every flat surface, but they weren't Christmas cards. Wendy saw Dylan and Dawn looking at them.

'We've had condolence cards from people we don't even know. Letters from people, some who've lost their children in horrific ways, they've been so kind, so thoughtful and comforting. It's really helped. Mum would've loved them all. They'd 'ave made her cry. It's been worse because I wasn't ... I couldn't ... be with Mum. I just feel like I've let everyone down. I'm so sorry,' she said as her hand covered her mouth and she fled from the room in tears. Trevor's eyes were swimming too.

'I'm sorry, she has good days and bad, mostly bad, but so do I.' He shrugged his shoulders. 'I can't leave her to go back to work yet.'

'We understand, Trevor. All I can say from experience is that time does heal, but it doesn't take away the pain of these dark days. Can I ask you something? Do you know a Martin Spencer?'

'Yes, I do. Why? He's nothing to do with it, has he? We were mates at school.'

'No. No, nothing like that. His son, Christopher, was murdered.'

'God, that's weird. I only saw him ... October, at a school reunion. I did hear on the radio about a boy being found dead by the canal, was that him?'

'Yeah.'

'I never made the connection. Bloody hell, that's really shocked me. When you leave school, you have every intention of staying in touch with yer mates don't ya - but once you start work, you end up drifting in different directions. I've seen him knocking about occasionally, but we don't socialise or anything like that. Then we got invited to this reunion and I thought why not, let's go and have a look at some of the people I went to school with, and he was there.'

'How did you hear about it, the reunion?'

'I'd been on that website, *Friends Reunited*, a few times, updating what I was doing, working as a fireman and that.'

'Did you put on any pictures?' asked Dawn.

'Just one of Wendy, Daisy, and me showing off, like. You don't think the reunion's got anything to do with it, do you? Nothing happened; we only had a drink and a chat. There was no bother or anything like that. I can let you look at the website if you want. I think they've put a couple of dozen pictures on since, from that night. They were trying to catch everyone who went.'

'Who organised it and put the photos on ,Trevor, do you know?'

'A girl called Liz Green. She was always "the" organiser at school. You know, planning the school disco, the school play … she was there. Her contact number's on the website. Do you really think there's something there?'

'It's just another line of enquiry, but it does connect you with the Spencers. Or it may be nothing,' said Dylan. He didn't want to build Trevor's hopes up.

'I'll get my laptop and you can print off what you need. Liz'll have everyone's details, I should think. We had to get back to her if we were attending, for buffet numbers.' Trevor sat on the sofa busily booting up the computer.

'What about the schooldays, Trevor? Did you knock about with anyone else apart from Martin?' asked Dylan as Wendy walked back into the room and sat next to her husband. Her eyes were red from crying and her face looked flushed and puffy. Trevor put a protective arm around her and gave her a squeeze.

'Barry Sanderson, mainly. There were just three of us.'

'Nothing you can think of, anything, from back then that would come back and haunt you?'

'No, we were just ordinary lads. Sports, girls, and in that order too. Got it, I'll print it off for you. I hope this is of some use.' Trevor stood, waiting for the printer to finish, hands on his hips as he sighed. 'Martin's son, I never knew,' and then went on to tell Wendy what Dylan had just told him.

'Do you know, we didn't even exchange phone numbers. It isn't as though we'd anything in common after all this time.' He shook his head and handed the printouts to Dylan.

'Is there anything else that you've thought about, any incidents, any other events you've been to, any people you know who died in suspicious circumstances, anything?' asked Dylan.

'We've sat for hours, trying to come up with something, but we just keep drawing a blank. I'm sorry, but if you see Martin will you pass on our condolences, please?'

Dylan nodded. 'We'll be in touch before the funeral. In the meantime if there's anything you think of, don't hesitate.'

Dawn and Dylan left and drove back to the station.

'There is a definite connection between the two dads, but what's the motive?' Dawn asked Dylan.

'Don't know yet, but it's certainly a priority line of enquiry. We'll wait and see what Larry managed to find out. We could certainly do with some luck.'

Chapter Nineteen

Back at the office, they sat down to discuss the latest developments.

'There're two sites. One is *Friends Reunited* and the school also has one of its own, but I've come up with a name,' said Larry, looking pleased with himself.

'Liz Green,' Dylan jumped in.

'That's right. I gave her a call and said someone would see her later today to get a download of photos from the reunion. She said she'd try to tell us who's who and give us a list of names and contact numbers for those who attended.'

'I don't mind working later tonight. Ralph's out so I'll do that one if you like, boss.'

'That would be great, Dawn, thank you. The other friend of Trevor and Martin, Barry Sanderson, we need to know about him. You're working Christmas Day, aren't you, Larry? Boxing Day, Dawn?' They nodded. 'Everyone on the list who attended the reunion needs to be seen as soon as possible. There could be up to thirty people, according to Martin. Can you get the team who are working over the next two days to look at that for us? I'll see you Boxing Day, Dawn. Are you both in on the twenty-seventh? Here for nine a.m.?' suggested Dylan.

'Yes. What could've happened at the reunion that could possibly cause someone to kill like that? Our two said it was a quiet evening and nothing happened,' said Larry.

'We need background on them all. Let's stay positive, eh? Anything else?' asked Dylan.

'When you were out, the divisional administrator telephoned and left a message about the store again. She said you hung up on her, boss.' Dawn's eyes went skyward.

'Me? Never. I must 'ave got cut off,' protested Dylan. 'I'll go and have a look at the store for myself. John and Vicky reckon it would only take a day to move the exhibits to the void. If not, we can use the attic at Tandem Bridge.'

'Wouldn't have thought we would need to use that,' said Larry, lazily doodling on his pad.

'I might nip in nevertheless, just to check, in case we do,' Dylan said.

Liz Green was a bubbly lady with verbal diarrhoea, as Larry would have said and as Dawn found out, much to her amusement.

'How can I help you? Are you into the reunion thing? It seems so popular these days. I've always tried to keep tabs on my classmates and school chums. Their lives run parallel to mine, but oh, how different they've all turned out,' she grinned. 'Not what I expected, I can tell you. And now with *Facebook*, *Friends Reunited* and our school website, it's so much easier. Can I offer you a drink?' She spoke so quickly that Dawn didn't manage to get a word in edgeways.

'Tea would be lovely, thank you.' Liz kept a pristine home. She was definitely the 'ironing socks and undies' type. 'No, I've never been into that sort of thing myself, never had the time.'

'Oh, you should try it. I don't spend that much time on it, just update my profile once in a while, or if I've got some spare time I try to contact one or two "blasts from the past". I'm researching my family tree, too. Thirty years since we all left school, though, what a milestone. "Let's have a reunion," I thought, "The Class of 75".' She stood in a star-struck pose for effect. 'I was so pleased with the response. Milk and sugar?'

'Yes please.'

'Help yourself to the mince pies. They're just out of the oven.' Liz placed a full cooling tray in front of Dawn. *She can't be all that bad*, thought Dawn as she bit into a mince pie. She was definitely warming towards the woman. *She might rattle on a little, but she makes a good shortcrust*.

Liz Green had a computer station in one corner of the neat, brightly-lit kitchen. She beckoned Dawn over and offered her one of the two chairs that she had positioned ready so that they could both see the screen, talking all the while.

'Right, let's get organised. I've got a list of people in the class, some addresses and a few dates of birth. We've even got two with the same birthday, would you believe it?' She brushed her long, straight, brown hair away from her face and tucked it behind her ear, pushed her glasses up the bridge of her nose and picked up a piece of paper from the desk, handing it to Dawn.

'Okay, here's a list from 1975. Now this one,' she said, passing Dawn another sheet, 'Is the list of people who came to the reunion. The Club required numbers for health and safety, and food. We had three different meats, six pounds fifty a head. Not bad, if you ever need a venue, it's good value for money.' She searched for her hankie in the front pocket of her blue floral apron. Wiping her nose, she said, 'You know how it is. Some people join in wholeheartedly, some not at all.'

Dawn helped herself to another mince pie; she could be in for a long evening.

'Some people update their website regularly. Put on recent photographs, like, and others just enter a brief resume. It's nice to see pictures though, don't you think?' Dawn nodded in agreement as she sipped her tea.

'The man who telephoned me said you wanted to talk to me about a murder, though. That's frightening. Who's been murdered, do I know them?' Dawn saw her chance to talk.

'Yes, well, you know the parents. In the last six months, Trevor Hind's daughter Daisy was murdered, and then, more recently, Martin Spencer's son, Christopher. You've probably read about it in the papers?'

'Oh, gosh, yes, but I never made the connection. How awful. Martin has put his details on the website. Just a minute,' Liz said peering at the screen for confirmation. 'He says he's set up a tile shop in town,' she said as she clicked onto the web page. 'Trevor, if I recall correctly, had put a picture of himself with his wife and daughter. Oh, god, you don't think it was someone in our class, do you?' she said as she held her hand up to her mouth.

'No, no, it's just the family's background that we're looking at. We can't leave anything to chance,' Dawn reassured her, grabbing another mince pie.

'You had me worried there for a minute. Look, some of these are photos from the night of the reunion. See her there,

119

the one with the blonde hair? It used to be so long she could sit on it. She married a lottery millionaire.'

'Interesting. Do you think I could have copies of the lists and the pictures, please, Liz?'

'Sure. It might take a while to print them off. Help yourself to more tea and mince pies whilst I do it for you.'

'Thank you. I'd like you to keep this to yourself at the moment, Liz. The last thing we want is for people to panic,' Dawn said, with her mouth full.

'No problem. I used to be a Girl Guide, you know, duty to God, serve the Queen and all that.' She laughed with three fingers pointed in a salute to her brow.

The printer made a constant burr as the head went from side to side, spewing paper onto the floor. Liz tried to retrieve it in page order.

'This is so good of you, Liz. I'll get you a replacement cartridge and some paper.'

'No, no, I wouldn't hear of it,' she said. Liz Green presented Dawn with the printed information she had requested, plus photographs with names added, all neatly stacked and placed in a folder.

'Thank you for your hospitality, Liz, I am really grateful to you. Merry Christmas.'

'Oh, that's no problem at all. I'm just glad to help and I hope those,' she said pointing to the folder, 'Are useful to you. Merry Christmas to you too.'

'Oh, final thing. Do you remember anyone having any major arguments or grudges at school? You know, really bad fall outs?'

'Kids row, don't they? But there's nothing that stands out in my mind as anything out of the ordinary, no,' she said. 'There were loud people, lads can be bossy, girls bitchy, but I was a bit of a geek at school, believe it or not,' she laughed. 'So I never really got involved.'

'Thanks again, Liz. And please keep this to yourself for now. We don't want people getting the wrong idea, do we? It's just a routine enquiry, but some put two and two together and make five.'

Chapter Twenty

That evening Dylan was home on time, but still with his bulging briefcase in tow. Carol singers stood in the porch, and he smiled as he listened to them.

'The dads know each other,' he announced to Jen as he took his coat off and hung it up in the hallway.

'Really?' Tea'll be ready in a minute if you want to come sit down, love. Want a glass of wine?'

'A bottle.' Dylan joined her in the kitchen, Max in his wake.

'If they knew each other, why didn't they tell you before?' she asked, as she greeted him with a kiss.

'They didn't realise they did,' he said cuddling her from behind as she stirred the contents of the pan on the stove. 'Mm, something smells good,' he said, pinching her spoon and tasting the gravy.

She smiled. 'But they do now?'

'Yes. They were at school together and went to a reunion back in October.'

Dylan relaxed over their meal. Jen didn't say anything, but he was quieter than usual and she knew he would be mulling over the new information.

Miraculously, he wasn't called out on Christmas Day. The turkey he'd imagined he could smell for weeks was delicious and, as it was the season of goodwill to all men, he assumed that meant dogs too, and plated Max up a turkey dinner, although he knew they would suffer later from the rancid smell of the dog breaking wind. It was only after he sat down following their Christmas dinner that he noticed how lovely Jen's decorations made the house and tree look. In fact, it was the first time he had been in the house long enough to sit in the lounge since the decorations had been put up. She had bought him a gold onyx signet ring along with a silk tie.

'It's a lucky tie,' she said.

He watched her every move and he caught her watching him, making sure he was taking it easy. She insisted he rest. Jen bossed him and he loved it that she cared so much. He felt lucky he had found her. She was nine years his junior and he didn't know why she had chosen him to be with, but he was so glad she had. It was the best bit of detective work he had ever done, finding her; he was sure of that.

The table was empty and the dishwasher full. 'Let's watch a DVD, eh? Mum and Dad sent me *Sense and Sensibility* for Christmas,' Jen said, as she crouched down to switch on the DVD player. She jumped back on the settee and settled in the crook of Jack's arm.

'Mm, it should be like this every night. Thank you so much for my present, I love it,' she said, holding her arm up in the air to show off the bracelet that Jack had bought for her.

'You're my best present,' he told her, kissing the top of her head and cuddling her tight. 'Have you missed going to the Isle of Wight this year and spending Christmas with your mum and dad? We could have a week there soon. What do you think?'

'You, have a whole week off work?' She turned to him in surprise. 'Don't make me laugh,' she said prodding him playfully in the stomach.

'No,' he laughed. 'I mean it, honest I do. Book it now if you like.'

'Yeah, sure, whatever,' she smiled snuggling up to him.

Dylan had to prise himself from bed for work the next day. Jen's body was so warm and inviting, and it was freezing cold when he tested the temperature outside the bedcovers with one arm and leg.

'Morning. Happy Boxing Day.' Dawn was already in the office when Dylan walked through the door.

'Good Christmas?' asked Dylan.

'Well, let's see, Ralph worked, drank too much, and slept most of the time we did have together, and I'm here today. So you could say it's business as usual. You?'

'Yeah, quiet, you know. Thought you two were trying for a family?'

'Not much chance for that, is there, at the moment. We don't see each other enough,' Dawn laughed. 'Press Office has been on the phone wanting to know if there's anything that we can give them to renew the appeals.'

'I was actually thinking we might do Crimewatch. We need to do whatever it takes to nail the bastard.'

'Whatever what takes?' asked Larry, as he entered the room, lobster red.

'You been on the sun bed again?' asked Dawn. 'Don't you listen to all the warnings about skin cancer?'

Larry pulled a face behind her back.

'I thought you were off today?' Dylan said, studying the Chief Constable's log to catch up on events that had taken place in the force over the last couple of days.

'Couldn't keep away. You know me, Mr. Conscientious himself.' He slumped in a chair and proceeded to read Christmas Eve's *Harrowfield Times*.

'More like Mr. Saddo hasn't got a life,' commented Dawn.

'Can you speak to the Press Office for me, Larry, and tell them we are thinking of doing the reconstruction?' asked Dylan.

'Yeah, yeah,' Larry said nonchalantly, turning over the pages of the paper.

'Now would be a good time.' Dylan's voice rose. Larry snapped the paper shut and reached for the phone.

'How did you get on with Liz Green, Dawn? Anything?' Dylan asked.

'She printed me off a list of people in their school year, and also gave me pictures and a list of who attended the reunion.' Dawn handed them to Dylan as she spoke.

'Fantastic. Firstly, let's get the names on those lists onto HOLMES,' said Dylan.

'She said the "do" was uneventful.'

Dylan brooded over the list.

'She remembered Martin, Trevor, and Barry as noisy, loud boys who knocked about together, but that was about it.

'Well, it's the only connection we've got, so let's see who else's on the list.' He passed the printed sheet over to Larry. 'Whilst you're looking at that I'm off to Tandem Bridge to look at the feasibility of using a room or the attic there for exhibits.'

Dylan intentionally took the route passing the locations where the bodies had been dumped.

The car park was almost empty when he arrived. He strolled across the yard thinking *what a lovely morning* as he breathed the cold, crisp air deep into his lungs. The sun was shining, but it didn't have any warmth. A perfect day for walking the dog and he was at work. Typical. The station was quiet. It being a Bank Holiday, only skeleton staff were working and he strolled around without seeing a soul. As he approached the attic, he saw two large rooms which spanned the entire area of the station. They were already racked, and although the ceilings sloped, there was plenty of standing room. Pleased with his find, he walked down the steps to his car. His mobile rang and echoed loudly in the empty reception area.

'Boss, it's Larry. The Spencers have just found what they believe to be part of Christopher's brace in a card put into the post box at the bottom of their driveway.'

'The bastard. Well, he's linked them for us now, hasn't he?' Dylan said.

'I'm going over there, so I'll ensure everything is preserved for DNA. Luckily Clive and Fran were there when they found it. Sarah is hysterical.'

'Who wouldn't be? Look, I'm on my way back to Harrowfield. Is Dawn still with you, Larry?'

'Yeah, she's still going through the lists and photos.'

'Tell her to get the kettle on. I won't be long. I'll see you there when you've been to the Spencers' house.' Dylan was only fifteen minutes away and Dawn was waiting for him with the warm drink and a mince pie.

'Well, boss, what a get this one's turning out to be. How evil can he get?'

'It's officially connected the two murders now, though. How you doing with the reunion stuff?'

'It's laborious, but I'll get there. It's got to be something to do with the dads now, hasn't it?'

'Got to be,' agreed Dylan

'This list has got thirty-two names on it and most of them we haven't seen yet. I'll make sure Barry Sanderson goes to the top of the pile. That's him there.' Dawn pointed him out in the photograph to Dylan; he was standing to the left of

Martin. The snap was no different from Dylan's own school group picture. The teachers were to the side with the tallest boys centre back. Girls in pretty school dresses sat elegantly in the front, legs to one side and skirts fanned out. Most displayed forced smiles and one or two had their eyes closed. The pictures of the reunion evening were so different. There were men and women with arms around each other. Everyone looked as if they were having a good time, a glass half-full raised in their hands.

'Hey, isn't that Harold?'

'Who?' said Dawn, screwing up her eyes to scrutinize the picture.'

'You know, Harold Little, the property man. The fella that's off sick with a twisted ankle. Here, have a closer look,' Dylan said, handing Dawn a magnifying glass.

'Yeah, I'm sure it's our "Little Harold" in the background.' Dawn laughed. 'Fancy that. Look, Liz has written some names on the back of another one he is in, hold on, let's have a look. She's written "Little Wilky".'

'Sure it's not "Little Willy"?' Dylan laughed. 'There's an "H. Wilkinson" on the back of the school picture, but not an "H. Little". How weird. He hasn't changed much has he? She's probably just mistaken.'

Larry walked into the office as Dawn poured the drinks. 'You must be able to smell coffee; I'll get you a cup.' Larry nodded as she passed him.

'A white envelope, boss, with a Harrowfield postmark. It's addressed to "Mr. & Mrs. Spencer". It's bagged and tagged and ready to go off to forensic on your say so. The card says "Happy Christmas". Right.' Larry scoffed.

'Take it over personally, will you. There should be someone working. How're Martin and Sarah, or don't I need to ask?'

'Absolutely distraught. Martin is angry and Sarah is beside herself. I've left Clive and Fran trying to console them. They simply can't understand how anyone could be so brutally cruel.'

'Me neither. Before you go, you know Harold Little, don't you? Would you say that's him?' Dylan slid the reunion picture and the 'Class of 75' over the desk to Larry.

'That's him, yeah. Oh, god, he's no kids, has he?'

'Don't know, but we better find out quick. If it is him, he needs seeing just like the rest of the class,' Dylan said grumpily. 'We've prioritised Barry Sanderson. We need to know if Barry has got kids too. What worries me is if they'd be next on the list if these groups of men are targets. Let's get the team to rattle the cages of the "Class of 75" and see what drops out.'

Chapter Twenty-One

The hearses drew up at the church. Daisy's coffin looked minute. Floral tributes spelled her name. The second car's tributes replicated the first, spelling out MUM and GRAN. Dylan stood close to Wendy and Trevor and watched the cortege behind the hearses shining in the morning sun. The highly polished cars gleamed and the combination of the church setting and the fragrance of the flowers as the coffins were carried forward through the cascading sunlight made him feel like he was in another dimension. Music spilled from within the church as teachers, friends, and townspeople surrounded the outside.

'Gosh, Mum, you and Daisy didn't realise you'd so many friends, did you? Look after each other now won't you?' Wendy whispered to the coffins as were carried by.

Dylan thought he saw Wendy's heart lift for a second as a spasm of joy came over her face. As he walked into the building the scent of the magnificent flowers was intoxicating, the colours so varied, the blossoms so perfect. It was a quiet, loving service that moved people to tears. Trevor gave an emotional eulogy with Wendy standing by him for support. Victoria, one of Daisy's school friends, read out a short poem on behalf of the school. They had all come to pay their respects. It was time for the coffins to be transported one last time, to the graveyard. As they were laid to rest side by side, Trevor had to hold Wendy upright. Dawn used her hankie, but not because she was hungry this time. Dylan tortured himself with the fact that he didn't know why and by whom Daisy had been murdered; it was a thorn in his side. He needed to find this murderer, for the families. The jigsaw was missing some important pieces and until he found them he couldn't complete the picture.

Dylan suddenly had the urge to speak to Jen and he rang her as he lingered in the grounds of the church. 'Hi love, funeral's over,' he said. 'It was so sad.' There was a pause, but he knew she was listening. 'It made me realise something. This family had planned the funeral with so much love, but if I died no one would do that for me, except you. I wanted to tell you how much I love you.' He fought to swallow a lump that rose in his throat.

'Me too.' Was all she could say. Dylan knew she was in an office full of people by the noise in the background. He hung up.

As soon as he got back to the incident room, Dylan rang forensic and read and re read the statements he had been given. His earlier sadness had turned into frustration; Dylan was like a bear with a sore head.

'What's happening? Any breakthrough?' he asked around the room. Blank faces met his. 'You won't find Daisy's killer sitting at that bloody desk. You need to be out there,' he yelled, pointing to the door. Not able to bring himself to say goodbye he picked up his coat and strode out into the night air.

Jen was waiting for him. She wrapped her arms around him and held him tight. He closed his eyes and enjoyed the moment. Neither of them spoke; they didn't need to.

'You're really quiet. Are you okay?' she asked as she reached out to him on the sofa that evening.

He nodded. 'Going to the funeral today made me think. What do I want to do with the rest of my life and who do I want to spend it with?'

'Gosh, that sounds ominous.' She looked at him, trying to make light of how heavy the conversation was getting, but he just cuddled her to him.

'I'm so glad I found you,' he said into her hair as he breathed in deeply. 'I just feel as if I am rolling from one murder to another and not getting on with my own life.'

'It'll be easier once you've got him, and you will.'

Chapter Twenty-Two

With the two investigations now merged, the uniform briefing room had to be used to get all the staff in. There was a packed audience as Dylan, Dawn, and Larry took their positions at the front for the debrief. As usual, Dylan went around the room and asked what each and every one of them had been doing. In turn, the officers updated the team about the particular line of enquiry they'd dealt with during the day. Some had traced and interviewed class members attending the reunion, but no one reported anything untoward on that night. One officer had been to see a psychic, Madame Romany. The officer told the assembled room that she'd been having visions, and she was sure it was of the murderer.

'I asked her to describe this man,' the officer said. 'She said he was a man of great stature, a scar across his face, long blonde hair, and he had been a Viking in a former life.' The officer mimicked the psychic, speaking dramatically, and throwing his arms about as he spoke. 'I asked her if she would be able to identify him again. She replied with a surprised look that it shouldn't be a problem as there weren't many Vikings in Tandem Bridge.'

The room was in uproar.

'She also said he visited her in bed most nights. Then she offered me an open invitation to come back and see for myself.' DC Sharpe had the whole room in stitches; a bit of light-heartedness, but a genuine enquiry nonetheless. It took the edge off the burden the room was carrying. 'And before you ask, boss, I'm not returning even for the good of the job. I'm not that brave.'

The ripple of laughter was like a Mexican wave around the room.

'Thank you for that, Terry. If you have second thoughts, let me know, you might need back up,' Dylan said.

Dylan walked back to the incident room. There was a note on his desk. He showed it to Dawn and Larry.

*ACC's secretary rang regarding the review team meeting –
everyone can make it tomorrow morning. 11.30 a.m.,
divisional conference room, Harrowfield Police Station. Lisa.*

Jen had a meal ready for him when he arrived home. 'I can
hear your mind ticking over. Relax, it'll sort its self out, you'll
see, love,' she soothed, patting his hand,. 'Go and put your
feet up for once. Read the paper while I wash up.'

The *Harrowfield Times* headline read CHILD SERIAL
KILLER STILL AT LARGE. He threw it down on the floor at
the side of the chair, lifted his feet onto the pouffe and rested
his head back on the headrest, hands folded on his lap as he
sighed heavily.

Jen knew he would be asleep before he finished reading
the paper. She'd watched him so many times open the first
page: his arms would drop to his lap, the paper still in his
hands; his eyes would close, then his head would fall to his
chest. The predictability of his actions always made her
smile.

But she was wrong this time; he'd not even started reading
it.

Another day, he told himself, as he drove into work the next
morning. He had the radio on and Terry Wogan was on good
form. He always made him laugh. The meeting with the team
was first on the agenda; they needed to go through the
format of the review. It had already been decided that he'd
cover the summary and the background, and Dawn would
cover the issues regarding the family and lines of enquiry.
They would play the DVD and show the relevant
photographs. The exhibits officer would be present to cover
what exhibits they had and tell them what was still
outstanding. The DS from the HOLMES team would be there
for logistics and to comment on actions that still needed to be
done. *If you fail to plan then you plan to fail* was one of the
sayings at training school, and it had stuck with him. The
divisional commander should be there, but whether he would
turn up or not only time would tell. Finally, they'd prepared a
detailed document, some twenty pages in length. There was

one for each of the review team members to take away, but they had to be returned for security reasons. Each numbered document and to whom it had been given was recorded. To avoid disclosure of information, no further copies could be made and all numbered originals had to be returned.

A buffet lunch was to be served at approximately half past twelve. *Lovely,* thought Dylan, *how the other half live.*

Assistant Chief Constable Edward Thornton was the review team leader. Previously he'd been known as 'Eddie' Thornton, until he made the rank of Chief Superintendent, at which time he'd sent an internal message, via e-mail, to everyone in the force announcing that he now wished to be known as 'Edward'. In his opinion, that was more fitting for the rank. Edward was tall with a very large stomach that hung over his belted uniform trousers. Silver-grey hair was swept across his balding head. Dylan had known him for a number of years, and boy did he love his buffets. His chief superintendent was Jackie Swindon, a rather slim woman in her late forties with a neat blonde bob. He knew little of her other than she was destined for a higher rank. The SIO was Jim Taylor. Dylan and Jim got on well. Jim had been an SIO for two years. Detective Inspector Tim Fixby, Detective Sergeant Barry Light, and Jenny Cooper completed the team.

Dylan was pleased with the chosen review team and he hoped that they would identify a line of enquiry that would lead to the killer. He wasn't bothered if it was something he'd overlooked that would embarrass him at this stage; he just wanted the murderer caught. His shoulders were broad enough.

Once the introductions were over, they commenced with the DVD. Firstly, it showed the moorland and the reservoir where Daisy's body had been found. Dylan took them through the findings and the document they'd been given. It took him back to his detective training school days where he'd spent almost four years teaching law, interview techniques, and the skills required of future SIOs.

There came a welcome break; lunch was being carried in and there was friendly chatter around the room. Dylan caught up with Jim on the things that were happening around the force.

'Time for a quick pee. Hey, listen to this, Jim,' Dylan said mischievously, as he walked past the ACC, whose plate was straining under the weight of numerous pies and sandwiches, topped off with his favourite: a family-sized custard tart.

'Can you get any more on that plate, Eddie?' Dylan spoke loudly. The room went quiet. Jim nearly choked on his cup of tea as Dylan left the room, not daring to look back as he was bursting to laugh. He knew he would get some glares over the table in round two of the review, but he couldn't resist.

The review came to an end; it had taken the best part of a day. If nothing else, it had given Dylan the opportunity to review events himself. It would be a month before he'd get feedback.

Back in the incident room, he wanted to know if locally there had been any prison releases, if so, who, and if there were any old cases of a similar nature. He was going over old ground and previous thoughts just to ensure that nothing had been overlooked. He was still in review mode, but was confident after talking to Dawn and the team and checking the computer system himself that all was being done that could be. It was just becoming more and more frustrating that nothing shed any light on the investigation. It was stagnating. The Hinds and Spencers must have bloody upset someone. The answer must lie there.

'What about the "Class of 75"? Have we seen them all yet?' Dylan asked Dawn.

'Not yet, but it's a priority.'

Chapter Twenty-Three

Dylan went straight to the property store. It was chilly, dimly lit, and austere with a musty smell that reminded Dylan of a second hand shop. It had a cold, stone-flagged floor and row upon row of battened wooden shelves from floor to ceiling holding hundreds of sealed bags. Boxes of all shapes and sizes, as well as larger, heavier items, stood on the floor in one corner. An old, padlocked, grey, metal cabinet similar to a wardrobe stood at the back of the desk that housed valuable items and the drugs from crime-related offences. Another long, thin, sturdy, and securely locked cabinet held crime-related firearms and ammunition. Each item was tagged with its own consecutive number. Detective Constables John Benjamin and Vicky Hardacre were rummaging through the 'Miscellaneous and Connected' property area.

'Now then, you two,' he called out loudly, startling them both.

'Hiya. Just checking the murder exhibits and files against the lists registered on the property forms. I bet these are some of your old jobs.'

'What you trying to say, Vicky. I'm getting on?' he joked.

'Never, boss. In fact, I like older men,' she flirted.

'Where're you thinking of moving these to?' asked John, ignoring Vicky.

'I know you said there was room in the void, but I've decided I want them to go to the attic at Tandem Bridge. Then at least they'll be out of the way of prying eyes. We could do an audit at the same time. Knowing Harold's obsession with record-keeping, it shouldn't be such a big job. Just wish he wasn't off sick,' Dylan said, moving a chair to one side so that he could get past.

'Don't know what these are or what they're doing 'ere,' said Vicky moving a cradle like an umbrella stand, filled with polished canes. The canes were beautifully made out of rosewood and had silver handles, but had no identification tag attached.

'They're old inspectors' canes, used long before your time. Probably stuck there because they are no longer needed and maybe even of value these days. Uniform Inspectors carried them round when I first started. They walked their beat with them under their arm, a bit like a sergeant major,' explained Dylan.

'They're beautiful but really heavy,' Vicky said, admiring the one in her hand.

'Now I do feel old, talking about the good old days,' Dylan mused. 'I can see lots of detected murder files, but how many undetected files are there in here, do you think?'

'There are only about six, boss. They're stacked by the desk. Reckon old Harold has been reading them,' said John.

Dylan stared at the cane that Vicky was placing back in its rightful place.

'Something similar to that would actually fit the type of weapon used for the murders,' he said thoughtfully.

'There's a bag at the back of the canes. "R V Wilkinson",' Vicky read from the packet. 'No crime reference or anything.'

'It's a good thing Harold isn't here. He'd have blown a fuse. I wonder who's looking after the store in his absence?' said Dylan.

'What shall I do with it boss?' Vicky stood holding the bag in her hand as if it were contaminated. 'Put it on his desk for when he gets back?'

'Wilkinson? I've heard that name twice in the last hour. Give it to me and I'll open it. It's only taped. Pass me a glove, will you please, John?'

Dylan picked at the tape. 'Nothing else for "Wilkinson"? You sure?' he continued as he carefully tore off the tape so it could be replaced easily. The contents of the plain, brown-paper evidence bag, no bigger than a carrier bag and no heavier than a feather, froze his body. His mouth went dry. His heart started to pump fast. 'Fucking hell.'

'Boss, boss, are you okay?' Vicky grabbed his arm. He looked first at Vicky then at John in total disbelief. 'Fucking hell,' was all he heard himself say again, quieter. He was rooted to the spot with the bag open in his hand.

'What is it? You're freaking me out now,' said Vicky anxiously.

'I've just seen the yellow and white striped football sock. I can see the name on the tag: "C. SPENCER".'

'Fucking hell,' John and Vicky said almost in unison. Adrenaline pumped blood around Dylan's body more quickly and for a moment he felt faint. He put his gloved hand into the bag.

'There is some cloth underneath it,' he said. 'And if I was a gambling man I'd bet it's something of Daisy's. John and Vicky stood like statues. Time stood still.

'Get scenes of crime here now. I'll call Dawn and Larry. We need to seal this store. In fact we'll also change the locks.'

'What is it? What's happened?' Dawn sounded concerned at the tone of Dylan's voice.

'We've just accidentally unearthed Christopher's football sock and some material from Daisy's dress, I think, in the property store.'

'Bloody hell. We're on our way.'

'What do you want us to do, boss?' John asked as Dylan hung up.

'Keep your hands in your pockets, mate. Let's go back to the door and make sure no one comes in here. We'll treat this as a crime scene, but I want to keep it under wraps for as long as we can so that we don't cause alarm.' Dylan was speaking his thoughts aloud. He dialled Jasmine's number. 'I need you at Harrowfield property store urgently.' Dylan didn't remember hearing her answer. He replaced the phone.

'Vicky or John, here.' He held out a five-pound note. 'Don't care which one of you goes, but get some coffee from the canteen will you? I think better with an intake of caffeine.'

'I'll go, boss.' Vicky took the money and headed off.

'What a turn up, eh? Somebody's got some nerve.' John whistled in amazement. 'A copper? One of us?'

Dylan shrugged his shoulders as if to say, *let's face it, who knows?* He took a few steps over the stone slabs to the canes. The store was deathly quiet and the air so full of expectancy that he could hear his shoes making a crunching sound on the gritty floor. The canes were lined up like soldiers on parade. There were five of them, but he'd not noticed until now that one was missing. The cradle held six.

Dylan and John hovered. 'You don't really think it's a copper, do you, boss?'

'Well, it's got to be someone with access, John. Someone close.'

Vicky returned to the entrance of the store with a tray of steaming mugs. Dawn and Larry arrived and John let them in before locking it from the inside. A light tap told them that Jasmine had arrived.

'The divisional administrator was on my back regarding the lack of space in here,' Dylan told them. 'We looked at Cage C to see how many murder files and exhibits there were, with the intention of cataloguing and moving them to Tandem Bridge. Vicky came across a brown-paper exhibits bag that wasn't tagged. Inside was a striped sock labelled "C. SPENCER" and material that could be from Daisy's bridesmaid dress.'

'Shit, pardon my French,' said Jasmine.

'I haven't taken anything out of the bag yet, but look over there.' Dylan pointed to the canes. 'Old inspector canes with two inch spherical knobs on the end. Any one of them could match the murder weapon. One seems to be missing. I want us suited up, and then the room photographed along with Cage C, the canes, and the bag.'

Jasmine and Vicky set up the camera on its tripod. John got the exhibit bags out of the case Jasmine had brought with her. For onlookers the activity would not raise concern, because it's usual for scenes of crime officers to photograph and examine items in a property store. The store was filled with nervous excitement, but it went as quiet as the grave when everyone went into professional mode. Jasmine photographed the bag marked *'R. V. Wilkinson'*. Then very carefully, with gloved hands, she took the yellow and white football sock from it. The tag was visible. Dylan heard everyone take in a deep breath at the sight. The sock was placed in an exhibit bag, sealed and labelled for future identification. Next, Jasmine plucked out a piece of jade green silk cloth; wrapped inside it she found a white lace heart. The mood was sombre but elated at the same time. Items were systematically photographed, labelled and bagged.

'Photograph the canes. I'd like them seized as exhibits, please,' Dylan said.

Dylan, Dawn, and Larry went over to the property clerk's desk. This was where Harold Little sat. At the side of the desk were murder files and their attached summaries. Without disturbing them, they each looked at the top pages. One was for a hanging, another for a hostage demand that went wrong. The items also needed photographing in situ.

'Liz Green was adamant that the man in the picture is called Harold Wilkinson, not Little. She described him as a bit of a loner,' Dawn reminded Dylan and Larry.

'Harold's not a murderer,' said Larry.

'What does a murderer look like? The bloody exhibits have been in the store, his bloody store all the time. Dawn, we need to go through every file that's here. It may have some bearing on the murders. Harold's computer will need checking and we'll have to force these drawers on the desk by the look of it. They appear to be locked and I can't see any keys, can you?' The occupants of the store looked around the room, searching for the keys, but they were nowhere to be seen. 'Harold is off sick at the moment and I don't know when he's due back, but just remember, other civilians and police have access to this store. It could be that someone has taken this exhibit, not labelled it, and left it for someone else to book in. We'll seal the store now, though, which means that people are going to start asking questions. Can I leave that with you?'

Dawn nodded.

'I'll go and see Beaky in admin and get what I can from Harold's personal file. See if that tells us anything about him.'

'No problem. I can't believe it. Right under our noses all the time,' Dawn said through clenched teeth.

'One of the team should be seeing Barry Sanderson about now,' Dylan reminded the team as he walked out of the store.

Chapter Twenty-Four

There was a spring in Dylan's step as he took the stairs two at a time on his way to the administration department. It was a small office with five desks. The girls were laughing, passing round a tin of chocolates, and they offered them to Dylan when he walked into the room. He scanned the room for Jen, but she was nowhere to be seen. The administrator's office was situated at the far side of the room. The door was furnished with a brass plaque bearing her name, AVRIL SUMMERFIELD-PRESTON, and was closed as usual. Through the little, head-height window, Dylan could see her with her feet up on the desk, laughing, as she spoke on the telephone.

He knocked on the door and walked straight in. The strong smell of perfume hit him, and he coughed. His immediate entrance took her aback.

'I'll have to go. Someone very rudely just barged in,' Avril told her caller. 'I'll get back to you in a minute.' she hung up. 'Waiting to be called in would have been nice,' she remarked.

'The call obviously wasn't work, then,' he replied. 'I've come about the property store.' He spoke directly, the only way he knew for dealing with a person like Avril.

'Actually, it was Chief Superintendent Hugo-Watkins on the phone.'

'Really.'

'You might know, the amount of extra exhibits is causing me no end of trouble and affecting the running of the station. The clerk is off sick. Allegedly he tripped over one of the bags down there. Now there'll be form-filling, an accident report, and no doubt a personal injury claim. This is a big health and safety issue for me.'

'What's the clerk's name?' he said, ignoring her speech.

'Harold.'

'Full name?'

'Harold Little,' she said, looking curiously at him. 'Why?'

'How long has he been here?'

'About five years. Why?'

'Do you have his personal file?'

'That's nothing to do with you, Inspector. Harold is a civilian. My staff, not yours. I myself interviewed and appointed him.'

That's no endorsement, thought Dylan. 'I don't want this to go any further than this office. The property store will be closed for the next few days as it's a potential crime scene. There's evidence connecting the two child murders in there, and I need to eliminate Harold and anyone else who's had access in his absence. Now, do you have his file please, and do you know any other details that may assist the enquiry?'

She swallowed hard, but her expression didn't change as she walked to a tall, grey, metal filing cabinet and pulled out one of the heavy drawers. Encased were files on every member of civilian staff, containing all their personal and work related details. She tossed the file to him nonchalantly.

'This is most irritating. What's going to happen to all the property now?' she said.

'Any property brought in from this moment in time will have to go into temporary store. I'll let you know where once that's been agreed.' He stood up to leave.

'You can't take that with you. I need it back,' she said, flustered 'I can't let a personal file go out of my hands without a signature.'

'What do you need me to sign?' he said. She passed him an authorisation slip.

'Bloody protocol,' he moaned as he scrawled his name. 'I'll need it 'til at least tomorrow. Don't, whatever you do, breathe a word of this to anyone, and I mean anyone, including police officers.'

He left through the main office, keyboards clicking, printers humming, telephones ringing and the kettle boiling, but still no Jen. It was all so normal in admin and yet things were beginning to move at a pace with the enquiry.

He walked briskly to the upper floor where the station boss for Harrowfield had his office. Phil Warrington was a homely man with big, red, rosy cheeks and a stomach that said he liked his beer.

'How're things, Jack? How're the murder enquiries going? You'll choose a quieter life one day and run a division,' he laughed warmly, beckoning Dylan to sit in one of the comfy chairs around the coffee table. Dylan and Phil had known and worked with each other, with mutual respect, for years.

'Up until the last forty-eight hours, nothing was giving at all on either of them, but, and it's very early days yet, we think we might be on to something. Avril had been nagging me about the property store because it was fit to bursting with the murder exhibits.'

Phil held his hand up. 'That's her job, Jack, but I understand it's the last thing you need at the moment.'

'As it happens, Phil, it may have been a good thing. I've had to close the store. It may be that there's potential evidence for the murders secreted in there. I've just got the personal file of the storekeeper from her, although she wasn't for parting with it. Can you believe she had me sign for the bloody thing?'

'That's Harold Little, isn't it? You think he may be involved?'

Dylan nodded.

'You'll tell me what's going on when the time's right, I'm sure, but I'd be grateful if you let me know first if you think anyone from the division is involved.'

'I assure you, Phil. I just need to firm some things up first, to be one hundred per cent sure. There's only Avril and you who know anything at the moment, and I'd like to keep it that way for as long as possible.'

'Best of luck, mate. I'm grateful for you keeping me up to speed, and if you need anything else let me know.'

'Thanks, Phil,' he said, shaking his friend's hand.

Back in the store with the other officers, Dylan allocated tasks. 'We need to get the lock changed for this door. Can I leave it with you, John, to arrange it with a local joiner? Invoice the incident room: I don't want Avril to have another other reason to have a go. Oh, and all the keys to us. We'll also need the keys for the cabinets from her and a sign needs to be put on the door.' While he talked, Dylan wrote in large letters on a piece of printer paper.

PROPERTY STORE FULL, CLOSED DUE TO HEALTH AND SAFETY REASONS
FOR INFORMATION ON DEPOSITS OR COLLECTIONS PLEASE RING HARROWFIELD HQ INCIDENT ROOM ON EXT 71146

'Deposits will have to go in a makeshift temporary store here in the void. I've cleared it with Phil Warrington. Inform the van man that when he collects the post from Tandem Bridge he needs to deposit their property to the void, too. Collections from this store will have to be dealt with by incident room staff. Avril and Phil know about what we're doing, but they're the only ones in the know apart from us six. Oh, I've also managed to get Harold Wilkinson-Little's file.' He put an emphasis on the 'Wilkinson'. 'How're you doing down here?' Dylan asked.

'We've already forced the drawer to his desk, boss, and there're one or two printouts from the *Friends Reunited* website, along with details about Martin, Trevor and Barry. There're a few scribblings, but none are particularly legible.' Larry handed Dylan the papers which were already in plastic see-through exhibits bags. 'We've just about done all we can at the moment. The sock and dress material are being dealt with by SOCO, and they'll be dealing with the printouts, too, once you've finished with them.'

'The canes?' asked Dylan.

'Each one has been photographed and bagged separately, boss,' said Vicky. 'They aren't half a weight collectively.'

'Jasmine, you all done?'

'Yes, for the time being.'

'Great. Dawn, anything?'

'Yeah, I've been looking at the logistics of doing a full search and an audit in here. We'll need to check every bag, so that means a week's work for about four staff. He may have hidden something else, so we can't take a chance.'

'We've no choice, Dawn, have we? But for the first time in weeks we may have a breakthrough.' Dylan hoped so, anyway. 'Right, everyone back to the incident room for a scrum down. We'll decide our next move and catch up with the team. Anything on Barry Sanderson yet?'

'No,' said Larry, 'but I'll get someone in the incident room to check the progress on that enquiry.'

'Vicky, are you staying in the store with John or coming with us to the incident room?'

'No competition, boss, you know that,' she said cheekily. 'I'll stay here with, John.' She cracked out laughing. It caused the others to laugh too. It wasn't that the comment was all that funny, but it felt good to laugh. Laughing was something that none of them had done in a long while.

'I'll remember that, Vicky,' he said, pretending to be hurt.

'I love it when you're cross, boss,' she teased, still grinning.

They headed back to the incident room. Dylan whistled. The development was a welcome breakthrough, and he knew it would have the same effect on the rest of the team. When the time was right he would tell them.

He sat and called Jen. 'I'm back in my office, love. We're having a really good day How about you?'

'Fine, something's obviously perked you up.'

'Ah, ha. Possibly. I'll let you know later if it turns out as good as we expect it to. Ring you when I'm leaving for home.'

He felt upbeat. Okay, he didn't have a motive yet or any reasons, but what he did have was a hell of a lot more than before. It could be Harold or one of a hundred people who'd accessed the store, but it certainly was a step in the right direction.

Harold was the property clerk, so he was the obvious place to start. He received, labelled, and sealed bags and boxes of property from people. This wasn't labelled. He was meticulous; Dylan knew that much. So was the item there without his knowledge? The only sure thing was that an item from both murders, trophies, had been found. Prove who put them there and the murderer or murderers would be known. They'd only been discovered by chance, hidden. The murderer thought they were in a safe place, locked away in a police station.

Chapter Twenty-Five

'Thank you, god,' he whispered. Dylan wasn't particularly religious but this was the piece of luck he'd been missing and he knew it.

Dylan, Dawn, and Larry sat and discussed the day's developments in detail late into the evening. They didn't notice the time or the dark creeping up on them, they weren't tired.

Little's file had been photocopied three times. 'WILKINSON' was his middle name.

> *Harold Wilkinson-Little*
> *D.O.B: 1.5.1960*
> *Address: - 12, Sycamore Drive, Tandem Bridge.*
> *Vehicle Reg: - T412 NRT – Suzuki Carry Van 1.3ltr*
> *Previous employers: - Administration Dept at the local Council Office, Librarian at large bookstore, Lost Property Clerk for British Rail.*
> *Starting date Police: - 3.4.2000*
> *In case of emergency: - Mrs Pauline Wilkinson-Little*
> *Comment by Interviewer: -*
> *Excellent interview. By far the most outstanding candidate. A fine, upstanding person who will be an asset to the service, mild-mannered, polite, eager to please, and respectful.*
> *Signed: Avril Summerfield-Preston*

'He's only forty-five. Jesus, he looks sixty,' said Dawn.

'He's got to be our main focus. We need the Spencers to visually ID the sock,' said Dylan. 'Same with the material for the Hinds, please. We need someone to do a recce on Harold's house with a view to surveillance until we're ready to move in on him. I want any known intelligence we have about him; family, vehicle, even parking tickets and speed cameras.'

'What do you want us to tell the family, boss? They're going to ask where we found the stuff,' said Dawn.

'For the time being, we're going to say that we found them by chance in a storeroom, but nobody's connected to them. Enquiries are continuing and there are a lot of people to see, which is the truth.'

'Do you want to do the Hinds, Dawn? Larry, the Spencers? That way I know it'll be done right. I'll get someone from the surveillance team over here and all the relevant paperwork for approval. Meet you both back here in an hour.'

Nobody needed asking twice. The chairs screeched back keenly, life had been injected into them: were they getting close?

Dylan had been updating the policy book with the day's events and scribbling the directions and actions he wanted the team to take. Now, he was waiting for Inspector Ben Wright, force surveillance. The team outside his office working steadily away knew something was afoot. A coffee was placed on his desk.

'Thanks, Lisa,' he said, watching her go. Eager eyes awaited her return.

'Nothing,' she shook her head. 'He didn't give anything away,' she said sadly, as she slipped back into her seat in the incident room.

Dylan was pondering his next move when Dawn returned.

'Might have known you'd be sitting and drinking coffee whilst we're all out working our butts off.'

'Privileges of rank, Dawn. One day you'll do it, hopefully sooner rather than later,' he beamed.

'Positive ID from the Hinds.' They asked a lot of questions and I told them what you said and that we'd have to wait for forensics examination.'

'Great. You've just reminded me, I want these exhibits up to forensics tomorrow, and I want them priority. Early start for someone. Our killer probably didn't expect them to be found so soon, so we may get lucky.'

'I'm off to get some coffee. D'you want a refill?' asked Dawn. Dylan nodded.

Larry walked into the office as Dawn walked out. 'Yes, please,' he called after her.

'No question whatsoever with the Spencers. Sarah gave me an unused name tag showing C. SPENCER, which I've exhibited. Both of them were excited by the thought we'd found their son's killer, but I assured them there was a vast amount of work to do yet.'

Vicky and John marched through the door at a pace. 'All sorted, boss. Three keys,' said John, as he placed them on Dylan's desk.

'The sock and the dress material have been positively identified. Not that we doubted it,' Dylan told them smugly.

'I think you ought to know something, boss,' John said, his voice taking a serious note. Dylan was all ears. 'When I went to get the keys for the cupboards in the store from Avril, she was on the phone. I heard her ask for Mr Hugo-Watkins and she went on to discuss the exhibits we found.'

'The stupid, stupid woman. She was on the phone to him when I went to see her. She was told how important it was not to speak to anyone about this. I'll have that woman's guts for garters before I'm finished. I know there've been rumours about them, but I never thought she was so … so thick.' Dylan's expression could have cut steel.

Dawn entered the room and closed the door behind her. She had heard the ructions from the incident room. Police stations had thin walls and scandal and rumour spread like wildfire. *If only intelligence on criminals did the same,* Dawn had thought more than once. The office outside, although looking busy, was very quiet as everyone hoped to catch a snippet of the conversation from within Dylan's office. A word, a sentence, a name, and the tongues would be off; it was all so exciting for everyone.

They were just waiting for Jasmine. Dylan could sense the elation being suppressed. Smiles kept appearing on the assembled faces. They wanted to rush out and grab Little now. Dylan could see them all fidgeting and moving bits of paper because they needed something to do.

'Larry, Barry Sanderson, anything yet?'

'The officers will tell us all at the debrief. What I do know is that he lives on his own, is divorced with two children that he doesn't see, and until recently he had a dog that became sick and died suddenly.'

'Did the officers say he admitted to knowing Trevor and Martin?'

'Yeah, he said he went to the reunion, hadn't seen them since his schooldays, and can't think why anyone would particularly target them. Neither could he think of anything that'd happened at the reunion, either.'

Jasmine arrived and took a seat. Dylan outlined to them how he saw the next seventy-two hours taking shape.

'We now have a positive ID on the sock and the material, linking the two items with the murders. We also have the fingertip and the brace that were sent to their homes. Our property store man, Harold Wilkinson-Little, has a link to the fathers of both children and the reunion they went to. He's our prime suspect. We've gone from having nothing and now have just taken one giant step. What we don't know is the motive. Spencer, Hind and Sanderson say nothing untoward occurred at the school reunion, but potentially there's something that caused a usually placid man to become a vile, evil killer.'

'Here are the files Little's been reading, the old murder cases. I know there's a hanging in one of them. Maybe he got some ideas from them,' Larry suggested.

'You could be right, which may account for the mismatch of injuries to the bodies. We need to go through the files and exhibit them. We also need to locate the murder weapons, that's if they're not the same in both cases. The inspector's canes are an ideal size and might be involved, and one of them appears to be missing from the cradle. Where is it? Could that be it?' Dylan was thoughtful. 'So we still have a long way to go to nail him, but what a difference a day makes, eh? He's been under our feet all the time, or maybe seen the exhibits brought in.' He shook his head in amazement as if nothing surprised him anymore. 'I'm having round the clock surveillance on him from this evening. We can't risk him going out and attacking someone else. Ben

Wright from the surveillance team is on his way. Early trip tomorrow to forensics. Anyone volunteering?'

'I'll go,' Vicky said.

'Thanks. We need to start thinking about getting his vehicle searched and lifted onto a low loader to go to forensics. He may have transported Daisy and Christopher in it. Did he do the murders on his own? He's only small and doesn't look very strong, but it's a thought. We need to identify arrest and search teams for his house, and someone to deal with his wife. I want the search to be in depth. We need to be sure we don't miss anything. I know it could take hours, but it's necessary. Where are we going to take him and the property we seize? Any ideas?'

'There's an unoccupied room just on the corridor from the incident room. It's secure, and nearby so that could be ideal for the exhibits,' Dawn said.

'Can you arrange that for me? What if we use a cell here? I know it's unusual but if we use the female one at the very end of the row away from anyone?' said Dylan, hopefully.

'That would work okay. What about constant supervision, sir?' Dawn enquired.

'It's something else we need to do.' Everyone had been very quiet and thoughtful, taking notes of actions they personally needed to do and also trying to absorb all that was happening.

'Come on, team effort. I'm doing all the talking,' said Dylan. They remained silent.

'Okay. I'll interview with Dawn. We all have in depth knowledge of the murders. Jasmine, from the scenes of crime side, how many staff will you need? Remember I want all the house filming, his vehicle, photographs and exhibits.'

'There'll be three scenes of crime officers working on the day, so that should be more than enough.'

'I'll speak with the custody staff, so they're ready to accept a prisoner. I'm thirsty, let's have a comfort break, then we'll discuss what we'll tell the team.'

Legs stretched, bladders emptied, and drinks made, they were back in the office and eager to get on with the job at hand, each and every one of them wanting to feel this evil child killer's collar as soon as possible. Increasingly the incident room staff sensed something was bubbling, but didn't know what. They were circling like vultures hovering around a wounded animal waiting for it to drop. They wouldn't expect Dylan to tell them, but after all their hard work they were straining at the leash.

Hard and fast evidence was needed. The pressure was on and a prime suspect in sight. Dylan was going to grab the nettle and go for him. He hoped to gain evidence through an interview and the search of his property. It was his decision and his alone.

'I'm thinking, the day after tomorrow for the arrest, providing we get confirmation that he's at home and hasn't been locked up already by the surveillance team, who'll do what's necessary if it looks like he's at it again. They'll ring me if they've any doubts, but we need to have our teams ready and briefed at tomorrow's debrief. We've a lot of work to do, but I'm sure we'll all sleep better when we get him behind bars. Anybody got any questions or views, problems, issues? Larry?'

'Should we update the review team?'

'Good point. I'll speak to someone direct. Dawn?'

'What're we going to tell the team?'

'They should all be here for the debrief shortly. I'm going to give them a quick overview of what's happened and arrange a debrief tomorrow for four o'clock, when I'll be able to give them more information and tell them what their individual roles will be.'

'Are you gonna want any uniform presence at the house?'

'Yes, Dawn, definitely.'

'Okay then, decision made,' Dylan said, slapping the palm of his hand flat on the desk in front of him. 'Let's do the debrief.'

Chapter Twenty-Six

'Now, everyone, what I'm going to tell you remains in this room. I want nothing, and I mean, nothing, discussed outside.' There was total silence. People glanced at each other to see if any of their colleagues' expressions told them anything. They shrugged their shoulders and turned their heads.

'First and foremost, both murders are now being merged and tomorrow's briefing will be a little earlier, at four o'clock. You'll understand why after I've finished,' he continued. 'Earlier today we recovered what we believed to be Christopher Spencer's missing football sock, which has since been positively identified by the family.' There was a gasp. 'Recovered along with this was material we believed to be from Daisy's bridesmaid dress, also IDd by her family. They were found in a bag together.' Never mind hearing a pin drop, only the sound of breathing and Dylan's voice could be heard as the assembled crowd stood like marble statues.

'You'll have to accept that at this time I can't tell you everything, but it's anticipated that we'll be making an arrest in the next twenty-four hours. I don't want you leaving this room and asking others what they know. We've done a vast amount of work recently and we're not, I repeat not, going to spoil that with careless talk. I know I've only given you part of the information I hold, but there're reasons for that which will become apparent tomorrow. I could've said nothing at this stage, but I felt you deserved to know at least that. Let's hope that continuing enquiries prove to be as positive. I'll see you all tomorrow.'

Normal service resumed slowly and the noise level returned, but anticipation and excitement hung in the air. Dylan was right: he could have said nothing, but he realised rumour spread quickly. That's why he had taken the team into his confidence, a gesture acknowledging their hard work and commitment.

Ben Wright arrived and Dylan explained the reasons for the surveillance he was requesting. Hopefully, from that night until seven-thirty the day after tomorrow, Harold Wilkinson-Little would be having his every move monitored.

'I'll have to check the area to see if a surveillance van is feasible,' Ben explained. 'There is also the option of a double-crewed car or motorcyclist nearby should he go on the move.'

Dylan gave him his mobile number and asked him to update him as to what was feasible after he had done a recce. He thanked him, as Ben left to get on with the job in hand.

Dylan rang Jen to tell her he was leaving work. 'I'll call for a bottle of wine on my way.' Dylan was buoyant.

'I can't wait to hear all about it.' Jen smiled. She knew he was going to be a busy man over the next few days if all went well.

Later that evening, in the middle of their meal, Dylan's mobile rang.

'Boss, Ben Wright. I've had a look at the target house. His white van's on the drive so I've arranged for an obs van. It's a cul-de-sac, so it'll be easy to monitor him should he leave, on foot or otherwise. I'll probably tag on a surveillance motorbike and if he needs back up, he can always shout up.'

'Cheers, Ben, thanks for that. Hopefully I won't need you for long.' Dylan squeezed Jen's hand across the table. 'Right madam,' he said. 'Let's take Max for a walk, the exercise and fresh air will do me good.'

'Oh, I'm so pleased it's working out for you Jack, at last.' His arm was round her shoulders and he pulled her closer to him as they walked. 'It's been a difficult one, hasn't it?'

'Yeah it has, but how can you tell?' He stood still and faced her. She gently ran her fingers over his face.

'Oh, little things like your eyes are clearer now and less hooded. Your face seems less lined, less stressed.' She reached up and kissed the tip of his nose. They walked hand in hand. 'And it's good to know that in a short while I'll have you back again.' She hugged him as they walked through the woods away from prying eyes. 'When it's finished, can we go on holiday?' she asked.

'Too true we can, I need some time to spoil you.' He looked down at her and smiled lovingly.

'Good,' she said as she kissed him.

The next few hours were going to drag for Jack. He couldn't wait to grab the murderer's collar.

Chapter Twenty-Seven

The elation, excitement, and anticipation could be felt in the incident room as Dylan walked through the next morning. Never before had he seen it looking so busy so early.

'Morning, sir,' Lisa said cheerfully as she placed a cup of coffee on his desk. He had a long 'to do' list after waking at four o'clock to scribble reminders blindly on bits of paper. Finally he'd given in, switched on the light and written them on a pad instead. Jen had groaned and muttered something about him being insane and then promptly fallen back to sleep. He couldn't disagree.

His first call was to the review team.

'Is no other bugger in before nine?' he growled as Larry entered the room.

Last night's rancid ale oozed from every pore in his body. 'Morning,' he mumbled with his head down as he stood in Dylan's doorway. He swung his leg idly, kicking out into fresh air like a sulking teenager. He looked as if he had slept in the suit he had on, the little knot in his tie dragged down to allow his top button to be open.

Dylan was not impressed but carried on talking as if he hadn't noticed. He wasn't in any mood for a confrontation; he had too much to do. 'I've left a message for the review team telling them that there've been developments, but no details, so if anyone rings and I'm not here that's what it's about. We've a lot to do today, Larry, I hope you're fit?'

'Yeah, just need a minute or so to come round,' he yawned, shaking his head. Dylan would have liked to shake it for him.

Dawn flounced in bright and breezy. 'Morning,' she hollered cheerfully. 'My god, have you been out all night? You look like shit.' Larry ignored her. Dawn pursed her lips, 'Ouch, touchy,' she mouthed to Dylan.

'Anything new, boss?' Larry asked.

'No. Dawn, will you check with the cells and make sure they're ready?'

'Consider it done, sir.'

Dylan picked up the phone. 'Ben, it's Jack Dylan. Is our man still at home?'

'Yep, no movement. Is your strike time still tomorrow at 07.30 hours?'

'That's right. I'll be seeking confirmation from you that he's still on site at seven.'

'I'll get one of the obs men to call you, unless anything happens before.'

'Thanks, Ben, and tell the boys and girls I'm grateful.'

'Dawn, will you speak to Clive, Fran, and Janice and let the FLOs know what's happening? Remind them the information is not for the Spencers' or the Hinds' ears at the moment. You can update them once we know more.'

'Will do.'

Larry sat very still in his chair; he leant forward and held his head in his hands, belching loudly.

'For God's sake go have a shower and get something to eat, whatever it takes. You're no damn use to me in this state.' Dylan raised his shoulders and sighed deeply. Without a response, Larry slid off his chair and dragged his feet out of the office. Dawn's head remained down and her eyes were fixed to her work. She knew Dylan understood better than most bosses what his officers had to deal with on a daily basis and he made allowances, but she also knew Larry had annoyed him and that wasn't a wise move.

'I'm remaining calm and focused,' Dylan announced, sitting up straight, splaying his hands on his desk and breathing in deeply as he tried to stay composed. 'It's a shame all detective sergeants aren't like you, Dawn.' He yawned as he exhaled. 'I'm going to try and get hold of Francis Boscombe, our profiler, and see if there is anything he can help us with.'

'Well at least he's linked the murders for you,' Boscombe confirmed. 'He's also kept trophies, which I suggest means he has some grudge against them, or wants to hurt someone close to them.'

'Mm ... our thoughts too.'

'Regarding the interview strategy, what sort of approach do you feel would get the best response from the murderer?' asked Dylan.

'I suggest softly, softly.'

Dylan was contemplating the interview as he replaced the receiver; Dawn spoke, breaking his reverie. 'Are we going to let the FLOs tell the families of the arrest, once we have him in?' she asked, her chin in her fist, her elbow on the desk.

'We'll have to; otherwise they might hear it on the TV or radio. Give the FLOs the go-ahead once we've made the arrest and tell them we'll update them as soon as we can. Stress that it might be some time before we can tell them any more. Boscombe didn't have much else to give us that we didn't already know. I don't know about his suggestion of a soft approach, though.'

Vicky was back from depositing the sock, material, and other exhibits at forensic when Larry returned to the fold, looking much better than when he had left, much to Dylan's relief. The last thing he needed was unnecessary distraction. Dylan flashed him a yellow card as he walked in the office, like a referee would as a warning on the field. Larry nodded in acknowledgement. Usually Dylan would have blasted him out of the water, but not today. It was a day to savour the mood of the impending arrest, so this time Larry was very fortunate and he knew it.

The meeting to discuss the interview approach and the arrest commenced. Dawn and Larry sat, pens poised, as Dylan began. 'I want the house covered front and back, then it'll be a knock on the front door.' Dylan tapped his fist on the table. 'He lives with his wife, Pauline. We will need someone to talk to her when he's arrested and taken from the house. Larry, how about you dealing with Mrs Wilkinson-Little?'

'Er ... do I have a choice?' Larry brushed invisible fluff from his dark trousers as he spoke. He reminded Dylan of a spoilt child at times.

'Not after this morning's episode you don't, no. You ought to think yourself lucky you're even coming on the lock up. Once she's calmed down, I presume you can come away. Remember, it's going to be one hell of a shock to her. I want you back here as soon as possible and she can be seen later for a statement. I'll make the arrest for both murders. I intend to treat him with kid gloves unless he kicks off. After all, I want him to talk to us and it'll be a lot easier in interview if he does. Dawn, I'll have you with me in the interview. We'll see what he starts off saying and then play it by ear. I'd like to deal with the murders in order, but we'll see how it goes. It's nearly briefing time. Anything else you think we need to cover?' he asked them both.

'Media, boss. Are we going to have a pre-arranged statement to be released at a specific time?'

'Yeah, I thought so, I drafted this. "A forty-five year old man from Tandem Bridge was arrested today in connection with the murders of Daisy Charlotte Hind and Christopher Francis Spencer." However, we won't release it till late morning. Right then, let's tell the team what's going to take place tomorrow.' Dylan was keyed up and eager to get on.

Walking along the corridor to the briefing room, he could hear the team's laughter, mimicking, teasing, and fun. *I'm going to have to hold the reins tight on this lot,* he thought. Once they knew, it would be like showing a dog a rabbit. Dylan himself was on a high; he was smiling inside, but his grin could not reach his lips. He had to hold a solemn face, the serious approach. He had arrested a murder suspect many times before, but that didn't stop him from wanting to see the surprised look on Wilkinson-Little's face when he felt his collar. Dylan could already feel his adrenaline pumping just at the thought of it, but he had to suppress it to make sure he remembered everything he had to say at the briefing. They'd worked so hard to get this far and nothing was going to spoil it now. He didn't want any mistakes or any transgression that could prejudice the case.

Jack Dylan and the two detective sergeants strode into the room. The noise cut to silence. The room itself was indifferent, unaffected by the enormity of it all. There were desks and chairs strewn about haphazardly so everyone could fit in. Larry closed the door and joined Dawn and Dylan at the front of the audience. Dylan spoke.

'Tomorrow morning at seven-thirty we will arrest a suspect whom we believe to be our murderer. He will be brought here to Harrowfield HQ. We have recovered Christopher's sock

155

and also part of Daisy's bridesmaid dress, which have been positively identified by their families and are now with forensic.' The room remained perfectly still. 'The target is Harold Wilkinson-Little.'

There were instantaneous murmurs and mutterings around the room, heads turned, people whispered into each other's ears behind cupped hands. 'Yes,' Dylan continued, 'Most of you will know him. He is our property clerk. He's obviously been amongst us since the beginning of these incidents. Tomorrow he'll be with us in a completely different capacity. At this time his house is under surveillance. His wife Pauline works at Tesco. A lot of hard work has been done so far, but there'll be a lot more to do when he's in. Dawn and Larry will give you specific tasks. Remember, I want nothing but a professional approach.'

The meeting was closed and everyone buzzed around to find out what his or her role would be in the operation.

Dylan contacted Superintendent Phil Warrington in a confidential e-mail to let him know of the arrest, as promised.

Jen was pleased when Jack walked in early.

'Steak's on,' she called from the kitchen as she heard the door bang. 'You'll need your strength to get you through tomorrow, I hear.'

She placed before him a plate of sirloin steak with fragrant garlic mushrooms, carrots, broccoli, and mashed and roast potatoes, accompanied by a glass of red wine.

'Just eat,' Jen ordered as she sat down in the chair opposite him; if he started talking, she knew it would go cold. Jack smiled, leaned across the table, holding his tie to his shirt so as not to trail it through the gravy, and kissed her.

With the exception of a small piece of meat on the corner of his plate, Jack ate the lot. At his side, waiting patiently, was Max. Jack dropped the scrap of steak into the patient dog's mouth; it never touched the sides.

'That was wonderful, love.' He was always appreciative, which made Jen love cooking for him. 'What's for pudding?'

'I'm sure you've got hollow legs, mister. Treacle sponge and custard. I hope you've left room.' She was standing at the sink running the washing up water as she turned to him and smiled. 'Then you can go into the lounge, put your feet up and watch the news whilst you're reading the evening paper. I'll bring you coffee when I've cleaned up here.' Jack stood up from the table and went to snuggle up behind her, wrapping his arms around her waist and nuzzling his face into her neck. 'Did I ever say "thank you" for loving me?' he asked, kissing her neck softly. 'You spoil me, you know.'

'I like spoiling you. Oh, by the way I called in at Tesco, so there're plenty of bananas for you to take tomorrow, plus an apple, water, and two packs of doughnuts for the team.' Jen busied herself clearing the table. 'I bumped into my friend who works there. She used to look after Max for me when I went to Mum and Dad's before I met you. I haven't seen her for ages.'

'That's lovely, and guess what? That's where our man's wife works.'

'Eek. Oh gosh, I bet she knows her.'

'Well, it's not as if she's done anything wrong, poor woman,' Jack called as he walked down the hall and up the stairs to the bathroom. As he passed their bedroom, he noticed Jen had already hung his suit, shirt and lucky tie on the wardrobe door for the next day. He shook his head in disbelief. She really was amazing.

Five thirty in the morning and Dylan was buzzing, ready for off. He hadn't slept much, tossing and turning in anticipation of the arrest, but surprisingly he felt fresh and wide awake. The day felt cool as he left the house, there was a morning mist, and the slight breeze had a bite. It was so quiet and still; it felt eerie as he drove to work. Larry arrived as Dylan parked his car and they walked into the incident room together. Luckily it was a very different Larry from the previous day.

'Morning, you two,' shouted Dawn, looking over her shoulder from where she stood making coffee. *That's more like it,* thought Dylan.

As promised, on the nail the call came in from the Obs team.

'Boss,' said the caller in a hushed tone. 'Your target hasn't moved. Best of luck. We'll move away once your cars arrive.'

'Thank you,' Dylan said, and replaced the receiver. 'Arrest time, you lot.' he growled.

Chapter Twenty-Eight

Dylan and Dawn travelled in silence, each nursing their own emotions. They'd waited a long time for this day.

The small convoy of six vehicles moved slowly. Five plain vehicles and one marked car crept down the cul-de-sac, tyres crunching the gravel, until they each took their positions to surround the house. The officers moved forward as one to number twelve and stopped.

Dylan's knock was like thunder. The echo made the sound last. Lights illuminated neighbouring houses. Blinds twitched as occupants looked to see what the noise was about. A glow appeared to the side of number twelve's bedroom curtains. Dylan impatiently thumped again. A beam of light sprang through the half window of the front door.

'I'm coming, I'm coming, patience, please,' came a voice from within.

Dylan could hear the bolt drawn back. The key turned and the door squeaked open.

The boy-sized frame of Harold Wilkinson-Little stood in front of them, dishevelled, dressed in blue striped pyjamas and old tartan slippers.

'Can I help you? Oh, it's you Mr Dylan, sir,' he said politely, pulling his pyjama top together with one hand as he held the door open with the other.

Dylan stepped forward across the threshold. 'May we come in?' He pushed the open door wide with the palm of his hand, not waiting for an answer. Harold took a step back.

'Harold Wilkinson-Little, I am arresting you for the murders of Daisy Charlotte Hind and Christopher Francis Spencer.' Dylan spoke quietly but with authority, as he cautioned him. Little stood, his face expressionless, as he stared at Dylan and remained silent.

'What's going on, Harold? Who is it? Harold.' A woman's high-pitched voice cracked the tense atmosphere. Dawn silently handcuffed Harold and escorted him to the waiting car, as his wife Pauline appeared at the top of the stairs. Dylan directed the team into the house to start the planned search.

'What's happening?' she asked. 'What's going on? Where you taking Harold? He's not dressed,' she said, flustered.

Larry stepped towards her as she came down the stairs. 'Mrs Wilkinson-Little, your husband has been arrested for the murders of two children. We'll be searching the house and taking items away,' Larry said, as sensitively as he knew how. Leading her by her elbow, he took her through the hallway and into the small kitchen. Sitting her down, he found the kettle and filled it with water.

'What? He couldn't possibly. Tell me this is a dream. This is ridiculous, you've got it all wrong he … he … works for the police.'

She was in need of a cup of strong, sweet tea. Larry knew Pauline would also be a victim, and he wouldn't find it easy to console her. Not only had Harold killed two children and ruined the lives of those families, he'd also destroyed her life. Neighbours would point fingers at her. *That's her that's married to the child killer.* The house, her home, would more than likely become a target once it became common knowledge. Dylan and the team would do their level best to get support for her. Time would heal, maybe, but Harold had left her with her own life sentence: the tag of being the wife of a child murderer. The question people would always ask would be, *did she know?*

Larry sat with Pauline while the team searched. He tried to explain to her what they were doing, but in her dazed state, he could have been reading a shopping list. He knew it would all have to be explained to her again, later.

Harold's van was being lifted onto a low loader outside the house, and the orange light of the truck flashed in Pauline's face as she sat at the kitchen table. Pauline began sobbing, her cries muffled by the tissue she held. She told Larry she had a sister who she'd like to have with her. Pauline would soon learn that the man she'd shared her life with was a stranger; she didn't actually know him at all. There were so many questions she needed answers to, but only one person could tell her and that was Harold. Would she ever believe a word he said again? Although distraught, she began to realise that the police didn't go to these lengths for nothing.

Harold sat in the back seat of the CID car and stared straight ahead, as if a mannequin. They arrived at the custody suite of the station, where the sergeant went through a series of routine questions: name, address, and date of birth. Dylan and Dawn remained quiet, watching Harold's every movement.

'You will need a solicitor; do you have one in mind?'

'Yes, Brenda Cotton from Sykes and Co,' he said in a quiet voice, his head bent. His chin nearly touched his chest.

Dawn looked at Dylan. 'Have you been expecting us?' asked Dylan.

Harold stared straight ahead and spoke to the sergeant as if Dylan wasn't there. 'I know my rights. I haven't had breakfast,' he said, lifting his head up and speaking clearly.

'Oh, dear, what a shame. Breakfast's over,' the sergeant drawled sarcastically as he continued to fill in his paperwork.

'Harold, we'll get you breakfast. Is tea and toast all right?' Dawn asked.

'Thank you,' he whimpered. His lip quivered like a child as he turned to look at her. *Perhaps the soft approach will work,* thought Dylan.

Dawn was playing games, keeping him sweet until he was interviewed. Thereafter he would be the evil child-murdering bastard she knew he was. She managed to smile at him with this thought in mind.

'Your solicitor will be contacted and asked to attend at the police station as soon as possible. In the meantime, we need you to change out of those clothes into one of our overalls, until someone brings you alternative clothing. You'll go into a cell until some food can be arranged,' said the sergeant as he marched him down the corridor to the dedicated chamber that awaited him.

The cell had no natural light; it was dimly lit and furnished with a low, wooden, fixed bed base with a thin, blue plastic mattress on top. A metal toilet stared at Harold from where he sat on his bedstead; it had no seat. Although the cell was dismal, claustrophobic and bare, it was still too good for a murderer. It would remain a mystery to Dylan why criminals were looked after so well, even after conviction in prison.

161

Harold would be under constant supervision, which meant the cell door would be open and a uniformed officer would sit outside on a chair. It was known as 'suicide watch' and was in place because nobody knew what Little's reaction would be to his arrest. The officer would be under instruction to record any comments the prisoner made: they might be useful in interview. However, the police officer could not reply, or the defence could claim it was oppressive and an actual interview.

'Sarge, don't upset him before we've interviewed him, please,' said Dawn, in an attempt to appeal to the custody sergeant's better nature now Harold was in a cell.

'I won't.' He tutted and rolled his eyes.

'We're serious, sarge,' Dylan growled.

'I know, I know ... kid gloves,' he reluctantly replied.

'One double murderer in the cells.' Outside in the corridor, Dawn dramatically punched the air.

'Just got to prove it now,' replied Dylan.

'He must have planned to have Brenda Cotton from Sykes and Co when he was arrested. Don't you think?'

'Was he expecting us? Who knows. Bacon butty?' Dylan asked licking his lips at the thought. He could smile now he had a prisoner.

'Maybe.' she said thoughtfully. Then, 'Oh god, yeah, dipped in tomato juice, please.' Dawn dabbed her mouth with her hanky while picking up the phone to ring Harold's solicitor.

'Brenda Cotton speaking, can I help you?' A loud, clear, crisp voice came over the phone.

'Brenda, Detective Sergeant Dawn Farren here, how're you?'

'Busy.'

'Well, I'm going to either ruin your morning or make it. We've arrested a man this morning in connection with the murders of Daisy Charlotte Hind and Christopher Francis Spencer. I think you may be aware of the cases?'

'I've seen it in the papers and on the news.'

'He's asked for you as his legal representative.'

'Right, who is he? Someone I've represented before?'

'Don't know, but he obviously knows of you. He came straight out with your name. It's a Harold Wilkinson-Little.'

'Name doesn't ring any bells,' she said thoughtfully. 'I suppose you want me as soon as possible?'

'Yes, please, and could you contact the cell area to let them know you're aware of the request?'

'I'll have to re-arrange a few appointments, but I'll be there as soon as I can. Should I ask for you? Are you going to be interviewing?'

'DI Dylan and myself, yes, but if you want to speak to your client first, ask the desk sergeant to ring me when you're done and I'll come down to meet you.'

In Dylan's experience Brenda Cotton was sound; in fact, he would go so far as to say he liked her, she was fair.

'What do you think of our man?' Dylan asked Dawn as he tucked into his sandwich.

'Um, very cool. Fancy complaining he'd had no breakfast. How does his mind work? Forty-five, but he looked like a little old man stood there in his pyjamas this morning. It was weird. Wasn't it like he was waiting, knowing he was going to be arrested?'

'Did you see any signs of his twisted ankle?' Dylan was curious.

'No, did you?'

'No, but I did wonder if he'd hurt himself when he was up on the moors dumping Daisy's body and not in the property store.'

'Have we heard from Larry?' asked Dawn.

'No, but I don't expect to for a while. It's going to be hard for his missus to take it all in. Actually, I'll ring him now,' Dylan said, reaching for the phone. 'We need to make sure the contents of the van are seized before it's taken away to the lab.'

Dawn mimed *coffee* as she stood in the office doorway. He nodded positively as he keyed in Larry's number.

'Hello, boss. It's been like telling the woman her husband's dead. She's in denial, but her sister should be here before long.'

'I know I'm teaching you to suck eggs, but can you make sure that the van is searched before it goes to the lab?' Dylan instructed.

'It's already on its way to the nick prior to the lab, so it can be searched and property seized there if you can catch them. The neighbours are already showing an interest. I've suggested to Pauline that she goes to stay at her sister's for a few days to let things settle down.'

'Good idea. It would also give us time to put an intruder alarm in.'

'She isn't in a fit state to give us a statement right now, but I've noted her comments and told her we will need to speak to her again. Anyway, it shouldn't be too long now before I'm back, once the sister's arrived.'

'Do you know how the search is going?'

'It's well on its way. Inspector Baggs is here, so I'll be able to leave them to it.'

'Could you let me know once you've told the families?' Dawn asked the FLOs on her return. 'Then we can release it to the Press. I'm sure we'll be getting a call soon from one of the papers asking questions. The neighbours are bound to ring the media about the police activity.'

Dylan and Dawn sat drinking their coffee quietly, both deep in thought. Dylan couldn't sit still for long, though. He enjoyed the interviews, and the team were all energized and sitting in anticipation now the word had gone round that Little was in.

'Can I be cheeky, boss?' Lisa said, as she walked into the office to empty the 'out' trays.

'You usually are,' Dylan said light-heartedly as he smiled at her.

She blushed. 'Does he look like his photograph we've been given from his personal file?'

'Yeah, he does Lisa, he's not changed much, but I'll get you a more recent one. Do you not know him from the property stores?'

'No, I've got no reason to go in there and the station is such a big place. I'm still finding my feet to be honest. I'd only just started when the first murder broke, so it's my first big case. It's so exciting,' she said as she left the office, a grin on her face.

Like Lisa, a lot of the team had been involved for the duration and they wanted to know more about the man who could do this kind of thing. Who could blame them?

Dylan's thoughts were all over the place and he couldn't concentrate. He was itching to get the interviews started and he could sense Dawn felt the same. He wondered if Harold would talk, and if so what would he say? The telephone rang, and they both reached out for it. Dylan was the quickest, or was it just he was the nearest?

'Michelle from the Press Office. I've had a few calls wanting to know what all the police activity is about in your area. What do you want me to say?'

'I knew this was coming. There has been an arrest. The families are being informed. Give it thirty minutes and then you can release the agreed statement. There'll be nothing else from here for a long while, so when I've anything to tell, I'll call you,' said Dylan.

Brenda Cotton had just asked the desk sergeant to contact Dawn; she'd spoken to her client.

'No wonder we get indigestion,' Dawn said, choking on the remainder of her sandwich and gulping the dregs of her coffee. Larry walked in.

'Pauline's sister is the spitting image of her. They asked over and over again if they could see him. Neither of them could believe he would do such a thing. He'd always vehemently abhorred violence, they said.' Dylan listened with interest. 'They're in shock. They were sitting with their arms wrapped around each other, sobbing, when I left. I told them we would update them when we could.'

'Fine, Larry. Is she going to stay at her sister's?'

'Yeah, they were just going to pack a few things before leaving.'

It was eleven o'clock. In the first instance they'd only twenty-four hours to interview Harold. If they needed more time, it would have to be authorised by the divisional commander.

The interview room was rectangular and held a table that was fastened to the wall and chairs that were bolted to the floor. There would be no throwing about of tables and chairs in this interview. Microphones were fastened to the wall above the table. They would pick up the slightest noise. In the corner of the room was the tape machine, a twin cassette deck perched on a custom-built shelf. The seals on new tapes would be broken at the beginning of every interview in the presence of the prisoner and his solicitor. At the end, they would be signed and dated by all present. A long, fluorescent ceiling light illuminated the room; there were no windows and only one door. The only natural light came through a small peep-hole at eye level in the door, which faced into a sunlit corridor. Around the centre of the wall was an alarm strip, the panic button should any officer need urgent assistance.

The first interview was about to commence.

Chapter Twenty-Nine

Dylan stood waiting in the interview room, the air of anticipation making adrenaline course through his veins. The sudden creaking of the un-oiled hinges attached to the heavy interview room door interrupted his thinking. Harold Wilkinson-Little, dressed in a white paper suit, shuffled into the room with Brenda Cotton closely behind, and then Dawn, who closed the door.

'Harold, sit in that chair furthest from the door, please,' pointed Dawn. The usual place for a suspect. Brenda sat alongside and Dylan and Dawn took their seats opposite the pair. This positioning of the four allowed the video camera to be focused on Harold.

Little looked almost child-like in the coverall. Dylan thought the description of him as the size of a jockey quite apt. He appeared to be such a timid individual, but they knew otherwise. How looks could deceive.

The formality of breaking the tape seals and placing them in the machine began. Everyone present in turn identified themselves.

'I'm Detective Sergeant Dawn Farren. It is eleven-twenty a.m. on Wednesday the eighth of March, 2006, and I am in the cell area interview room at Harrowfield Police Station. Also present are ....' Dawn nodded and each person present spoke their name for the purpose of voice recognition.

'Detective Inspector Jack Dylan.'

'Brenda Cotton, solicitor.'

'Harold Little.' He spoke so quietly he could hardly be heard, his head bowed once more to his chest.

'Could you speak up, Mr Little, for the purpose of the tape, please?' Dylan asked.

'Sorry, Inspector Dylan,' he said clearing his throat. 'Harold Little,' he said once more, in a somewhat stronger voice and with his head raised, eyes forward.

'Is that your full name?' Dylan enquired.

'Harold Wilkinson-Little,' he corrected.

Dawn then spoke the caution, informing Little of his right to remain silent should he so wish. They went on to confirm his date of birth, his home address, and the details of his vehicle. They also confirmed that he resided with his wife, Pauline at the address he had given. Dawn had spoken briefly to Brenda prior to the interview to inform her of the arrest and disclose the findings of items from the two murdered children. She intimated that Harold had said very little at all, other than stating that it wasn't his fault.

It had been decided that Dylan would talk and Dawn would sit quietly. Gone were the days of pressure in interviews when two people talked at once. *The Police and Criminal Evidence Act* had seen to that. It was now classed as oppressive and unfair to the prisoner. No more 'good cop, bad cop' routine. Dylan started by simply going over Harold's background, letting him speak as he wished. Although Little was talking softly and calmly, his face remained expressionless. Dylan noted Harold's hands tightly clasped together. He could see Dawn biting her lip and he knew she was chomping at the bit to get stuck into Harold's ribs. Dylan knew that feeling all too well, but discipline in interview technique was a must.

'Which school did you go to, Harold?' Dylan asked in a friendly manner.

'Harrowfield,' he said. He was talking, responding, although his head was still down and he was not looking at Dylan, therefore avoiding any eye contact.

'Most people do that live around here, don't they?' Dylan continued.

'Yes', Harold replied with a nod, still looking down at his clasped hands on his lap.

'I never really liked school, how about you, Harold?'

Little lifted his head, just slightly and stared at Dylan and Dawn. *Did I strike a nerve*, Dylan wondered, as he observed Harold's body language. The way he was repeating certain twinges and movements indicated to Dylan that he was either lying or very uncomfortable.

'Well, let's say I was glad when I could leave. I wasn't very academic.' His speech was quick, and he fidgeted from one cheek to the other in the chair.

'What weren't you good at, Harold? Maths? French? I was poor at languages.'

'Most things.'

'What about friends? Didn't they make it all worthwhile?'

'No. I didn't have any.'

Again, his speech was fast; he appeared bored, but his body language and the way he was speaking said otherwise. He was squeezing his hands so hard that his fingernails were going white.

'Can I go to the toilet, please?' he asked.

'Of course.' Dylan stopped immediately. He spoke to give the time and the reason why the interview was being suspended for the purpose of the tape. When Harold returned, he would have to recommence the formal procedure. Interviews were all about patience and recording everything that occurred, speech was automatically picked up. The camera saw actions such as a 'V' sign, but the interviewer also gave commentary. Dylan was tempted to make him wait before letting him go to the toilet, to let him suffer, but he didn't. It was going to be a long day.

'Is he going to do this every time it gets to a point he doesn't like?' Dylan asked Dawn quietly, exasperated, as they waited.

'God knows.'

'Least he's talking. I wonder why he didn't attack the parents rather than the children if it's them his argument is with? It doesn't make sense.'

'What do you always tell us? "Where is the rule book for murderers?".'

Minutes later Harold returned, sat down, and thanked Dylan and Dawn politely for being so understanding. What a Jekyll and Hyde character he was turning out to be.

'You okay to continue then?' Dylan was sympathetic, but his face looked anything but concerned.

'Yes, thank you.'

'Before we had the break we were talking about school, if you remember, Harold. You said you didn't have many friends. Was it really so bad?' asked Dylan.

'What's this got to do with the murders? Look, you've arrested me for murders, haven't you, and I've murdered no one. I wouldn't murder a child. I like children.'

Dylan ignored his outburst. 'You went to a school reunion recently, didn't you? Now if school was so bad, why would you do that?'

'I don't know the children. You've got it all wrong.' Harold stuttered, as if he hadn't heard Dylan speak. 'I work for the police in the property store, but you know that. I work with the police. You've got it all wrong. It's not me. This is terrible, terrible.'

Dylan nudged Dawn gently to lift an exhibit bag from the floor beside her. Because of his outburst, Dylan had decided to introduce the brown paper bag they'd found in the store.

'You see, Harold, we found this bag on a shelf in the store, your store. As you can see it says on it quite clearly "Wilkinson" in black marker pen. That's your middle name, isn't it? Who wrote that on the bag?' Dawn held up Exhibit JB1 for him to see. 'Was that you?' asked Dylan.

He made no reply and, lips pursed, Little stared blankly straight forward.

'You are meticulous about things in your store, aren't you, Harold? Your records and accountings are second to none. How many times have I heard people say so?'

Little smiled. 'Thank you, Mr Dylan, sir.'

'Do you remember booking this in? The name would mean something to you, but not others.'

He made no reply.

'Okay, then, who else could have put it there?' asked Dawn.

Harold remained silent.

'Why the silence? Can't you explain this bag being there, Harold?' Dawn continued.

He coughed. Shuffled in his seat. There was an air of expectancy, but Harold's breathing remained shallow as he maintained his silence.

'You've been reading old murder files in the store, haven't you?' asked Dylan.

Little made no reply.

'Why the silence Harold?' Dylan asked. 'If we've got it all wrong, tell us why. This is a chance for you to put it right. Speak to us.'

Still Little made no reply.

'The bag with "Wilkinson" written on it, explain it to us, Harold.'

Dylan decided it was time to stay quiet and Dawn followed suit. After what seemed like an age, but was probably no more than one or two minutes, Harold broke the silence.

'Mr Dylan, sir, I have nothing to say other than I'm not the person responsible for the murders and I don't want to answer any more of your questions.' He spoke in a hushed tone.

Dylan's eyes bored straight into Harold's. His mind was spinning. *You arrogant bastard,* he thought. He was sorely tempted to drag Harold across the table and rip his head off. 'If you're not responsible, Harold, explain to me how there's a labelled bag in the store marked "Wilkinson", your middle name, that doesn't belong to any other case?' he said, through gritted teeth.

Harold smirked. 'No reply.'

Dylan was boiling over inside.

'You know the fathers of both the murdered children, don't you, Harold?' Dylan asked.

'No reply.'

'Did you know their families?' asked Dylan.

'No reply.'

'Did you speak to the children's fathers at the reunion?'

'No reply.'

Dylan terminated the interview and Little was returned to his cell.

'We'll resume in an hour. Is that okay with you?' Dylan asked Brenda Cotton.

'Yeah, sure, I've already written the day off.' Brenda smiled. 'I'll just go and grab a coffee in the canteen.' Dylan nodded.

'Dawn. Office,' Dylan hollered as he strode in the direction of the incident room. Dawn hurried to keep up with his pace. 'Arrogant bastard, he's enjoying this,' Dylan ranted.

'I thought at one point there that you were gonna climb over the desk and hit him' Dawn puffed.

'I nearly did,' Dylan fumed.

Chapter Thirty

Just over an hour later Dylan and Dawn were back in the interview room with Harold Little and his solicitor, the camera once more focused on Harold. Dawn again reminded him of the caution and everyone present went through the procedure of saying who he or she was for voice recognition purposes.

'Harold, in the previous interview you became silent or said "no reply". We are simply trying to establish the truth, and we may be able to do that a lot quicker with your help,' Dylan said.

'My help, my help. I've been handcuffed, dragged from my home in my night attire, accused of murder, and you want my help?' Harold seethed.

Brilliant; a response, and one that shows he's not the quiet little man everybody believes, thought Dylan.

'Okay, Harold, let me explain. We needed to arrest you and you know why. Because of what we found in the store. Your store,' Dylan said. 'Also, you have a connection to the children's fathers.' Dylan spoke slowly and calmly. His eyes searched Harold Little's for a reaction.

Silence ensued. Harold shuffled in his seat before he spoke and he avoided eye contact with Dylan as he did. 'I can't be blamed for what's in the store. I've been off sick so … so lots of people will have had access. As for the school reunion, everyone there knew the children's dads. You didn't need to arrest me. Why me? I would have answered your questions without this … this humiliation. You've probably cost me my job, my life as it was, and you want me to help you?' he raised his voice once again.

From Dylan's point of view, Harold was playing the victim.

'Harold, you know we are searching your home. Your vehicle, clothing, and footwear will be seized and examined forensically along with anything else we feel there's a need to. You know how thorough that search is going to be, don't you? Are we going to find anything else that links you to the deaths of these children, Harold?'

Harold remained silent, although Dylan felt he was considering what he'd said. 'You've read old cases in the store, Harold, haven't you? Those murderers all made mistakes. It's likely you have done, too.'

'No reply.' Harold spoke clearly and firmly.

'When you don't like something I say, Harold, you don't answer me.' Dylan continued. 'Have you got a bit of a temper, Harold?' Harold glared at Dylan, but he remained silent. 'Tell me about your schooldays, Harold. Were you a model pupil? You are such an organised person now. Some people describe you as meticulous. That would be an asset at school, wouldn't it?'

Silence prevailed. 'Bet you were teacher's pet,' Dylan taunted.

'Pet? Pet?' Harold's reaction made them all jump. 'I hated school,' he spat. 'It was nothing but a breeding place for arrogant bullies.' Harold stopped suddenly.

Dawn spoke softly. 'Do you want to tell us what happened so we can understand?'

Harold glowered at her. 'How dare you even think for a moment you could understand?'

Dawn carried on talking calmly, quietly, cleverly repeating the word 'school' in almost every question she asked. Dylan watched closely as Harold Little started to fidget once more in his chair. He could see sweat beads appear on the man's forehead. Harold was wringing his hands again and Dylan knew that Dawn's questions were getting to him. Without warning, Harold stood up and banged the desk with clenched fists. 'Stop this. Stop it now,' he snarled.

'Sit down,' Dylan said.

'And you're gonna make me?' Harold sneered through clenched teeth. If only he knew how tempting it was to Dylan.

'Do it,' Dylan said, towering over him with authority.

Harold sat. His solicitor seemed shaken by Harold's outburst but said nothing.

'Mr Dylan, you're no different from the others. I don't want to speak to either of you anymore.' Harold turned around and faced the wall like a sulking child.

' "The others", Harold, who are "the others"? What were they like?'

Harold remained silent.

Dylan and Dawn repeated the question to give him the opportunity to answer.

'Didn't you expect to be caught yet, Harold? Is that what's really annoying you? Have you unfinished business you hoped to have dealt with by now? More children to kill?'

'That's unacceptable, Inspector Dylan,' Brenda Cotton said.

'Whatever,' Dylan replied as he terminated the interview. It was lunchtime and he was hungry.

Harold didn't take his eyes off Dylan as the gaoler took him by the arm and led him out of the interview room. Arrangements were made with Brenda Cotton to return at four o'clock.

'Don't think he likes us much, boss.'

'What makes you think that, Dawn?' Dylan smiled as they queued for their lunch.

Harold's house was still being searched. While they ate their sandwiches, Dylan and Dawn spent the next twenty minutes on the phone in the office trying to get updates from the search team, forensic, and the incident room. They needed something else to get stuck into Mr Little with, to really put him under pressure and get him to speak to them.

'Make sure the vehicle goes on a low loader. I want soil samples from the wheel arches.' Dylan told Inspector Baggs.

'Sure. Just about to get an update on the van; I'll call you back,' he replied.

Dylan looked at Dawn. 'Nobody said it was going to be easy. It's early days. I know it's him, though. We just need a bloody motive, and then we can hopefully start to open him up.'

Dylan's phone rang. 'Boss. Vicky, just ringing to let you know that inside Mr Little's van, wrapped in a black bin liner and wedged above the side door, we have found what appears to be a cane, similar to the ones in the store.'

175

'Right. That's really interesting. Get it off to forensic as a priority will you? Tell them I want it to go to the top of the list.'

'Will do,' Dylan heard her say as he put the phone down.

'That's looking a bit tasty, Dawn. They've found a cane secreted in his van.'

'Why's he kept it?'

'Maybe he was going to use it again, or return it back to the property store.'

Dylan walked to the gents before going back into interview. He texted Jen. It was just about the only time he'd been alone lately. *It's gonna be a long haul – he's not bending. Love you Speak ASAP x.* He didn't wait for a reply; his mind was set ready for the mind games with Harold Little.

Chapter Thirty-One

The interview room stank of sweat, and Dylan could feel the oppression in the atmosphere as Dawn went through the caution and voice recognition for the tape.

'Okay, Harold, we mentioned your time at school in the previous interview and you got annoyed. Let's talk about the reunion. You went to that, didn't you? You're on photographs that were taken on the night,' Dylan said.

Harold's expression was blank. 'You know I did, so why are you asking me?'

'Because I'm trying to understand, Harold, if school had been such a nightmare, then why would you go to a reunion?'

There was no response.

'I just don't understand why you'd go.' Dylan repeated.

'I wanted to see if people had changed,' he replied, which surprised Dylan. He hadn't expected Harold to speak so early in the interview.

'And?'

' "And" what?' answered Harold.

'Had they changed? Anyone in particular?'

'No. It's not a crime to go to a school reunion now, is it? I didn't even stay that long.'

'Can I just ask, Inspector, where you're going with this? My client doesn't deny going to the reunion. I fail to see the relevance of your questioning,' Brenda Cotton said.

Dylan rounded on her quickly. 'Well, if you allow me to continue, it'll become clear.'

Brenda frantically scribbled something on her notepad. Dylan smiled, it probably said *arrogant bastard,* he thought.

'Why didn't you stay?'

'My wife's not well.'

'Did you see Trevor Hinds and Martin Spencer there?'

Harold remained silent.

'It's a simple enough question, Harold,' provoked Dylan.

'I'm thinking. I believe I did.'

'Did you speak to them?'

'Why? Should I 'ave?'

''I don't know. I'm just asking,' Dylan responded.

Awkwardly he answered. 'Look, I went, didn't stop, and came home. My wife's ill. I wasn't going to enjoy myself, was I?'

'I fail to see why you even went. You hated school; your wife's ill … why even bother?' Dawn piped up.

Harold glared at her. If he thought it bothered her, he was wrong.

'Well?' Dawn pushed.

'I've told you. Don't you listen, lady?' Harold turned, trying to put Dawn in her place. His breathing became more pronounced.

Dylan shifted in his seat and took over.

'Harold, let's move on. Your van's been searched and it will be examined by forensics. However, inside, secreted above the door, we've found a cane, wrapped in a bin liner. Where's it come from, and what is it doing there?' Dylan stopped and waited.

Harold bit his lip.

'I'm waiting,' Dylan said.

'It actually belongs in the police store. I just borrowed it, took it home, because I found a rat in the garden that keeps getting into my shed. I thought it would be ideal to hit the rat with. I didn't use it.' He looked straight into Dylan's eyes. 'Ask Pauline, if you don't believe me,' he shouted. His words were deliberate and laced with menace.

'Why wrap it in a bin liner and wedge it above the door?' Dylan came back.

'Out of sight. I was going to return it, but then I hurt my ankle. No one uses them anyhow. They've been in the store for years.'

'You have an answer for everything, don't you Harold?' Dylan backed off slightly, knowing he would bring him back to the subject.

'It's true.'

'It's absolute rubbish and you know it. You're a murderer. You've killed two young children. Was that the murder weapon?' pushed Dylan. Harold stayed silent, but Dylan could see from his hands, his sweating and the glare in his eyes that he was angry.

'An innocent little girl, Harold. Tell me, had you been watching the house?'

'What house? No,' he shouted at Dylan.

'Did you kill her, Harold?' Dylan growled.

'No,' he shouted back.

'Why did you take her clothes off, Harold? Do you like young girls?' probed Dylan.

'No, no,' he shouted.

Dylan thought he was about to explode.

'I want to object to the way you are questioning my client,' Brenda Cotton butted in.

'Noted,' Dylan said, as he quickly moved on to the next question. He leaned across the desk. 'Did you keep part of her dress as a trophy, Harold, so you could relive the event over and over again when you were alone in your storeroom? Is it all about sex, Harold?' Harold Little jumped to his feet and slammed his fists on the table. Dylan had wound him up. The heat in the room was overwhelming. Sweat stood on his brow and upper lip.

'You, you're no better than the others ... you're a bully. None of this is my fault ... none of it. I would like to go home now.'

'That's not possible at the moment and you know why, Harold,' Dawn spoke quietly. 'So please sit down.'

Harold gave her his usual stare, but sat down as she requested.

'Can we take a break please?' Brenda Cotton asked.

'We'll start again in thirty minutes,' Dylan said as he leaned over to switch the tape recorder off.

Dylan sat with Dawn in the office going over and over the interview. 'I wanted him to boil over,' he said.

'Yeah, in between the evil eye he kept throwing at me,' laughed Dawn. 'He'd an answer for the cane being in the van, but to kill a rat with? That's rubbish, we know it, and so does he.'

'But he did squirm a bit.'

'He wasn't comfy, that's for sure, but he was right about one thing: you're a bully,' she chortled.

The next interview was a non-starter. He offered 'No reply' to every question put to him for half an hour. Dylan and Dawn covered all the points of each murder. Harold rhythmically rocked in his chair. His eyes had turned glassy.

'That's it for today. You'll be detained overnight and we'll continue with the interview in the morning,' Dylan stated. Harold hadn't expected to be kept in overnight; Dylan could tell by his face.

'Early start tomorrow, nine a.m. first interview?' Dylan confirmed with Brenda Cotton.

Dylan knew only too well that the next interview was crucial. Little would have been in custody for over twenty-four hours. He needed to apply to get a further twelve hours detention from the divisional commander; after that he would have to charge him, release him, or put him before the courts. He needed more: he needed forensics.

Dylan's head was spinning. Had he jumped too soon? He'd expected Little to fall apart in the interview. How wrong could he have been. Would a night in the cells bring him around?

'I want every item of property seized from Harold Little's home gone through with a fine-tooth comb,' Dylan told the team in the incident room. 'Nothing, and I mean nothing, is to be left to chance. I want answers now. We haven't got time. We have a murderer locked up and there is no way I want to let him go. No way at all.'

Chapter Thirty-Two

Dylan hadn't slept much. He'd discussed the events of the day and the forthcoming interview with Jen in bed until the early hours of the morning. She had eventually fallen asleep in his arms.

The clock struck nine; and the make or break interview was about to begin. Dylan took a deep breath and paced the corridor, waiting for Harold Wilkinson-Little to be brought to the interview room.

'I wonder how he'll be after a night in the cells, Dawn?' Dylan said, as the door opened and the gaoler let Harold and his solicitor into the corridor leading to the interview rooms. Harold was staring at the floor as he shuffled along and he never looked up.

Apart from the occasional 'No', his answer to all the questions they put to him was 'No reply'. The buzzer on the tape interrupted the interview. Forty-five minutes had passed and the tape was about to end. Dylan was churning inside. He hated being beaten and at this moment he knew he hadn't sufficient evidence to charge Little. He terminated the interview and left the room. Harold was returned to his cell.

'Are you releasing my client or charging him?' enquired Brenda Cotton.

'I'm just going to make a phone call to forensics, and then I'll make that decision. If you'll give me ten minutes?' Dylan said, leaving Brenda in the custody suite.

'What a bastard,' Dawn said running after Dylan, who marched down the corridor.

'He's had too much time to think and plan, Dawn. The last thing I want to do is bail him, but I might have to if forensic haven't come up with anything. Whilst I'm on the phone to the lab, will you get hold of the surveillance team and see if they're available? I don't want to lose any more time on Little's detention clock than we have to.' Dylan tapped his teeth with the top of his pen. 'God, it's like ringing a call centre,' he said out loud as Dawn's call was answered before his.

'Bastards, whose side are they flaming on? They haven't even looked at the cane yet. Can you believe it?' Dylan sat with his head in his hands; his fingers grasping a clump of hair.

'More bad news, boss. The surveillance team are tied up all week watching an armed gang around the clock.'

'Fucking hell. Okay,' Dylan sighed. 'We'll have to bail the twat for the time being. Can you arrange obs on his home by some of our staff, Dawn? Get a couple to follow him from the nick to make sure he goes straight there.'

'No problem.' Dawn walked to the door of Dylan's office.

'And Dawn?'

She turned. 'Yes, boss?'

'Keep smiling, kid, we'll get there,' he said half-heartedly. 'Once we've sorted out his bail, we'll get the team in and update them. Then we must speak with the family liaison officers.'

'I know,' she replied, seeing his pain.

Dylan bailed Harold Wilkinson-Little. He signed for his personal possessions and as Harold left the cell area without a word, he stopped, turned, and smiled. Dylan could feel the muscles twitching in his face as he strained to stop himself from showing any emotion. He felt his stomach do a sickening churn. Dylan was glad he'd taken the chance and had him in. The team needed to feel his collar and he was sure in his own mind that Harold was the murderer. He could have him followed, but he now had to tell the families of the victims his prime suspect was released without charge. They would be thinking that at last Dylan had the killer. He couldn't tell them he was sure the murderer was Harold. How could he justify to them the reason for his bail if he did? Visions of little Daisy and Christopher laid out on the slab haunted him. He'd stared right through Harold to the image of the corpses.

Back in the office, he spoke to the FLOs to let the families know that enquiries were continuing, but they couldn't at this moment in time connect the man who'd been arrested with the murders.

Dylan was positive with the enquiry team at the briefing, as he talked through Little's attitude and responses in each of the interviews.

'Harold Wilkinson-Little is still our main focus. When we get more evidence, especially from forensic, his feet won't touch the ground before he's back inside,' he said.

'Are you really sure it's Harold?' DS Larry Banks asked in the privacy of the SIO's office. 'He seems so meek, he's got no previous criminal history, and he's coped with the interviews. I'm not sure.'

'It's him, all right,' snapped Dylan, angry that his judgement was being questioned.

'Okay, okay, it was just a thought. You're always telling me not to wear blinkers or make assumptions,' Larry replied.

'I know, but I am satisfied with this one.'

'You're certain it's not Meredith, then, boss?' needled Larry.

'If he's of interest to you, Larry, then get me some evidence. We've got a lot of links with Harold Little, so let's keep focusing on him at the moment, eh?' Larry was aggravating Dylan.

The rest of the day was a slog through paperwork. Dylan's pride was hurt. He'd had to let a murderer back out onto the streets. He was tired. He needed to re-charge his batteries; he needed a cuddle of reassurance from Jen. Deep down he knew that at the forensic laboratory they had to go through procedures and they couldn't rush their processes, but patience wasn't Dylan's greatest strength.

His mobile phone had been on silent all day because of the interviews. 'Six missed calls and a voice mail, all from Jen,' Dylan said, worried.

'Jack, Mum's been in a road accident. She's in hospital and it doesn't sound good,' she'd told the machine. 'I'm at the airport … been trying you since.' Dylan could see her pushing through crowds as he tuned into the noises in the background. 'Look, I have to rush off, sorry. Look after Max … speak soon.' The line went dead.

Dylan grabbed a lager out of the fridge. He broke the seal and the froth foamed over the top of the can. 'Shit,' he yelled. Max scurried under the kitchen table. The house felt cold and empty. He sat for a moment on a kitchen stool as Max crawled on his belly from his hiding place to Dylan's feet.

'Sorry, mate. What a shit day.' He sighed as he stroked Max's head. 'I wonder how Jen and her mum are.' Max barked. 'All right, I'll get you some tea before I ring her.' Max responded with a wag of his tail; he knew the word 'tea'. Dylan hadn't the stomach or energy to make any food for himself as he mixed Max's. Placing the dish on the floor with one hand he picked his mobile up with the other to ring Jen.

'Hello love,' he said, before he realised her mobile was turned off and it was her answering machine message talking to him. Resigned to the fact that she was probably at the hospital, he typed a text: *Give me a call when u can X.*

'I'm off to the chippy, Max,' he shouted. *Am I really talking to the dog,* he thought, as he picked up his coat and left. For once his mind was off murders, he was thinking of Jen. *Poor lass, having to go all that way down south on her own; I should have been there for her. The bloody job.*

Dylan jumped. The pie and chips repeated, and he belched loudly as he sat up in the chair. A phone was ringing in the distance. He must have fallen asleep.

'Jen?' he said, as he picked up the receiver.

'Jack. Are you okay?'

'I'm fine, love. How're you? How's your mum?'

'I'm at the hospital.'

'I thought you must be. I've been ringing, but your phone's been off.'

'Oh, Jack, I wish you were here. I don't know what to do. Mum's in intensive care. She's wearing a mask … they've got drips and tubes in her … monitors stuck to her. They keep taking her away for tests, but she's dying, Jack. I just know it.' Jen sobbed.

'Oh, Jen. I'm so sorry I can't come. With the arrest and that ….'

'I know.' Jack heard Jen's grief, and he felt as though someone had just squeezed his heart. His stomach flipped. 'And Dad's … just crying … he's clinging to her. They've had to prise his hand from hers … and he wails …. I think they may have to give him something to sedate him. What am I going to do, Jack?' Her sobbing became more intense and as he closed his eyes he could see her standing in the hospital, biting her lip and trying not to cry, tears spilling from her eyes and cascading down her face.

'I'm sorry, Jen, I'm so sorry,' Jack said, as he replaced the receiver. He cried like a baby, for Jen, for her mum and dad, for Daisy and her parents, for Christopher and his, and for feeling so inadequate.

'

Chapter Thirty-Three

A white frost had blanketed the park overnight, but was beginning to melt as Dylan walked Max the next morning. He could see his breath steaming before him, even though the sky was pea soup from a foggy mist. The ground was muddy and wet underfoot, so he stayed on the path around the playing fields.

What the hell am I doing here at half past five in the morning? he thought, and shivered, as Max jumped and barked excitedly at his feet. Dylan threw him a ball and Max ran through the grass, sliding dramatically in the mud to catch it. Dylan couldn't help but smile as Max ran back to him, his coat wet and his eyes shining as he offered Dylan the slimy ball.

'We should be with Jen,' Dylan told Max.

Breakfast was a cup of strong coffee to warm him as he fed Max and put the washing in the machine. God knew how it worked; Dylan certainly didn't, but when he got a day off he'd work it out. Until then he'd at least a dozen clean shirts in the wardrobe. He threw Max a chew. 'I'll try to get back soon, mate,' he said as he left the house for work.

'It's got to be him,' Dylan said out loud as he pored over the previous day's interview transcripts and checked the lists of items removed from Little's house, his van, and the property store. *There has got to be something,* he thought. The bastard made no attempt to hide the bodies, but if he wanted people to know what he'd done why not come clean in the interviews? He'd had plenty of opportunity. Was Dylan wearing blinkers? Had Larry been right to challenge him about Little's innocence?

Jen rang; he got up from behind his desk and pushed the office door shut. He noticed people's heads turn at the sound of the door closing; it wasn't something Dylan did often.

'I thought I'd just try and catch you. I'm at the hospital with Dad. There's no change.'

'It's so good to hear your voice,' Dylan said. 'I just wish I could do something.'

'There's nothing anyone can do. The nurses are lovely, and we just sit and pray for a miracle.' She laughed a hollow, tired laugh that told Dylan she was trying so hard to be brave. 'You eating?'

'Of course.' Typical Jen, worrying about him at a time like this. 'I'm fine and so is Max. You just take care.'

'Look, I've rang my friend Penny. You know, the lady who works at Tesco? She's going to come and take Max out and feed him whilst I'm away. You've got enough on your plate.'

'But I can look after him,' Dylan protested.

'Yeah. Sure. I never know if you'll get home, never mind having poor Max crossing his legs. No, honestly I've made my mind up and rang her. Max is used to her, and she has a key so there is nothing for you to worry about.'

'Okay, if you're sure. I love you.'

'I love you more, but I must get back to Mum and Dad.' And with that she hung up.

Two o'clock and Dylan realised he hadn't had anything to eat all day. He felt light-headed and his temples had begun to throb. *Too much caffeine,* he guessed. Jen was right. He could hardly look after himself, never mind the dog; and it was a weight off his mind.

'You look pale, boss,' Dawn said. 'You okay?'

'Just a headache. You haven't got any paracetamol, have you?'

'Sure,' she said heading off to her desk. 'I've just had a call from the obs team. Little hasn't left the house,' she called. 'They tried to ring you, but you were engaged.' Dylan swallowed the tablets she gave him with the remains of some cold coffee. 'I noticed you'd shut your door. Anything important?' she enquired.

'No. Actually, I think I'll head home.'

'In the middle of the afternoon? You've either got a secret lover or you're really not well,' she exclaimed. Realising it was the latter, she said, 'Do you want me to drive you?'

'I'll be fine.' He couldn't help smiling at her. If only she knew she was right on two counts. 'I'll be on my mobile if you need me.'

'Let me know if you need anything,' she called, as he left the office.

God, did he look as bad as he felt?

The short journey seemed to take forever. His head was fuzzy. He felt hot then cold and his mouth felt dry. Max greeted him, furiously wagging his tail as he let him out. He poured himself a glass of cold water. Standing still in the kitchen, he watched Max in the garden and, as he turned, he swayed and nearly fell. *Boy, I feel odd,* he thought, as he steadied himself.

'Penny's coming to take you out mate. Someone else to fuss over you. You'll like that won't you?' he told Max, as he threw his jacket over the back of the chair and rested on the settee.

Once again, the telephone woke him. It was dark and he was freezing cold. He felt Max on the floor at the side of the settee as he grovelled in the dark for the phone.

'Were you asleep?' asked Jen in reply to his gruff hello.

Chapter Thirty-Four

Jen's dog walker, Penny Sanderson, worked two jobs. She was bringing up two children on her own since Barry had left and she needed all the money she could get. This invariably meant that fourteen-year-old Becky was often left in charge of seven-year-old Troy, much to the girl's annoyance. It wasn't too bad on a Saturday morning though, she conceded, as she could take him to the Ice Skating Rink in Harrowfield, where Mr Meredith ran the youth skate. Both children's school friends went and Becky could sneak off with Carly for a quick fag in the toilets while discussing the latest crush or crisis in their lives.

'Troy, are you ready? We've got to go now,' Becky screamed at the top of her voice.

Troy was still sprawled on the settee in his pyjamas, watching TV.

'Come on, just put your tracksuit on,' she yelled impatiently, throwing it at him from where it was heaped on the living room floor.

'I haven't had breakfast,' Troy whined.

She put her hands on his shoulders and looked him straight in the eyes. 'Look, I'll get you something from the newsagent's, right?'

'Thanks, Becks,' he said pulling his clothes on with vigour.

Becky and Carly busily texted back and forth to work out who was going to be at the skating rink and where they were going to meet.

'Let's have a look at you.' Becky turned Troy round. 'Have you brushed your teeth?' Troy looked puzzled. She'd just asked him to be quick, hadn't she? Becky fussed around him, pulling his clothes straight and whizzing the brush through his hair, just like Mum did.

'I'm starving, Becky,' Troy moaned.

'Run, otherwise we're going to miss the bus,' Becky shouted, as she pushed him out of the door and slammed it shut. They ran for the ten past eleven to town.

'You promised, Becky,' Troy whinged as Becky dragged him past the newsagent's and onto the stationary bus waiting at the stop.

'Standing room only,' called the bus conductor as he rang the bell. Troy's stomach growled noisily.

The bus dropped them outside the ice rink. As the doors of the bus opened, the smell of fish and chips wafted towards Troy. *Food at last.* Becky kept her word and soon they were all sitting on the wall scoffing chips outside the chippy. Troy's unruly blonde hair blew in his face; he tucked it behind his ear and licked his fingers, savouring the taste of the salt and vinegar.

The girls giggled uncontrollably when Pete and Gary called to them as they swaggered across the road. Becky threw Troy her scraps and jumped off the wall to greet the boys. Carly followed.

'See you've got your young 'un with you,' said Pete.

'Yeah, but he won't be no bother. He's got some mates coming,' Becky assured him. The last thing she wanted was Pete to think she'd got Troy hanging round her all session.

'I've got the money to get him in, so if we go first and sneak him in through the fire exit at the back, we can spend it on a packet of fags,' she said, giving Pete her brother's entrance money. 'Troy.' She beckoned him off the wall to join them. 'You wait at the fire exit and we'll open the door from the inside like before. Remember?' she asked.

'But why can't I go in the front like you?'

'Just do it,' Becky hissed, as she escorted him by the elbow towards the doors. If he showed her up, she'd kill him when she got him home. Pete and Gary went to buy the cigarettes. Carly waited for Becky by the entrance.

'Wait there,' Becky demanded as she shoved Troy in the porch of the fire door.

'Come on, Becky, there's a queue. We won't get in at this rate,' Carly shouted from the corner of the building.

'I'm coming,' she shouted back. 'Don't move, and listen for us to shout you,' she told Troy before running off to join the others.

Did she think he was stupid? He waited as he was told. Five minutes, ten minutes … he impatiently kicked the door. They were taking forever. Where were they?

'Troy. Troy,' came the voice and Troy turned and saw him. 'Hiya, mate. What're you doin' there?'

The fire exit door scraped open, making a scratching sound on the flagstones beneath.

'Troy, get over here. Quick,' Becky whispered as loud as she dared. There was no response. 'Troy, stop messing about. I'll flaming well kill you if you don't come here now,' she hissed. Still there was no reply. Becky peeped out of the open door as best she could without setting off the alarm. Troy wasn't anywhere to be seen.

'Here, let me look,' Carly said, pulling Becky back by the sleeve of her coat.

'I can't see him, either. What we gonna do now, Becky?'

'Where's he bloody gone? I told him to wait. We'll have to go back out and find him,' Becky said in a huff, as she carefully closed the door and ran to the main entrance. Waiting to get the backs of their hands stamped, Becky was fuming. 'Did you see that Helen Tracy sniffing around Pete? The tart, if her zip gets any lower her tits will knock him out,' she said.

'And if Sharon's skirt gets any shorter, you'll be able to see her belly button,' Carly remarked. 'I just knew she was after Gary.'

'I'll kill our Troy if he's lost me a chance with Pete. How long have I fancied Pete for, eh? I tell you Carly, I'll fucking have him.'

'Yeah, and they've probably smoked the fags too. I'll kill him for you.'

Outside, they ran round the building. Troy was nowhere to be seen. They screamed his name. It was no good. He wasn't there.

'Mum is going to skin me alive if I've lost him,' panicked Becky, out of breath. 'Carly, what am I gonna do? I'm dead meat.' Becky's voice shook, she was worried. 'Troy never does this. He always does what I tell him. Well nearly always,' she conceded.

'Call the police, Becky, they're good at finding people, aren't they? I would.'

'I'm gonna 'ave to, aren't I? He's gone,' said Becky, her eyes brimming with tears.

Carly hugged her friend. 'Yeah, it's probably best to let them do it from t'rink. Police'll listen to them,' Carly said.

'Where's me little bruv, Carly? Where is he? Do you think somebody's got 'im?' Becky cried.

'I don't know. Becky. I don't know what to say.' Carly stood shaking.

Chapter Thirty-Five

Dylan crawled into bed. He could smell Jen's shampoo on her pillow. It smelled like bubblegum. Resting there, he felt close to her and as his eyes closed, he fell into a deep, fitful sleep.

'Hello? Hello?' A woman's voice calling from downstairs broke into his dream.

'What the hell?' Dylan sat up and immediately lay down again. 'Argh,' he moaned as he held his head in his hands. He could hear Max running up and down the hallway. His eyes ached in their sockets, his neck was stiff and his stomach was sore. He'd forgotten Penny was coming to take Max out. In the hope that she wouldn't know he was in bed, he stayed as still as he could until the door slammed shut and he heard her feet trip up the path, Max in tow, barking playfully.

'Come on, pull yourself together,' he growled as he dragged his feet to the side of the bed and slowly sat up. His head spun. Standing under the shower normally refreshed him, but this morning his stomach churned. He felt nauseous and his legs felt like jelly, then they went from under him. Sitting on the floor of the shower cubicle with water gushing over his head, he heard his mobile ringing in the distance. Dylan crawled on his hands and knees, grabbed a towel from the radiator, and dried off as best he could. Pulling himself up using the hand-basin, he poured himself a glass of water and sat back down on the floor, sipping it slowly until he began to recover.

Max was in the kitchen eating his food when Dylan opened the kitchen door. He'd not heard Penny return or leave. Even though he didn't feel like eating, he put two slices of bread in the toaster. His mobile rang again, and he reached into the back pocket of his jeans.

'How you feeling?' asked Dawn.

'Rough.'

'Well don't come back and give whatever germs you've got to me,' she laughed. 'I've got some news that might make you feel better though. Forensics 'ave just called and they tell me that they've found a trace of human blood on the wooden shaft of the cane recovered from our Mr Little's van. And wait for this; it's enough to do a DNA profile.' Dylan listened intently. His heart raced. 'The blood group is "O positive", so it's common, but it's the same as Christopher's. They've also found traces of skin and blood on the van's door, so they're doing the necessary tests on those.'

'Good, yeah. That is good,' Dylan said absent-mindedly as his toast popped up out of the toaster. He picked the spots of mould off the crust. 'Keep me updated, will you? I'm going to stay here today.'

'Will do. And get yourself right. We may be interviewing again sooner than you think,' she said cheerfully.

Dylan should have been elated as he stood there buttering his toast, but no way could he raise his game. He walked into the lounge, turned on the television, and flopped on the sofa. Wearing his big woolly jumper and sheepskin slippers, he figured he'd be warm, but it felt like 'a goose walked over his grave', as his old mum would have said, and he shivered. Sky's twenty-four hour news channel droned on in the background and, oddly enough, he found himself enjoying his breakfast. He pulled the dark-brown, fur throw from the back of the settee and covered himself up with it. No sooner had he shut his eyes than his phone rang.

'Boss, the obs team have lost Little somewhere in Harrowfield town centre,' Larry told him. 'And I've had to divert staff to the ice rink; a seven-year-old lad's gone missing. It fits the pattern. Shit.' Dylan heard a car horn sounding. 'Get out of the bastard way. Police. It's an emergency,' he heard Larry shout.

'You're fucking joking.' Dylan sat bolt upright, discarding his cover.'

'Not only that, but his name is Troy Sanderson.'

'Fucking hell. His dad's name?'

'Don't know.'

'Well, fucking find out. I'm on my way,' said Dylan.

Dylan's mobile rang en route. 'Damn.' He hadn't got his hands-free set up. It would have to wait.'

Larry's screeched his car to a halt. He ran towards the uniformed officers who were in deep discussion with two young girls in the foyer of the ice rink. The girls were tightly grasping each other's hands, tears trickling down their puffy faces.

'Has Troy's description been circulated inside?' asked Larry.

'Yes, sir,' replied a uniformed officer.

Above them the loud speaker buzzed and a lady coughed then spoke. 'The police are here because a little boy who goes by the name of Troy Sanderson has gone missing. He's got blonde hair and is wearing a blue tracksuit. He was last seen outside the ice rink about forty minutes ago. Anybody with any information about his whereabouts, please come to the reception desk.' The tannoy screeched a piercing wail, fingernails down a blackboard, and Larry cringed.

Dylan's car drew up behind a marked police vehicle with its light still flashing. Getting out, he walked as fast as he could towards the huge glass doors that led from the street to the foyer of the ice rink. He could see Larry leaning on the sweet counter taking notes.

'Well?'

'Barry.'

'Jesus wept. No sign of Troy yet?' Dylan asked, as he introduced himself to Becky and Carly. Dylan's mobile rang. He pressed the red button to cancel the call.

'No, sir, not yet,' said Larry.

'Try not to worry,' Dylan told the two frightened girls. 'We're doing our best to find him quickly.'

'I 'ope so. My mum's at work and I'm supposed to be looking after him. She's going to skin me, isn't she Carly?' Becky's lip quivered.

'Do you come here often?' Larry asked. Dylan cringed. 'Er, I mean ....'

'Mr Meredith gets school discount for us, so lots of us come every Saturday morning. I need to tell you something, Mister,' Becky said shyly.

'I'm all ears.'

'We were gonna save Troy's money to get in by sneaking him in the back door,' she admitted sheepishly.

'For sweets?' Larry asked.

'Cigarettes,' Carly said quietly. Becky started to cry, sobbing on her best mate's shoulder.

'Get Dawn to collect Becky's mum from work,' Dylan ordered Larry. 'Do you know where Mr Meredith is now?'

'I've been told he left for today, sir,' the uniformed officer said, as he walked in on the conversation.

'Send a car to Meredith's house,' Dylan instructed the officer. 'Now.'

Becky ran into her mum's arms.

'Mrs Sanderson, can we get Mr Sanderson for you?' Dylan asked as he reached to shake her hand.

'Penny, please. No, no. We're divorced,' she replied.

As Dylan retreated from the group to answer his ringing mobile, he could see Penny gently comforting her daughter while talking to Dawn. There were three missed calls from Jen. Dylan could hear Larry talking on his radio as he approached him. His head was spinning and he swayed, grabbing Larry's arm to steady himself. 'Where the fuck is Little? What happened to the obs?' he asked.

'But Meredith …?' asked Larry confused.

'Larry, enough is enough.' Dylan held up his hands. 'Listen to me. You're jumping to conclusions.' Larry looked stunned. 'Number one priority: find the young lad. Let's have an organised search. Number two: find me Harold Little. Circulate him again and start from where he was lost. I want a street by street. Shop by shop. Number three: put Meredith's car details out over the radio. If anyone sees it, tell him or her to stop it and search it for occupants. Number four: find Barry Sanderson.'

A lady came towards the pair offering warm drinks from a tray.

'You're a lifesaver, love, I truly mean that,' Dylan said, sipping the hot sweet tea. She smiled before moving on to offer some to the rest of the group. Dylan looked at Larry. 'What street was Little on when you lost him? Has anyone thought about trying to contact him? He may be at home by now.'

'I don't know.'

'Town centre CCTV. Have we anyone looking at the tapes?' Larry stood, pen poised, a blank expression on his face. 'Any problem with that Larry?' asked Dylan.

'Boss, you all right?' Larry asked, as if seeing him for the first time.

Dylan was pale, his eyes sunken and rimmed with grey circles. His legs shook, but a sniff of smelling salts from his inside pocket made him throw his head back and his eyes water. 'Hell fire,' he stuttered as he shook his head. 'I'll be fine. Just find me the boy, Little, Meredith, and Sanderson,' he said.

A uniformed officer approached Dylan and Larry. 'Meredith's not home. We've a unit at his house, sir,' he said.

Dylan drew a deep breath. 'I don't fucking believe it. Does Meredith know Little?'

Chapter Thirty-Six

Pete and Gary strolled down the road, pushing each other in fun. Troy followed. Penny ran towards them and scooped Troy up in her arms.

'Where have you been?' she cried. 'We've been out of our bloody minds.' She kissed her son and cradled his head.

'We've even got the police,' Becky said.

'I saw Dad and he gave me the money to get in, legal like. We thought you two had gone t'toilet to do your hair and stuff, so Pete and Gary let me hang round with them. Look, I got my hand stamped.'

Becky yanked him into her arms and held him tight. 'You scared the death out of me. I thought some creep had got you like the others and I'd lost you for good.'

'Where's your dad now, Troy? Do you know where he was going when he left you?' asked Dylan.

'Probably to the nearest pub, he said he needed a drink. He's always pissed.'

'Hey, watch that language, young man,' his mother said, clipping Troy's ear. 'I might be glad to see you safe and well but I won't stand for that.'

No longer needed, Dylan spoke with Larry and Dawn. 'Make sure there's no possibility of foul play and then leave it to uniform to deal with. I'll see you back at the office.'

'Boss, just go home. You look shocking.' Dawn stroked his arm.

'Actually, yeah … yeah, you're right. But keep me updated regarding Little, Meredith and Sanderson. I'm on my mobile.'

'Sure,' Dawn called as she walked over to Troy and the rest of the happy group.

'You can remove the tape and clear the scene now,' Larry called out to the officers on site.

Dylan stopped his car en route to get some money out of the cash machine in the high street. His bank was on the opposite side of the road to where he'd parked and he got out of the car gingerly. The traffic flashed past him and he pressed his body back against the car. His head felt woozy and his vision was blurred. A gap in the traffic would have allowed him to make a dash across the road, but he was rooted to the spot. He told his legs to move, but they wouldn't; it was as if his feet had been glued to the ground. There was no more than fifteen feet to walk, but he couldn't. He felt himself growing hot under his shirt collar and his face burned. He broke out in a sweat. His heart started pounding and he felt dizzy and sick. *Oh, my god, I'm going to pass out,* he thought.

He swayed, but managed to turn and grab the door handle and, pulling the door open, he collapsed into the driver's seat. Shaking, but in the safety of the car, he began to feel silly. *Pull yourself together,* Dylan told himself. But it didn't work. He sat quietly for a moment to see if it passed. His ears rang, his body shook, and he was sweating profusely. He undid his tie and the top button of his shirt. Luckily Jen always kept a bottle of water in the glove compartment and he fumbled for it. Sipping it slowly, he felt the cold liquid trickle down his throat. He tried desperately to control his breathing. *Breathe in to the count of six and breathe out to the count of six,* he told himself.

Finally, he admitted defeat; there was no way he could get to the cash machine. Dylan decided he would try to get home instead. Everything seemed to be happening in slow motion. He felt drained, exhausted. He drove slowly, but felt as if the car was going round a permanent corner. He leaned toward the middle of the vehicle to try to counter the effect. He tried to steer towards the pavement so he'd a line to follow, then almost drove into the kerb. At that moment his stomach churned as if someone had punched him. The adrenaline flowed. *What the fuck is happening to me?* He finally made it to Jen's house and staggered out of the car. Pushing open the front door, he stumbled inside. His phone bleeped a message as he took it out of his pocket, intending to ring for a doctor.

Mum's, he read as he collapsed face first onto the floor.

'Have you got any pain? Do you need me to call the doctor or an ambulance?' Penny asked as she stooped over Dylan's prone body.

'No, no,' Dylan protested, his hand in the air. 'I just want to go to sleep. I'm tired,' he mumbled, as he closed his eyes. Max barked excitedly and jumped around his head. Dylan could hear Penny on the phone.

'Ambulance, please, I've found a man collapsed in his home,' she said. 'Hello, hello, what's your name?' she asked Dylan as she stroked his head. 'I only know him as Jack,' she told the emergency operator. 'I'm sorry, he's not responding.'

Dylan kept hearing her voice as he drifted in and out of consciousness, it sounded as if she was talking to him down a hollow tube. As Penny rolled him onto his side, trying to put him into the recovery position, she realised the man she was helping was DI Dylan, who had helped find her son Troy. What on earth was he doing at Jen's?

The doctor was a tall man with greying hair, delicate hands, and an air of quiet authority. He did the necessary tests, checked Dylan's blood pressure, took a blood sample, looked in his eyes and ears, and performed an electrocardiogram (ECG).

'I'm fine now,' Dylan protested, trying to get up off the trolley.

'Let me be the judge of that,' the doctor said, as he pushed him back down. 'Blood pressure is a little low, temperature's a little high, but there's nothing untoward.'

'You don't understand, I've got a murderer to catch.'

'Your father died of a burst heart when he was sixty, is that right?' the doctor asked, reading from Dylan's notes.

What was he saying? That Dylan was going the same way, so young? He felt numb. His head hammered. His heart raced. There were wires and electrodes fastened to his chest.

The doctor hummed to himself as he waited for the printout from the ECG machine. 'Due to the fact that you've a family history of heart problems,' he told Dylan, 'I want you to have an ultrasound scan.' He was already picking up the phone to get Dylan transferred to the X-ray department. Dr Roebuck was a neurologist. He wasn't a person who pulled punches, he gave the facts as they were. 'This sounds like a slight stroke. Let's get a scan done.'

Dylan gulped. *A stroke.* His heart sank. *Fucking hell,* he thought.

He was pushed on a trolley to the X-ray department, following the yellow line marked on the floor.

'It's like the Wizard of Oz,' the porter said cheerfully.

Dylan was transferred from the trolley to a bed. At the press of a button it moved in slow motion and Dylan felt himself going backwards into the hollow of the circular scanner.

'Try to relax, Mr Dylan,' said the radiographer.

Dylan was trying to relax; *after all,* he kept telling himself, *what is the point of getting worked up?* Easier said than done, though.

'Think of nice things,' the radiographer said, and visions of the sea rolling onto a sunny beach filled his mind while soothing music played around him. By association it hit him then. Jen's mum: what had happened to Jen's mum? What did the text say? What was he doing here when he should be with her? He struggled to raise himself off the bed.

'Steady, Mr Dylan, nearly finished,' said the radiographer. *Thank god,* thought Dylan, flopping back on the bed. He had to speak to Jen.

'My girlfriend ... she needs me,' he said.

'The doctor will be with you in a minute,' said the radiographer. 'Try not to get upset.'

Dylan's mobile was dead, so he replaced it in his jacket pocket. He couldn't even read the text.

Fifteen minutes later, a nurse carrying a large envelope wheeled him into Dr Roebuck's office. The doctor took the negatives from the envelope and placed them on a light board. He cleared his throat as his eyes scoured the negatives.

'Clear, clear, clear. Nothing untoward here,' he said, bringing his glasses to the end of his nose as he turned to face Dylan. Dylan hadn't realised he had been holding his breath until he exhaled.

'So tell me,' said the doctor, 'What've you been doing recently? Working hard, no doubt. I've heard you on the radio, read about you in the papers, and seen you on the news. How many hours a week does that entail?'

'I need to go to my girlfriend right now.' Dylan started to get out of the wheelchair.

'Hold on there,' said the doctor, placing his hand on Dylan's arm. 'Answer my questions first, then you can go to your girlfriend.'

Dylan relented. 'Dealing with murders,' he mused. 'About eighty hours a week, I should think.'

The doctor held his hands in the air. 'Enough. Enough. Neither you, I, nor any other mortal being, is superhuman, even if we like to think we are. I think your mind is just jamming with the amount of plates you are trying to spin. I don't need to tell you this, though. You're an intelligent man. Slow down. Say "no" and cut down the hours. Oh, and make sure you eat properly. Knowing you lot, you live off caffeine.'

Dylan looked sheepish.

'If you don't follow my advice, you're going to make yourself ill. Today's a warning. Next time, who knows?'

Talk about feeling he'd had his hands truly slapped; all Dylan could do was agree with him. He shook the doctor's hand, gratefully. Even though he didn't feel great, at least he knew he wasn't dying.

Penny Sanderson was waiting for him in Casualty.

'Don't worry about an ambulance,' she told the nurse. 'I've got my car. I'll take him home.'

'You're going to 'ave to put a lead on your fella to stop him from doing too much,' laughed the nurse, making the assumption the girlfriend he spoke about was Penny. Dylan shook his head, there was no point in going into detail, and Penny took the hint and smiled sweetly.

'This is really kind of you, Mrs Sanderson. I'm very grateful,' said Dylan as they walked to the car park.

'It's nothing after what you've done for us today,' she replied.

'If I hadn't been taking Max out, goodness knows how long you'd have been there. Isn't it a small world, eh? Jen didn't mention she was seeing anybody special.'

'We agreed … I thought it best to keep the relationship quiet until we saw how it went. It sounds daft now. Have you heard from her?'

'Yes, she phoned me. Her mum's critical. They don't expect her to live.'

Dylan held his head in his hands. 'Oh my god. The missed calls,' he groaned. 'Please don't tell her about this. She's enough on her plate at the moment. I'll ring her as soon as I can. Dying.' Dylan shook his mobile in his hand.

'Well, as long as you promise to look after yourself,' Penny said.

'Yeah, and thanks I really mean it,' was all there was time for as he got out of her car.

He walked in the house, clicked on the kettle, and plugged in his mobile to recharge. No sooner had he turned his back to get a cup out of the cupboard than it bleeped and then rang.

'Boss? Boss, where the hell 'ave you been? I've been trying to get hold of you. Thought you were going straight home,' said Dawn.

Chapter Thirty-Seven

'Dawn, just give me five minutes, will you? I've a personal call to make.'

'No, wait. Don't hang up. I've had a call from forensic. We've a full DNA match for Christopher Spencer with the blood on the cane from Little's van,' she told him.

Dylan looked up to the ceiling. 'Thank you, god,' he whispered.

'Boss, you still there?'

'Yeah, Dawn. Fantastic, just the news I needed. At last they've given it priority.'

'I rang Little's home and he picked up, so we know he's in. Larry's chomping at the bit to go lock him up.'

'Tell him to stay put. Do you want to go with me?' He smiled as he imagined the glee on her face.

'I wouldn't have spoken to you again if you'd done it without me,' she said.

'Pick you up at the nick in fifteen minutes,' Dylan said, looking at his watch as he turned the key in the door. 'You arrange the uniform car with two officers to come with us. I'm not having that murdering little shit in my car,' he said as he threw his mobile on the passenger seat beside him and sped off.

Dylan knocked at the door. Harold Little opened it cautiously.

'Not you again. This is harassment,' he said, boredom in his voice as he tried to shut Dylan out.

Dylan put his size ten in between the door and the jamb and pushed the door open wide. Dawn followed him into the hallway. Dylan grabbed hold of Little by his cardigan and threw him against the wall. With his face almost touching Little's, he growled, 'I am re-arresting you for the murders of Daisy Charlotte Hind and Christopher Francis Spencer.'

Little's feet hardly touched the ground as Dylan cautioned him and then dragged him outside to the waiting officers.

'Cuff him and take him to the cells,' he ordered.

An officer handcuffed Little, then placed the palm of his hand on the crown of the prisoner's head as he lowered him into the police car.

'For a minute there I thought you were going to punch him,' Dawn said, as she dropped the house door latch and they headed for Dylan's car.

'Tempted. I was very tempted, Dawn,' said Dylan, throwing the gear stick into first.

'We should get at least one interview this evening, shouldn't we?' asked Dawn.

'Definitely. How was Larry when you told him we were going to arrest?'

'Sulking. He still thinks Meredith's the murderer. He says he doesn't think Little is strong enough. When the call came in from the ice rink today, I think he really thought that he was going to sort it without you.'

'You don't have to be strong if you've got a weapon,' Dylan said smugly. The news of the DNA hit had lifted him, there was no doubt, and although Dylan didn't feel a hundred per cent, at least he felt as though there was some progress in the investigation at last. Maybe just a few more interviews Maybe by this time tomorrow, Little would have admitted to the murders. He had to ring Jen. His mobile phone beeped: low battery.

This interview was different. This time they had solid evidence and, two hours after Little's arrest, Harold Wilkinson-Little sat in the interview room again next to Brenda Cotton.

'You have been re-arrested, Mr Little, due to fresh evidence,' Dylan said. 'I'm sure you'll remember from the last interviews that we'd recovered a cane from your van.'

Little listened intently but made no sound.

'If I recall correctly you said you'd borrowed it from the police station stores to deal with rats at your home, remember that?'

'Yes,' Little's whisper could hardly be heard.

'Was that a "yes"? Could you speak up for the tape, please.'

'Yes,' Little barked.

'Thank you. It's now been examined forensically and the blood of Christopher Spencer was found on it.' Dylan paused. 'How do you explain that, Harold?' Dylan leaned forward across the table. 'Well, Harold?'

'I told you. It's not my fault,' Harold replied. He screwed his hands tightly on his lap.

Dylan and Dawn sat perfectly still. Dylan's eyes bored into Little's as if he could pierce his subconscious for a reaction.

'It's their ...,' Little stuttered slowly, quietly.

'Whose, Harold?' asked Dawn, with compassion. 'Whose?'

'Nobody knows what I've been through. Nobody knows what I've suffered. Nobody,' whispered Little.

Dylan instinctively knew he was talking about his schooldays, but needed him to tell them on the tape.

'Who're you talking about, Harold?' asked Dylan.

'People just don't realise how bad it was,' Little said solemnly. 'I could be sick just thinking about it.' His face was expressionless; *trance-like,* thought Dylan.

'They called me names. They pushed me down. I still have nightmares. I wet the bed. My mother hit me ... she said I was dirty.' He turned to look at Dawn. 'I wasn't really, I wasn't.' A tear trickled down Harold's cheek, but he didn't attempt to brush it away. Dawn handed him her hankie.

'Thank you,' was all he said as he dabbed his eyes. He composed himself.

'The memories don't vanish, you know. Just like that.' Little clicked his fingers. 'They've ruined my life. Sometimes ....' He stopped, struggling with his emotions. He swallowed. 'Sometimes I wished they'd 'ave killed me. It would've been better than living with this pain.' Little held his fist to his solar plexus. His head was bent. He was pale and pitiful, thought Dylan but he wasn't fooled. He knew Little was still a vicious child killer.

'What sort of things happened to you, Harold? Can you tell us? Can you talk about it?' Dawn spoke softly so as to prompt, not disturb him. His eyes were lifeless.

'Didn't you tell anyone?' she asked supportively, her voice reassuring.

'I once tried to tell my teacher, Mr Whittaker. I thought I could trust him.' He swallowed again. 'They called him "peg leg". He knew what it was like to be called names, to be ridiculed, but it was a mistake. He laughed in my face ... he told me not to be soft.' Little shook his head. 'After that,' he said, 'I never listened to anything he told me because he didn't know anything. I was their plaything to do as they wanted, when they wanted. I was trapped.'

'Did your parents not help you, Harold? Didn't they speak to the teachers at school for you? Did you tell them how bad it was?' asked Dylan.

'You're joking.' He smirked, shaking his head. 'They were busy, always out. Mum worked in the corner shop during the day and cleaned in an office at night. Dad worked in a factory all day, called at the pub on the way home until Mum finished her cleaning job. Usually by the time they got in I'd be in bed.' Dylan and Dawn continued to listen. There was no need for questions. He was talking to them. 'I was the original "latch key kid". I didn't see a lot of anyone and that was the way I liked it. I stopped telling them anything and they didn't ask. Mum would say, "Oh, dear, dear".' Little mimicked his mother's whining voice. 'And dad would call me a wimp and give me a clip round the ear. If my clothes got torn, he'd hit me harder, saying I should stick up for myself and fight back.' There was a long silence, but just when Dylan opened his mouth to speak, Little spoke, so he shut it again and let him talk.

'We didn't have a lot of money and what we did have Dad drank away. They wouldn't spend money buying me clothes. You've really no idea have you?' Little asked. 'No idea at all. I'm not your murderer, Inspector.'

'Who are these people at school you talk about?' asked Dylan.

'Bullies, Inspector, bullies.' He raised his voice and Dylan raised his eyebrows. 'They were twice my size. I used to think they'd done their worst, that they couldn't do anything else to me, but then they found something more horrible, more disgusting. When I screamed, they laughed, so I learnt how to keep silent as I cried.' As if to prove he could do this,

207

tears ran down his face and Little cried without making a sound. It was eerie.

'Tell me, like I asked before, what sort of thing did they do, Harold, so we can perhaps try to understand?' Dawn used every ounce of compassion in her voice to try and get to the bottom of what had happened. But it was like pulling teeth. The room was still and quiet. The only sound that could be heard was the tape whirring as it continued recording. They waited in silence for a reply.

'One time, lunchtime, we'd just had Spam fritters for dinner … I liked them,' Little reminisced. 'They for no reason tripped me up in the playground and dragged me across the football pitch by my ankles, like a horse rider with his leg stuck in a stirrup.' Little nodded as though liking the simile. 'My head banged on the ground 'til my forehead bled. I remember passing people who were laughing and jeering … they pulled my shoes and socks off … then my trousers … they … stripped me naked. I was left cut and bruised … when they'd had their fun. I curled up on the grass and they … they came back and … urinated on me. I had to search for my clothes that they'd thrown. The teacher shouted at me for being late back for class. He said boys would be boys.' Little grimaced and swallowed hard, as though reliving the nightmare, a memory that was still raw. 'A note was slipped onto my desk. The teacher's back was to the class as he wrote on the blackboard. It said "you smell of piss". As I looked around, all eyes were on me. The boys grinned. The girls giggled. They all knew.'

'It must have been a horrible time for you. Harold, how old were you then?' asked Dawn.

'Fifteen.'

'So, Harold, that was about … thirty years ago?' Dylan said, unable to keep quiet any longer.

Harold threw his head back. 'It feels like yesterday,' he hissed, as he jutted his head forward. His eyes stared into Dylan's with pure hatred. Dylan didn't react, but held his stare.

Softly, Dawn spoke to him, although her heart must have been racing at the verbal attack, Dylan thought. He could see her breathing heavily. 'There's no need to shout, Harold. Was this a one off?'

The Walter Mitty character turned his glare away from Dylan and his face softened as he looked at Dawn.

'That was just one occasion … just one.' He'd dismissed Dylan as if he didn't exist, but it didn't bother Dylan; he would bide his time. He couldn't and he wouldn't let Little take over the interview.

'Where are your parents now, Harold?' Dawn asked, trying to change the subject.

'Dead. Died in a fire. Friday the thirteenth,' he shrugged. 'Unlucky for some,' he smirked.

'Parents and teenagers, eh?' said Dawn. 'Did you get on with them any better as you grew up?' It was obvious to Dylan that Dawn had been taken aback by his response.

He made no reply. *Did he start the fire?* wondered Dylan.

'I know it's upsetting for you, Harold, but could you please tell us more about your dreadful treatment at school. You know, specific things,' coaxed Dawn.

Little studied for a moment or two. He was motionless, as though he was going to clam up once more, but suddenly he lifted his head as if he'd just remembered something. 'On the way home they grabbed me, pushed my face to the floor into dog shit. Then they prised my mouth open and put some in my mouth. Once, they stood me on a wall and put rope around my neck, saying they were going to hang me. They kept hitting me behind my knees.' Little put his hand to his mouth and retched. 'Oh, my god, I think I'm going to be sick,' he said, suppressing the secretion. He clasped his hand tighter and gulped. His hand still hovered around his mouth.

'Do you want a drink of water, Harold?' asked Dylan, as he leaned back, half expecting Little to vomit on the table. Some details he was describing were undeniably similar to Christopher's death; the last thing Dylan wanted was for the interview to be interrupted now.

Little shook his head and within a moment appeared calmer. 'No,' he said, swallowing repeatedly. 'They just laughed. To them it was fun. I never did anything … I'm okay.' He waved his hand in protest as he coughed. 'It's like this all the time … I can still feel them hitting and burning me.' Harold was sweating; beads of perspiration trickled down the sides of his head. He patted his brow with Dawn's hankie.

'Burning you?' quizzed Dawn.

'They used to forcibly hold out my hand and use a cigarette lighter to burn me, or stub cigarettes out on me.' He held his right hand out as if being instructed now to do so, palm up.

'Were there a lot that involved themselves with this, or just one or two? Who were these bad children? Who did this to you?' Dawn's questions came fast and furious.

Dylan sat in silence although the voice in his head was urging Dawn to slow down.

'I know them … I see them … I do … I see their faces. They still laugh at me …. Why did they do that to me?' Little asked Dylan and Dawn. 'It's their fault. It's all their fault.' The dam broke quite suddenly. Great, tearless sobs rattled in Little's chest. Slumping in his chair, he struggled to speak. He lay his head in the crook of his arm on the desk and wept.

'Harold. Harold.' Dawn's voice grew louder as she tried to rouse him. 'Do you want to tell us, Harold, the names? Who did this to you?'

'I … he … they ….' Broken sentences made him difficult to understand.

'I think my client needs a break, please,' Brenda said as she observed Little.

'Okay,' accepted Dylan. He didn't want it to get to the stage where Little's solicitor would ask for a police surgeon to examine him. A doctor could render him unfit to interview.

The interview was terminated. Dylan exhaled a long sigh and arched his back to stretch his aching spine as Little was led back to his cell.

'Come on, I'll buy you a drink, Dawn,' Dylan said. 'So far, so good,' he remarked as they walked amiably along the corridor. 'I don't want some quack saying he's off his head. I want him to tell me why he killed those children.'

'Do you think he's genuine?' Dawn asked Dylan.

'What?' he shrieked, as they swung through the doors of the canteen.

Chapter Thirty-Eight

'Chilling, ultimate and full of menace, the dark suspicion that nobody is safe until the killer is apprehended, murder calls for redress like no other crime.

'Homicide represents the supreme test for the detective.'

Dylan read the words aloud from the scruffy bit of paper he'd kept in his interview folder since becoming a detective. He felt like shit, but the adrenaline rushing around his body at the anticipation of the impending interview with Little was keeping him going. He took his mobile out of his pocket, then remembered it was dead as a doornail.

Little shuffled in; Brenda and Dawn followed. Little looked marooned in his misery. His brow was furrowed and Dylan could see the artery pumping in his neck.

'You were telling us before about the terrible time you'd had at school. You said people were laughing at you at the reunion, so what happened then, did you lose it?' asked Dawn.

'What do you mean, lose control?' asked Little.

'Yes.'

'No, I'm not like them.'

'Harold, who is *them*? Will you please tell me who you're talking about?'

'You know who the evil bastards are.' His voice grew louder; he was holding back tears. *Is it anger or sadness?* wondered Dylan.

'Tell me who did what to you. Name them,' Dawn said.

'I thought after all these years they would want to apologise to me. But no, no, they just laughed as they stood drinking their beer. After all these years it's been … an open wound to me and they just rubbed salt into it. Nothing … nothing had changed.' He shook his head as if in disbelief. 'Do you know, they even remembered it in such detail,' he said gravely.

'So did that make you want to do something about it, Harold?'

'They hadn't suffered like I had.' Little grew agitated.

'You wanted revenge?' Dawn asked.

'Don't even go there,' answered Little.

211

'But why, after all these years?' Dawn asked.

'I thought they'd have changed or forgotten. I'm scarred. There isn't a day goes by when I don't suffer a panic attack or break out in a sweat with the flashbacks.'

'So are you saying if they'd changed, or apologised to you at the reunion, everything would have been okay?' Dylan queried.

'I didn't say that. I didn't say that, did I? Stop putting words into my mouth. Thirty years I've suffered,' Little stormed.

'Calm down, Harold, we're only trying to understand what went on. Did you want to attack them?' asked Dawn.

'How could I? They're bigger … stronger … than I am, and they always will be.'

'Could you not have challenged them at the reunion about their behaviour at school? I mean, now everyone is older, wiser and more mature, they might've understood.'

'No.'

'Okay, so how many people are we talking about, Harold? Did you hate all the class, the whole year, everyone?' Dylan asked.

'No. Nobody liked me. I know they thought I was strange. I didn't hate them. I just didn't have any friends because ….' He stopped, choking back tears.

'Because?' asked Dawn.

'Because nobody wanted to be seen with me in case they got treated like I did.'

'Is the reunion the first time you've seen these people, since school?'

'No. 'Cause I've seen them. But I was hardly going to go up and say "hello", was I?'

'Why? Do you think they'd hurt you now?' Dylan asked quietly.

'A bully's a bully. What they did to me wasn't just a schoolboy prank. I know what they're like, don't I? With respect, you don't, Inspector.'

'So why did you think they'd be any different at the reunion?'

'Well, like … there'd be people about, and anyway I was going to let them know I worked for the police. Once they knew that, they wouldn't try anything again, would they?' Little said smugly.

'You said they'd made fun of you. Did they do anything specific to you at the reunion?'

'No. I just overheard them laughing.'

'Had they changed much? Did you recognise them? Did they recognise you?'

'I recognised them and they recognised me, all right. I'd seen them and their pictures on the website.'

'Are you going to name them now? You don't owe them any favours, do you, Harold?' Dawn felt the time was right to ask.

Little said their names fast as if it would conjure them up in the interview room. 'Martin Spencer, Barry Sanderson, Trevor Hind, Billy Fletcher.'

Dylan carefully watched Little's reaction. The revelation was an anti-climax. Billy Fletcher? Dylan hadn't heard of him, but he knew very soon he would know. He would be raising an enquiry to see who Billy Fletcher was.

'So what did you do to get back at them?' Dawn continued, probing and prodding him for an answer, as if Little had just announced the names of his favourite group, not the names of his torturers.

Dylan saw Little's eyes flicker and knew he was picturing the boys.

'I made up my mind. They would pay this time. I wanted them to suffer like I've suffered day in, day out since.'

'The visit to the reunion got you so upset? So angry? How were you going to make them pay?'

Three questions at once Dawn, thought Dylan. *Slow down.* But he did understand her frustration. Little's face had turned grey and he fingered his wedding ring. He ignored the questions, looked at Dawn, and spoke as if they were having coffee in a street cafe.

Turning his head on one side, he asked softly, 'How is my Pauline? Is she okay?'

'She's with her sister,' Dawn said quietly.

'His wife's ill.' His solicitor spoke up for him.

'I'm sorry to hear that, Harold. She'll be worried sick, won't she?'

'Yes, I know. I didn't think it would happen yet.'

'But you expected it at some time?'

He didn't reply.

'Come on, Harold, let's put an end to all this. Tell us in your own words what happened.'

He sighed and his shoulders sank. Dylan held his breath. A smile of triumph creased Little's face. He was savouring the moment as if the taste of sirloin steak had just reached his lips.

'I decided I wanted to hurt them as they'd hurt me. I watched them in their perfect lives, playing happy families. We couldn't have children, you know. They hadn't suffered, like me. Pauline … it's not fair. It isn't fair. They made my life hell, why should they be happy? They didn't even know. Martin Spencer's son played football. Do you know, he had a son and he didn't even bother to go and watch him play football?' Little tutted in disgust. 'I watched him for weeks. Trevor wasn't fit to be a dad and when he realised how lucky he was; it was too late, wasn't it?'

'So what did you do?' Dylan asked as the tension built.

Little closed his eyes and Dylan knew that he was seeing the scene as if it was being played on a video. 'Simple, really.' His eyes sprang open. 'It was a lot easier than I thought,' he said smugly. 'I followed him 'til I knew his routine. Saturday was football. He dropped Christopher off, but I knew something he didn't know when he left him that day. He wouldn't see him alive again.'

'So what did you do then?' asked Dylan.

'I went to his shop and stabbed the tyre of his parked car. It was so simple. Then I drove back to the football game and watched and waited. I parked the van behind the trees by the gate. Christopher was kicking a stone on the ground, laughing as he talked on his mobile. He heard me at the last minute, but I hit him on the back of the head with the cane to keep him quiet. He fell to the ground like a sack of shit.' Little was visualising the scene with great clarity. He looked straight through Dylan and Dawn, who sat directly opposite him. He appeared younger as contentment flourished on his face; he was smiling slightly as he began to tell of Christopher's murder, reliving and enjoying the experience.

'Did you kill Christopher?' Dylan asked.

'I told you. I was watching. I was so close I could hear him talking to his dad on the phone. I could almost feel his breath. I had to be quick. I dragged him and then bundled him onto the floor of the van.'

'Wasn't he heavy?' continued Dylan.

'No.' Little appeared surprised by the question.

'Where did you go?'

'You know where you found him.' Little appeared bored; his fantasy lived out once more.

'Why hang him, why the dog dirt?'

'I told you. That's what they did to me, his dad, Martin.'

'You took things from Christopher, didn't you? Why?'

'I wanted to hurt Martin Spencer. I wanted to make it last, to go on and on. I've read murder files in the store, you know. I'm no worse than those murderers and I'd good reason. The killers in them files ... they were evil.'

'What do you mean when you say you wanted to keep hurting Martin, Harold? How did you do that?'

'By post.'

'What did you post to him?'

'A card with his son's brace ... well part of it ... they aren't meant to come out, them bloody things. That sorted Martin Spencer out for this year.' He laughed a cruel, frenzied laugh, threw his head back and opened his mouth wide. He slapped his hands on the desk in front of him. No longer did he portray the image of a poor victim, but an evil predator.

'Did you take anything else?' Dawn asked.

'One of his socks. I was going to send it to Martin next year,' he said, smiling, obviously pleased with himself. 'When they thought it was all over, I was going to turn the screw again.'

Little was enjoying this. Dylan could see his eyes dancing with possibilities.

'You know we recovered the sock in the "Wilkinson" bag, don't you?' Dylan asked.

He looked taken aback as though he'd just realised he'd said too much.

'Right,' was all he said.

'Christopher was an innocent young boy. He'd done nothing to you,' said Dawn.

'Well, I know that feeling, don't I? I was innocent. What'd I done wrong, Inspector? It's his dad's fault not mine.'

'So just to be absolutely clear, you're telling us, after watching and waiting, you killed Christopher to get back at his dad?' confirmed Dylan.

'I can see now why you're an inspector,' he said, cocking his head in a bird-like fashion.

'What about the other lads from school?'

'Barry Sanderson's a waster. He's sick, an alcoholic. Thank you, god.' He spoke to the ceiling as if calling to god almighty. 'But I poisoned his beloved dog. He buried it in the garden, but I dug it up. He was going to get it back in a parcel,' he said sniggering. Dylan let him talk. 'Billy Fletcher, he got killed a couple of years back, a hit and run driver. He saved me a job. I wish I'd have thought of that, and fireman Trevor and daughter Daisy. That was fate lending me a hand; I got divine help with that one.'

'How's that?' asked Dylan. For a moment he looked as if he contemplated holding back, but then realised he had said too much, come too far.

'Right place, right time. Ah, poor little Daisy,' he pulled his lips in an unhappy grimace, but sounded chuffed with himself all at the same time. He appeared to be really enjoying himself now.

'So what did you do to Daisy?'

'I watched the house just one night, like you said. I like to be organised. I'd only just got there after work and she appeared pretty as a picture at the door and ran down the street, alone. Now tell me, why would you let a child go out in the dark alone? Some parents she had. She had to come back, didn't she? So I waited,' he said with menace in his tone.

'What did you do?'

216

'I parked my van at the side of the road and waited. When I saw her coming, I got out, I hit her over the head when she passed, and threw her in the van.'

'And?'

'She was dead, so I drove up towards the reservoir and dumped her body.'

'Is that where you hurt your ankle?'

'No, no that's a health and safety issue. I've got a claim in for that. That happened in the store. Bloody administrator, I should have seen her off ... the way she spoke to me.' He was talking now as if he was a powerful individual and capable of anything.

'But you didn't just dump Daisy's body, did you, Harold?' teased Dylan.

'I know what you mean .... Yes ... okay, I removed her clothes. I wanted them to know that their daughter was dead but needed them to think that someone had raped her first. I'm not into that sort of thing, but I thought it would add to their pain, rub salt in it like ... when I was stripped, you know, before ...?'

'You say *their* pain but Daisy's mum and Christopher's mum hadn't done anything to you, had they? They don't even know you and neither did Daisy nor Christopher.'

'Ah, but their pain would have given Martin and Trevor pain, too. You reap what you sow, I'm afraid, in this life. It's their fault, not mine.' Little was indignant and had absolved himself of all responsibility, which mystified Dylan to watch. Little truly believed he had done nothing wrong, but was paying back a debt, a huge debt of bullying.

'What about the fingertip?'

'Well, that was an accident. They do happen. It trapped in the door when I flung her in the van, so I thought I'd make good use of it by sending it to them,' he laughed. 'Waste not, want not, call it recycling.' The smile was set on his face like an ugly joker.

'And once you'd done it with Daisy?' Dylan enticed.

'Christopher was a piece of piss,' Little tittered.

217

Chapter Thirty-Nine

'Jen? Jen, is that you, Jen?' Dylan could hear the desperation in his own voice.

'I'm sorry I can't take your call right now. If you'd like to leave your name and number I will get back to you as soon as possible,' her answering machine said before it bleeped for a reply.

'Jen, he's coughed,' he yelled excitedly. 'I wanted you to be the first to know. I love you. Ring me.' He terminated the call, feeling deflated and sad. He missed her.

The next interview with Little was at nine. Dylan had an hour. He struggled into his suit trousers, which he'd thrown over the dressing table chair the night before. Right now he had to get to work.

Dylan wanted to get into Harold Little's ribs in this interview. He was fired up, ready to go. He read the statements submitted by the officers dealing with Martin, Trevor and Barry as he walked along the corridor to the interview room. Dylan stretched his legs as he strode out and it felt good. He knew psychiatrists would argue for the defence at the trial, but he was confident with all the planning Little had done, he would be found guilty of murder. Dawn ran to catch him up.

'Right, updates from the team,' Dylan said, thinking aloud as he walked with Dawn. 'Martin Spencer says at school they once stripped Little off as a joke on the playing fields because he'd been bullying some younger kids. Trevor Hind says he remembers teasing him because he was a bit weird.'

Larry knocked on the interview room door as Dawn and Dylan took their seats.

'Morning, you two. I've just had a word with the officer that interviewed Sanderson, and I think you should know that he remembers them threatening to hang Harold Little. He said it was just a prank. Some prank eh?'

'So, he was bullied, but would that fester for thirty years, or did he want to show them he was now big enough to get his own back?' Dylan said.

Dylan opened the questioning. 'Harold, last night you admitted murdering Christopher Francis Spencer and Daisy Charlotte Hind, is that correct?'

Little's lip curled. 'You're the expert.'

'Yes, but you're the one who actually killed them, aren't you?'

'You tell me,' he spat out, nonchalantly flicking his fingernails.

'Harold, if your beef was with Martin and Trevor, why didn't you damage their houses, Martin's shop or their cars? Why go for their children and why to the extreme of murder?'

'I wanted to hurt them,' Little growled.

'So why didn't you wait for a dark night and the element of surprise? Why their children and not them?' Dylan continued to question him.

'I can't fight them, can I?' he asked Dawn, speaking once again as if Dylan didn't exist. Dawn was controlled and remained silent.

'But armed with a weapon, even a gun, you could have dealt with them easily. It didn't have to be the kids, did it, Harold?' Dylan was adamant he was going to make him talk to him.

'I've told you once, why,' Little snapped. He spoke through gritted teeth, his mouth hardly moving. Once again, it was directed towards Dawn.

'So you picked on somebody small, a defenceless child, an easy target to hurt, to kill. You're nothing but a bully.' Dylan goaded him, enjoying every minute of his discomfort. 'You just wanted to kill children, didn't you? This is you wanting to become a big man isn't it? The school incidents are just a lame excuse.'

Harold slammed his clenched fists on the desk 'No,' he shouted. 'I wasn't, I was kind. I hit them hard so they wouldn't feel anything. They didn't suffer like I had. It was Trevor and Martin that I wanted to suffer.'

'But Christopher did suffer. He didn't die till you hanged him. He died from hanging. That's no pleasant death, is it?'

Little's nostrils flared. His eyes were piercing as he looked at Dylan. He pushed his neck out and his head lunged forward in an attempt to frighten Dylan off. Dylan didn't flinch. He sat perfectly still and stared him out.

'He was unconscious,' Little said, retreating back into his seat. 'Knowing that would make it worse for his dad.' He appeared to revel in that fact. His voice had become deeper, more aggressive, and more sinister.

'Worse for his dad, or just more pleasing for you to have that feeling of power, Harold, which one was it? Where did you get the rope from, Harold?' Dylan continued.

'Work. The property store. Right from under your bloody noses,' he sniggered.

'You pulled out his brace and smeared dog dirt in Christopher's face. That was just pure evil.' Dylan could smell the excrement as if it were right under his nostrils.

'No. It was necessary.' Harold was calm, defiant in his reply.

'Necessary? How could it be necessary? Necessary for what?' Dylan demanded from him.

Dylan could see Little squirming, shrinking visibly before his eyes into the wizened, evil, little man he was.

'I wanted his dad to see the dog shit. I wanted him to smell it on his son. To know what it was like for me.' Little sneered at Dylan with pure malice.

'You must have been planning this for some time, from before the reunion?' Dylan questioned.

'I'd thought about it,' he admitted. 'But seeing them again, laughing at me made me realise ….'

'And the sock, you kept it in the store in a bag labelled "Wilkinson"?'

'Under your very noses again, yeah,' he sniggered.

'But you didn't expect us to find it yet, did you?'

'Wasn't bothered.' He shrugged his shoulders. He was indignant.

'Yes, you were, or you wouldn't have hidden it.'

Harold didn't reply.

'So what about Trevor's daughter, Daisy? You obviously planned that as well.'

He didn't reply to Dylan's question.

'Do you know, Harold, little Daisy was going to be a bridesmaid for the first time. That little girl was so happy, and you killed her, you killed her for something that happened years ago.'

Little remained silent.

'They may have made your life hell, but you still have a life. You're a grown man, for god's sake.'

Dylan appealed to him. He didn't make a sound.

'Come on. What's Pauline going to say when she finds out that you stripped a little girl naked after you killed her? And then because you'd got away with that, you murdered a little boy.' Dylan tried to rile him, to get a reaction and it worked.

'Leave her out of it, do you hear me?' he snarled, breaking his silence with aggression. 'You understand, don't you, Sergeant?' he said softly as he turned again to Dawn.

'No, I don't, Harold. Inspector Dylan is right and Pauline has a right to know what kind of man she's married to. Do you know what I think? You've killed for the sake of killing. You've read about murders and then you thought you'd do it, but it could only be with children because you're a coward and you're a bully, a far greater bully than the others ever were.' Dawn spat the words at Little. The ally he must have thought he had in Dawn had just deserted him and he must have known at that moment she'd just been playing a game with him to get him to talk to her. He was raging. He jumped up from his chair.

'You think you're dead smart, don't you? You think you're always right, but you're not. You're just arrogant,' he spat on the desk. His solicitor jumped. 'Police,' he shouted as he spat again.

'Sit down,' Dylan told him.

'Are you going to make me? I'll kill your kids.' Harold glared at Dylan.

Brenda raised her hand and intervened. 'Sit back down, please, Harold,' she said, trying to calm him.

'Do you actually care about your wife?' asked Dylan.

'My wife?' His eyebrows raised, he looked surprised at the question.

'Yes, do you actually care about her?' Dylan asked again. 'What will she think of you?'

'It doesn't matter what she thinks now, does it?'

'Where're Daisy's clothes?' asked Dylan.

Little didn't reply.

'Why the plastic bag over her head?'

'Recycling,' he laughed.

'Don't you feel sorry for the children at all?' questioned Dylan.

'Did anyone feel sorry for me?' Little pulled his hands through his greasy hair, obviously exasperated by the intensity of the questions being fired at him.

'So all your planning, scheming, watching and waiting were all about revenge?'

'What do they say? He who laughs last, laughs longest,' Little whispered with a smirk upon his face.

'You've shown no remorse whatsoever for killing two children. Now, looking back, don't you have any feelings at all?' asked Dawn.

'No.' His voice was matter-of-fact. 'It's my turn now.' He raised his upper torso in defiance as he spoke directly to her.

'Will you still be laughing when people see you as a horrible, evil, child murderer? Everyone will hate you. Is that what you wanted?' said Dawn.

He made no reply.

'Why keep the murder weapon in your van? You reckon to be so organised, why didn't you destroy it?' Dylan asked.

He made no reply.

'Your school days were nowhere near as bad as you made out, were they, Harold? You've just tried to find excuses for being a coward, a child murderer. The school reunion was just your evil way of selecting innocent children to murder,' Dawn said keeping up the pressure.

Harold Little jumped to his feet. 'I'm sick of listening to you now,' he raged.

'No, you're just annoyed because you've been caught and don't like to hear the truth. You thought people would feel sorry for you. What they did to you at school does not justify killing two little children thirty years later. You're an evil killer.

Is that Harold Wilkinson-Little leaving his mark on the world? You're still a nobody, Harold,' Dylan told him.

Harold turned and screamed at Brenda, who almost leapt out of her chair. 'I want out, now. Get me out of here,' he shrieked.

Dylan calmly terminated the interview.

'The feeling's mutual,' Dawn muttered under her breath as she slid off the chair.

Little was returned to his cell, not because he demanded it, but because they had nothing more to put to him at that moment. Dylan knew he had a vast amount of evidence against him, sufficient to charge.

Tired but elated, Dylan and Dawn walked back to the office. 'What're you thinking, Dawn?' he asked.

'Mm … premeditated murderer who chose children because they were too small to fight back. Although he used the element of surprise anyway, didn't he?'

'I totally agree. Do you want to charge him, Dawn, whilst his solicitor is still here?'

'Oh, boy, do I. Thank you, Jack.' All of a sudden the tiredness was insignificant and he smiled. Dawn's face glowed as she took off to the cells at a pace.

'My office when you've charged him,' Dylan called after her. She waved as she turned at the cell area door.

Larry was sitting doodling on a pad in the office when Dylan walked in. 'Contact the FLOs will you, Larry, and ask them to inform the families that we are charging him.'

'Yeah, sure, boss.'

'We'll have a debrief in an hour. Let's get it done then we'll grab a couple of pints, eh?' Dylan said, slapping Larry on the back as he passed him.

'Boss?'

'Yeah?'

'You were right. I'm sorry.'

Dylan smiled wanly. 'I suppose I'd better inform the chief constable and the force. Watch the bosses come out of the woodwork again now,' he chortled. 'Larry?'

'Yeah?'

'Thanks for that.'

Dawn read the two charges of murder to Harold Wilkinson-Little: that he did, charge one, murder Daisy Charlotte Hind, and that he did, charge two, murder Christopher Francis Spencer. He did not reply.

'Inspector Lever, Force Control.' A bright, clear voice answered Dylan's call.

'Hello, Inspector. Detective Inspector Dylan. One for the information of the Chief, all Divisions and the Press Office. A Harold Wilkinson-Little, forty-five years old, will appear before Harrowfield Magistrates' Court tomorrow charged with the murder of Daisy Charlotte Hind and Christopher Francis Spencer.'

'That's bloody great. Fantastic news. I'll do that with pleasure.'

'Thank you,' he said, as he replaced the phone, smiling like a Cheshire cat.

The packed room at the debrief was jubilant, like a room full of lottery winners all waiting for the presentation of the cheque.

Dylan spoke to them, his voice strong and triumphant. 'This has been a long and hard enquiry for all of us. It seems to have gone on for ages without any luck at all and then out of the blue this breakthrough. That's policing. You'll be pleased to know he's admitted both murders. He blames the fathers of the murdered victims for bullying him at school, thirty years ago. I have my personal thoughts on that and anyone who knows me can probably guess them.' The crowd jeered. 'He's been charged with both murders. I want to thank you all for your work over the past few months. This was a team effort and you can be proud of yourselves. Please thank your other halves for me. I know they will have had to be patient too. Well done everyone.'

A cheer went around the room.

'Just one more thing. Don't forget we still have a hell of a lot of work to do over the next week to collate the file, but the bar is open for those who wish to have a drink on me. Once again, thank you.'

The room emptied as quickly as if a fire alarm had just gone off. Everyone was on a high and was ready to celebrate the success. Dylan telephoned the cells to thank them and ensured that Harold Wilkinson-Little was on suicide watch; he didn't want him taking the easy way out.

'Cheers, everyone.' Dylan raised his glass as he turned from the bar.

'Cheers.' The shout echoed around the room. It was noisy. Everyone was loud.

Tomorrow he, Dawn and Larry would have to speak to the families, but first he had to contact the Crown Prosecution Service. They needed to know Harold Wilkinson-Little would be appearing in court, so they could prepare for the remand. He felt good.

The courtroom would be packed and there would also be Press and people outside. Local uniform would need to be increased in the area for the duration. Dylan's head was buzzing. He loved this part of the job best and at last the family had some sort of closure. The pints went down well and he felt his worries fall from his shoulders.

'Jen? We've charged him,' Dylan shouted in the noisy bar. Ecstatic in his drunken state, he wasn't bothered who knew about their affair. He'd even called her from the bar's extension.

'I'm sorry, Jack, I can't talk right now.' Jen's voice was sombre.

'What? Oh, come on, Jen, I'm sorry. I know I haven't been there for you. But you know what it's like when a job's running, love. We can spend some time together, now. I've missed you so much. I'm not bothered who hears me. Let's tell the world ... we're together,' he announced splaying his arms lavishly. He felt like he could take on the world. He'd got everything he wanted, a wonderful job and a wonderful woman. Dylan pulled the extension cord into the corridor so he could hear Jen better.

'Jack, you don't understand. Mum's died.' Jen's voice was sobering as it cracked with emotion.

'Oh, my god. I'm sorry ... I love you ...,' he stuttered, realising in that instant that his triumph meant nothing without her.

'Jack?' She jumped in before hanging up.

'Yes?'

'Jack, I … I think you should know … I don't know if I'm coming back.'

Jack Dylan arrived at Cowes Red Jet passenger terminal early the next day, a very unexpected visitor, and Jen's face said it all. Wonders would never cease. He wanted her to know that he needed her as much as she needed him and right now he knew where his place should be. Then, and only then, could they both decide what their future held - together?

CONSEQUENCES by RC BRIDGESTOCK is the second in the series of Detective Inspector Jack Dylan's books.

Detective Inspector Jack Dylan's list of things to do is getting out of control. He has two unconnected murders to solve of a small child and a young woman, plus a missing detective to find. Long hours are part of the job but does he have the time to figure out the pieces to the crime jigsaws, and save his relationship?

Top of his list is to find out who has used a toddler for target practice. The list of the boy's injuries is horrific and his team of detectives won't stop until the murderer or murderers are found. Their only solution is to find the culprit and put the murderer behind bars for a long, long time.

Detective Inspector Dylan also has to deal with a serial jumper – a man who keeps threatening to jump off high buildings; will he do it one day and is he involved with the child's death?

With the pressure mounting Dylan has to solve the murder of Liz, a young woman found burned alive in a public park. He also has to find out where half a million pounds of the young woman's money has gone and how his missing sergeant may be involved in the whole sorry mess. Usually the search for the murderer begins with the immediate family but the dead woman's husband is in prison. CONSEQUENCES shows the steps the detectives must take to find the answer to the question - who killed Liz?

CONSEQUENCES is a pacy thriller seen through the eyes of detective hero, Jack Dylan, who lets the job take over his life leaving his girlfriend behind with no one to support her when she thinks she has cancer. With so much already on his plate can Dylan save his relationship with the one person who keeps him grounded and sane, and even if he can is it already too late?

To be published by Caffeine Nights Publishing in paperback and eBook.

Lightning Source UK Ltd.
Milton Keynes UK
175767UK00002B/2/P